HONEY AND IC

A CROWN of PETALS and ICE

SHANNON MAYER
KELLY ST CLARE

A Crown of Petals and Ice, The Honey and Ice Series, Book 3

HiJinks Ink Publishing

Original illustrations by MB

Mayer, Shannon

St. Clare, Kelly

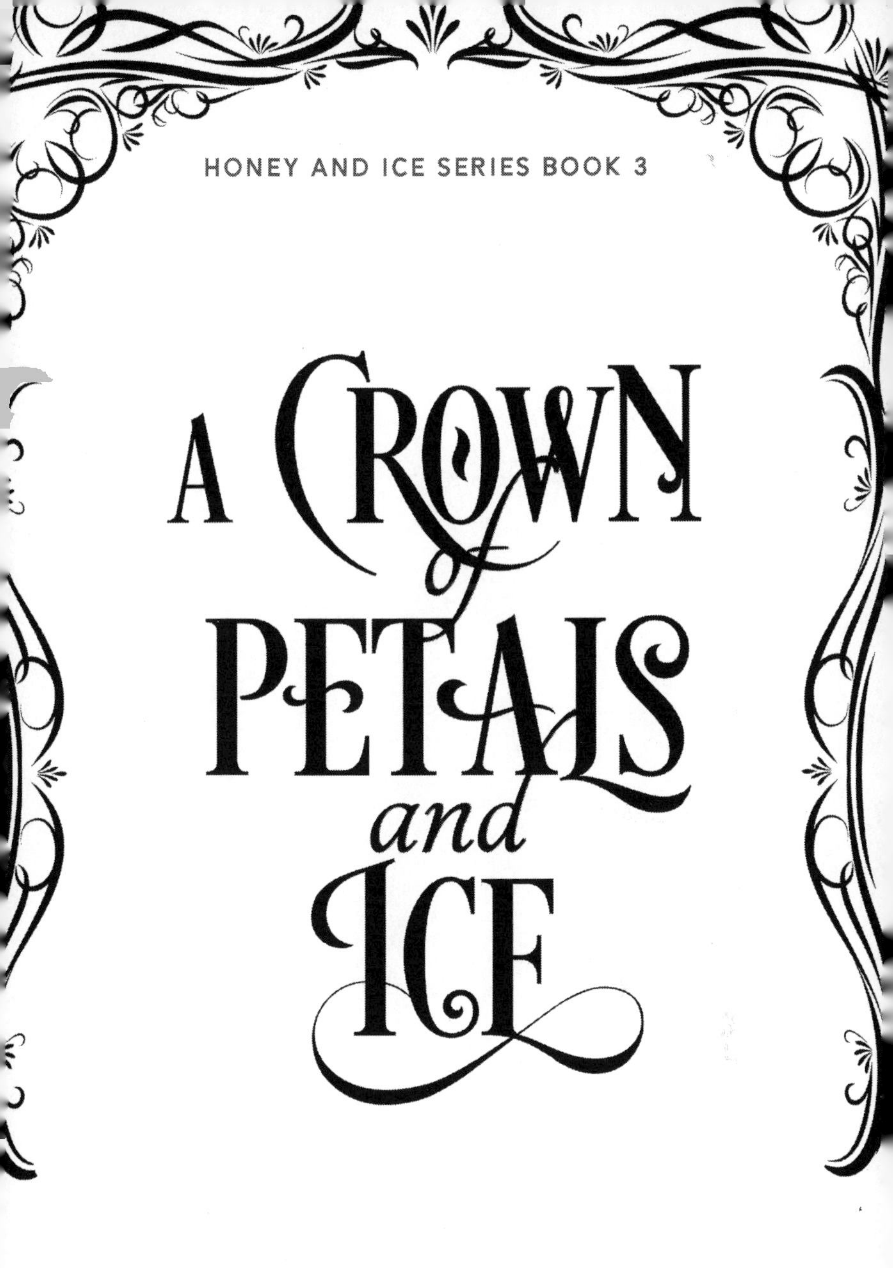
HONEY AND ICE SERIES BOOK 3
A CROWN of PETALS and ICE

As always, our thanks to our editors, early readers, beta readers and reviewers who have helped us to bring Kallik, Cinth, and Faolan and all the characters from this world, into our world. We could not have done it without you.

CHAPTER 1

I tried to sit in the high-backed chair as though I sat in it every day. As though studio lights were set up around me all the time. As though having at least two cameras zoomed in on my face from different angles was a normal occurrence. As though sleeping and existing in the royal suite of the Seelie castle was a run-of-the-mill thing.

The human interviewer, a brisk and oddly confrontational woman, looked me square in the eyes. "The human population is understandably concerned and anxious about recent happenings, Queen Kallik. What assurances are you able to give us about our ongoing safety?"

Here's the recap I couldn't tell the humans. Two weeks ago, the fae giant Rubezahl was catapulted into Underhill by Queen Elisavanna of the Unseelie, who sacrificed her life to send him away, but before he left this realm, he unleashed his outcast army on Unimak, destroying everything in his path, human and otherwise, on his way to the fae courts. That collateral damage was very much an issue given humans outnumber us fifty to one and possess a range of mass murder weapons.

"The fae in question was dealt with," I answered, the creeping feeling of deja-vu coming over me. "We are working to contain the aftermath, and thus far our efforts have been successful."

This was my first human interview since I was sorted and took up rule of the Seelie court, but the CTN or CMM or whichever agency this journalist was from weren't the first humans or fae to come hounding me for answers. My father's old advisors had coached me on the best response, and suggested this woman the best one to interview with. By now, I could say the words in my sleep.

The human leaned forward, pinning me with a cool look over her thick spectacles. "So, there's no way this fae being, this . . . *giant*, could return to wreak havoc and harm our children?"

I lifted a shoulder. "Not that I know of. Shouldn't rule it out, I suppose. He's old and powerful." And far more resourceful than anyone had given him credit for over his centuries' long life. He'd steadily brainwashed hundreds of outcast fae using his special tea in a bid to conquer the courts.

There was an audible intake of air from my Seelie advisors, standing in a row to my left. What? Right, wrong words.

"There is a known fae population in the Alaskan Triangle," she said next. "In recent years, the human death and disappearance toll in the area has catapulted to horrifying levels. Are your kind behind that too?"

I tilted my head, holding her gaze. "What are you implying?"

The interviewer blinked twice, then turned to one of the cameras and dialed her smile up to full wattage. “This is Emily from CNN, and we’ve just been up close and personal with the newly instated Queen Kallik. Up next, how to broach the subject of fae safety with our children. Also, in uncertain times, how will the human race protect our identity from infringement by outside species? Stick around for tonight’s special on retaining cultural autonomy.”

My brows nearly shot up before I remembered the presence of the other cameras.

Just . . . wow.

The cameras turned off, quickly followed by the lights. The journalist extended her hands to me, a wide smile still in place. “Thank you, Kallik.”

I stared at her hand, then shifted my gaze up to her face, a small part of me appreciating that she wasn’t one of the selfie-happy tourists we were usually exposed to on Unimak. The rest of me was offended by the supposition that we were some invasion humans needed to shield themselves from. “Queen Kallik, actually.”

Her smile slid away like ice on a hot tray.

I stood and turned toward the balcony, leaving my advisors to usher the woman out, and unclasped my cloak’s heavy chain from around my neck. I gathered the fabric and tossed it over the nearest piece of furniture—a piece that was a mixture between a bed and a chair. Rolling my shoulders, I turned my attention to the gold gauntlets chafing my wrists. Those landed on top of the cloak.

“Your Majesty—” an advisor whose name I’d forgotten bowed low, “—it is likely that your final comment will be misconstrued by the human populace. We should gather without delay to decide on a course of action and how to best answer further human inquiries.”

Leaning on the balustrade, I took in the view of the dividing river beneath my window. Seelie on one side. Unseelie on the other. Just like me. "You think they'll somehow misunderstand me and assume Rubezahl *isn't* coming back to harm their children?"

"No, Queen Kallik. We think they'll believe you absolutely."

I blew out a breath. "So, what's the problem?"

His shuffling footsteps were about as irritating as his hesitation. "Things with the humans are tenuous. We have discussed this at length."

Correct. I just didn't understand how lying benefited anyone. Rubezahl certainly wanted revenge against the courts, but he held as much hatred for our non-magical neighbors as he did for the fae who'd cast him out to the Triangle long ago. How would false reassurances protect them or us? They needed to at least be aware that the danger was lurking.

In summary, I was terrible at politics. Or maybe I just didn't give a shit. "I'll make a few calls tomorrow."

I'd planned to do that regardless. My advisors had given me an entire list that I was supposed to get through. Various human leaders and leaders of other races who hadn't 'come out' to humans yet—werewolves, vampires, witches and demons. Then there were the other fae courts.

Everyone wanted a piece of the new queen. The mixed queen.

The queen they hoped to manipulate.

The advisor lingered, and though I wasn't looking at him, my mind drew up the image of his mouth opening and closing like that of a fish.

"Leave me now," I announced. "Everyone. Clear the room. I don't wish to be disturbed again this evening."

Perks of being queen, people listened to menial requests without hesitation. Within a minute, I was blissfully alone.

Just in time too.

The sun was disappearing over the Unseelie mountain range to the east. Another castle, similar in shape to the one I now lived in on the west range, protruded dramatically from midway up the mountainside on the Unseelie side.

Halfway up was a balcony much like mine.

In the dying light, my eyes were just good enough to make out the dark shape of a figure—a man. I didn't need binoculars to identify him.

On the days Faolan and I didn't meet to discuss court issues, we'd agreed to have our moment here. I lifted an arm, and a beat later, Lan lifted his in answer.

My heart panged, but this was a necessary move. The Oracle may have declared me queen of *all* fae, but reality wasn't so accepting . . . or so simple. Our courts had operated in parallel, physically close yet *completely* separate, for centuries. Our societies were different, from clothing to etiquette and intra-court rules. To combine them overnight would be ludicrous.

So, in wake of Elisavanna's death, I'd selected Lan as regent of the Unseelie court. He hadn't wanted the role, but he was the only Unseelie I knew and trusted. The only other option had been for *me* to take up residence in the darker castle, and that would have required me to leave Adair and Uncle Josef to their conniving here in the Seelie court. A move that would prove disastrous for everyone. I didn't need to be the Oracle to see that.

I didn't want my leadership position any more than Lan wanted his, there was no question about it.

But I'd do my best regardless. Not because I believed myself the best option for a ruler, but because the Oracle had literally told me the only path to success was with me right where I was.

Goddess, what a mess.

I lowered my hand and stayed in place, watching the figure. He did the same. We often stood out on our respective balconies until the light disappeared.

Was this what King Aleksandr and Queen Elisavanna had done over the years? Had they longed to be together out in the open?

Had they even been in love when they decided to combine their essence and place me in the womb of a human?

They were both dead now, so I'd never know the truth.

The sun disappeared, and though Lan remained, even my fae eyes couldn't find him now.

"It won't always be like this," I whispered. Except damn, those incredible days in Underhill, when Lan and I hadn't needed to pretend away our feelings for one another, when we could touch and smile and just *be*, seemed like a long-ass time ago.

A happy sigh from behind me made me jump.

"Seriously the cutest," Cinth said.

Glancing back, I cocked a brow. "You think?"

"You guys come out here at dusk every night to wave to each other. Yes, I stand by my assessment. Absolutely adorable."

I took in my friend—and, with nearly as much scrutiny, the tray of baked goods she'd wisely brought with her. "Doesn't feel cute, I'll tell you that."

Her expression softened. "I know, Alli. But you guys are the real deal, and that's more than most find. It makes me want the same for myself."

A chuckle left my lips. "You want to settle on one man after all this time? Jackson's been trying to convince you for how long?"

"Maybe a decade. Just . . . it's nice to know someone has your back or is just *there* for you, no matter what." She shook her head. "Before I saw you two together, I didn't believe it was possible."

This wasn't a small admission from my friend. She'd never struggled to rake the guys in—in fact, they flocked to her like children to a parade, but aside from her on-again-off-again routine with Jackson, I'd never seen her take relationships very seriously. "I get you. That's what I feel with Lan." A security that I'd never known I wanted.

Unconditional love.

Not to say we hadn't had our ups and downs, but that was hopefully all behind us, aside from the opposite castle situation.

I reached for what looked like a peril—a pastry delicacy named for its ability to make you eat far more of them than intended.

Cinth slapped my hand. "Bad."

A laugh left me. "Did you just slap the queen of all fae?"

She snorted. "I used to bathe you. So yes, I fucking did. Got a problem with it?"

It was the only thing in the last several weeks I *didn't* have a problem with. "What am I doing wrong? Do I need to close my eyes for this one too?"

Cinth always brought me her latest inventions for me to sample, often with unusual requests.

After the Seelie head chef was rounded up as one of Rubezahl's outcast spies in need of isolation, I'd given my friend the job. Those who'd complained promptly shut the hell up when she made bruadar—a delicacy the fae had not seen on Unimak in years.

"I want to engage as many of the senses as possible," she murmured. Tray in one hand, she lifted her other hand and wiggled her fingers. A beautiful turquoise magic danced at her command, erupting into a mist-like rain that fell upon the perils like icing sugar. "*Now*," she hushed.

I was almost as reverent as I carefully selected a magic-coated peril and took a bite. The magic wove through me, a smooth, warm wave that first relaxed my face and then eased the tightness in my shoulders and back. Languidness paved the way for the delicious, nutty sweetness that followed like a cool breeze after a storm. I exhaled, savoring the taste and the feeling as they slowly dissipated.

"How did you do that?" I croaked after.

Her expression was smug. "Awesome, right?"

I should've known better than to inquire about her process. Even with me, she never revealed her cooking secrets. "Delicious isn't a good enough word to describe it. That was other-worldly."

She beamed down at the tray, and Lugh knew that I'd never felt more grateful for the normalcy my friend always brought to my life. "How did the human interview go?"

"Screwed it up."

Cinth grinned. "That explains why your advisors are in such a tizz."

My lips twitched. "Keeps them busy."

Though it would undoubtedly bite me in the ass tomorrow. And the next day. And the one after that.

"You're exhausted," she said. "I'll get out of your...way better than usual hair. See you tomorrow?"

"Sounds good." I waved as she bustled from the room, only stopping to carefully place another peril on a small, round table that probably had a fancy name.

Bed. At last.

Had to give it to these royals—talking, behaving, and looking a certain way all day was draining on a level training had never been. I took the gold circlet off my head and placed it on yet another table—a triangle one this time—then shed the layers of bright, high-quality fabric that a Seelie queen was apparently expected to wear. I'd refused dresses, and so they'd designed me collared tunics that were longer in the back than the front and belted tightly at the waist, which had the effect of ballooning out the lapels to give a dress-like appearance anyway. Whatever. If I could fight in it, I would be happy.

A half-hearted knock sounded, and I called, "No, thank you" without delay.

Poor maids. I only accepted their help in the mornings. They were nice enough, but I wouldn't put it past them to report back to my councillors.

Slipping into a simple white nightgown, I tucked a dagger under my pillow and laid out one of the swords the Unseelie queen, a.k.a. Mommy Dearest, had given me on the empty half of the bed. The other one went on the bedside table. Then, stuffing the rest of my first peril into my mouth, I settled into bed and let the effects sink me down into the softest bed I'd ever slept on.

My eyes fluttered closed.

My body grew warm and heavy.

And someone breathed on my face.

Wrenching back to awareness, I sat, dagger already in hand. And found myself blinking through the torso of a spirit. "Oh...sorry about that." I lay flat again, staring up at my guide. "You're back!"

She smiled, and I felt a buzz of familiarity. Some things forged strong bonds between people, and this spirit had once walked my path to defeat Rubezahl and preserve the connection between realms and failed. Something I expected to do daily.

"*Greetings, Queen of All Fae,*" the woman said, her voice echoing slightly.

I grimaced. "Just Kallik will do."

"*Yet the Queen of All Fae is what you are.*"

"Not what I want to be," I confessed in the darkness.

She nodded and floated to perch on the edge of the bed.

At her continued regard, I lifted a shoulder. "I'll get used to it. To be fair, I really didn't know what I wanted to do anyway. This is as good as anything. At least I don't have to watch my back now." *In the same way.*

I was no fool. I knew I still had plenty of enemies.

"You reached Underhill. I am glad. And you passed the test of Underhill's mouthpiece, the blooded fae."

Devon was Underhill's voice? For real? "Guess so. Not that it got me far."

"Farther than those before you." Sadness rode her words, and if I could've hugged her, then it would be happening now. I wasn't a hugger by any means. There was just something about her I *knew*.

I scratched my cheek instead. "I suppose. Rubezahl is gone for now. Things are better than they were."

The spirit shook her head. *"The giant merely bides his time, Queen of All Fae. Because he knows the price of losing access to the esteemed Underhill."*

Huh?

"That was all bogus though. Being away from Underhill doesn't cause madness. Ruby made that up so he could get everyone to panic and rally people to his side. It's—"

Her expression didn't alter.

I blew out a breath. "Tell me. What's the price? Or are you going to leave me hanging again?"

She smiled softly. *"Today is the last day I will see you, regardless of whatever path you choose next. I am not on any of them. Here is what I know and can share."*

I sat up again, licking my lips. This was unprecedented. I never got any answers without at least bleeding and getting punched a little.

"A fae bereft of Underhill is a weak fae indeed," she said. *"Weaker and weaker over the months, the years, the decades, until their magic is but a memory. For Underhill replenishes our connection to its energy and essence. This is her power. And Rubezahl knows it well. The fae on Earth have been cut off from Underhill long enough that they will soon begin to pay the price. That soon they will become a foothold for this darker, more sinister power."*

Dark and sinister about summed Rubezahl up. My mouth dried. "If this goes on much longer, the fae here will lose their magic?" I closed my eyes. "He's going to wait us out."

"Both of you have a choice as to your eventual meeting place."

That one was harder to decipher. I studied her for a time. "I can get to Underhill. That's what you mean. But are you telling me that Rubezahl can also get back here?"

The spirit dipped her head.

I pushed off the covers and paced in the room. He could get back. Shit. On some level, after the Oracle's ominous statement, I'd assumed that was the case. *The problem is not that he is locked. The problem is that Underhill must open or fae magic here will die. What do you think happens when Underhill is eventually opened, Dandelion?*

Otherwise, she wouldn't have spoken of paths. "You're saying that I'll need to take the battle to him?"

"That is yet to be seen." She moved to take my hand, but her fingers passed through mine.

My stomach clenched. I swallowed my other question, instead asking, "This is the last time I'll see you? Why?"

Her gaze met mine. *"Because you have passed the point where a guide can help. No one before you has made it this far. Now, the path forward is unknown to anyone who could help without hindering your success."*

Like the Oracle, who could see everything but was bound by such chains. "Well, for what it's worth, thank you. You saved us at the sanctuary by directing us to the land kelpie. I wouldn't be here without you."

"You wouldn't be here with me," the woman answered. *"And so, though it brings me pain to part from a sister, I go easier knowing my failure might have led to your future success. We would never have met at all if I had not chosen the wrong path."*

I stilled, then sat heavily on the bed beside her. "Sister?"

She tilted her head as though listening to something only audible to her, then nodded to whoever had spoken. "*Goodbye, Queen of All Fae. Your victory shall warm me. As it will the hearts of our parents, who gave up all in the hopes of saving our kind. You are the last hope now, dear one.*"

As she leaned forward, sound swelled from behind my closed door—the ring of clashing swords.

Well, shit, that wasn't good.

"*Goodbye, sister.*" She hovered, her lips over my cheek, and despite the obvious problem not far away, I sat unmoving, chest rising and falling.

"Goodbye," I croaked.

The spirit guide—my sibling from another era—began to fade, but as shouts swelled beyond my door, I recovered my senses. "Wait! Tell me. When will Rubezahl return? How?" If I knew that much, I'd be much better prepared.

She cast a look at the closed door, and as I did the same, the sounds of battle echoed to me from the other side, ringing with an odd quality. "*Dear one, he has already returned.*"

I'd been the queen of all fae for less than a week, and already my rule was being challenged.

Awesome.

I sprinted from the sunroom, tearing off the white nightgown before grabbing my leathers, tunic, and light armor off the back wall.

"Send for Bres," I yelled at the maid who popped her head in from a side room. She leaped out of my way as I strode past. "Tell him to meet me in the war chamber." Okay, so I'd never actually been in there before, but it was where my father and Bres had met regularly to discuss security.

I may have overheard an advisor or two mutter that the war chamber would be no more now that a woman was leading the Seelie. Asses. They'd learn the hard way if necessary.

I tied the thick, leather, spell-woven armor into place as I got moving, pausing only to snatch up my two swords. Armed and armored, I sprinted out an entrance on the opposite side of the clashing of metal. It grated to leave the fight to others, but I couldn't just think of myself now.

Servants scattered as I bolted through the castle. So many floors, so many unnecessary rooms, and I had to get through all of them as fast as possible, which wasn't easy since I didn't usually go out the back way.

"Get Josef to the war chamber," I shouted at an advisor who all but threw himself from my path to avoid being trampled. Although I didn't have any major fondness for my uncle, he'd been around longer than me. He might know something I didn't. "And send news to the Unseelie court that we're under attack!" I yelled over my shoulder.

"We are?" the advisor called weakly.

Maybe there weren't alarms going off or an army at the castle door, but I knew Rubezahl well enough to understand that wasn't his style. He'd be slick as ice in the spring thaw. He'd sent assassins to kill me.

He would hit us when we weren't expecting it.

"How the fuck did he get here so quick?" I muttered. The giant knew something I didn't about getting between realms.

I skidded to a stop outside the war chamber. Maps and books were strewn about. Orbs the size of heads lined the perimeter of the room, floating in a circular motion from floor to ceiling. They flickered through different scenes, some even showing faces. I'd been told they were used for keeping an eye on the realm and humans. The fae version of spy T.V., just more effective.

"Show me Rubezahl." I barked.

One of the orbs fluttered closer, spinning rapidly, the fog within it clearing to reveal a scene.

The giant I'd thought was my friend and mentor came into view, though the image was far too close for me to see what he was doing. I tried to tilt the orb so I could make out more of the surrounding area and less of his nose and the pipe clenched between his teeth.

To no avail.

"It won't focus," Bres said from behind me. "We don't know why, but we can't see what he's up to. None of the orbs ever show his face or actions."

Frowning, I shoved it away. "Rubezahl is somewhere on Unimak. His people are in the castle. I heard the clang of steel outside my door."

“In the castle?” Bres asked, exchanging glances with the others. “None of the guards have reported anything.”

But I’d *heard* it.

My brow cleared. Maybe that was my sister’s doing, another warning of sorts. The sounds of battle had echoed and rung in an unusual way. “I may be in error on that front, but Rubuzahl is on Unimak already.”

"I thought the Unseelie queen killed him." Bres moved around the big table and took the head seat. I didn't raise my eyebrows, though I wanted to. Taking my seat was a definite challenge.

"No." I leaned on the desk. "Her death propelled him into Underhill. It took everything she had to open a portal." At least that was what the Oracle had explained to me. The death of someone with powerful enough magic could cause a tear in the fabric between worlds. Even then, the portal had only opened because the solstice had caused a particular weakness between the realms that night. Elisavanna had known that, and she’d used it to buy us some time. Only it hadn’t given us nearly as much time as any of us had thought.

A week. One week. How the *hell* was he here already?

I was not ready for this battle—not yet.

"So where is he?"

The familiar voice was like jagged fingernails up and down my spine. I didn't bother to turn and look at the woman attached to it. "Adair, I didn't call for you. And you're lucky not to be languishing in the dungeon, so I suggest you get out of my sight before I change my mind and give you a new apartment full of iron."

"Truly, Your Majesty, I didn't realize that in offering my views on the policies of our great people I would be stepping on delicate toes."

When I faced her, she was in a deep curtsey, head bowed. I still wanted to smash her, on pure principle. "How did you kill my father exactly?"

She gasped. Her head snapped up so fast it was a wonder she didn't break her neck. "I did nothing of the sort!"

I locked eyes with her, letting my magic fill me, and she slowly broke eye contact to find a spot over my shoulder instead.

“We will discuss your lies another time,” I said softly. Although now Rubezahl had revealed his true colors, the majority of my suspicions had swung in his direction over my father's murder. *Both* had stood to gain from his death—*both* desired a throne.

Adair didn't need to know I was of two minds, however. She'd still decided to lock me in the dungeon and execute me via drowning after all.

Bres cleared his throat. "The giant, why do you think he's here? If he's here at all."

Goddess damn it all, he didn't believe me either, and now I was beginning to doubt my spirit sister's warning. There may be one way to find out. I blinked and yanked the orb back to me. “Show me the children of the moon."

An image flickered to life, showing me a legion gathered on the far southern tip of Unimak Island, a series of boats behind them. They were filled with outcast fae, known amongst themselves as children of the moon. Some I knew, most I didn't. Judging from the number of unkempt beards, the wild fae had joined them. I had no illusions about who was leading them. Rubezahl had returned.

I looked at Bres, taking grim satisfaction in the way his mouth hung open. "Now do you believe me?"

"You need to get your army in action, General!" Adair barked.

I whirled on her. "Fool. You think that you, someone who has spent her life simpering and smiling has the experience to deal with this? Get out. Now!" I put a little magical oomph behind my words, and white lightning danced through the room, smashing into Adair's ass. She screamed and bolted, almost knocking Josef over as he sauntered into the room, a half-full wine glass in one hand and a mostly empty wine bottle in the other.

"Niece, what can I do for you?" he asked as if discussing the weather.

I pointed at the orb. "We have company. I want you to go with Bres and find out what they're doing here. As emissaries. We're playing nice for now. Let them think we are wary of them."

Bres snorted. "You are a fool. You have an army on your shore, and you want to have a discussion with them?"

I smoothed my features as best I could. "A moment ago, you didn't even believe they were *here*. Might I suggest that we do this in a way that does *not* light up our world as a target for the humans?"

Bres's face tightened, but he gave me the slightest nod. "Of course."

I spun the orb so I could get a better look. The army wasn't racing toward the southern boundary, and they weren't setting up weapons. They *were* setting up a camp.

I wasn't naïve. They'd come for a fight, but if there was a possibility of negotiating this away and saving fae lives, then I'd do it.

I clasped my hands behind my back. "The two of you will go as messengers. Nothing more. Be careful, but you shouldn't be in too much danger. Rubezahl likes to seem . . . civilized. Just don't drink his tea and don't get too close.

That seemed to offend Bres further, but I was beyond caring what he thought. He'd been my mentor for years, but he'd lost my respect when he'd backed Adair's baseless accusations that I'd killed my father. "If I don't send messengers of a high enough rank, Rubezahl will be offended. For now, I want him quiet. I'll wait here and keep watch over the orbs. Should you need additional help, I assure you it will be sent."

Josef shrugged. "Fine by me. Good day for a ride, eh, friend?" He tried to slap Bres on the shoulder, missed, and stumbled.

I withheld a groan.

"Meet me at the stables," Bres snapped at Josef, voice sharp and temper very obviously close to the breaking point if the throbbing vein in his neck was any indicator. As soon as Josef was gone, my old trainer rounded on me. "What game are you playing?"

"Josef is high enough in standing that it won't offend Rubezahl but low enough that if we lose him, we've not lost much." I shuffled a few of the papers around on the huge strategy table, not because I really wanted to look at them, but because I wanted to appear . . . casual. "I have a few phone calls to make to see what other allies we might have out there."

"Allies? You mean the other fae courts? Ireland and Louisiana have not spoken to one another in over a century, and—"

"Go and talk to the giant. I will write a missive you can give to him."

When Bres didn't move, I took the seat at the head of the table that he'd occupied a moment before. "Dismissed."

He executed a sharp salute, turned on his heel, and was gone.

I'd won that round at least. I grabbed a blank piece of paper, a quilled pen, and a jar of ink. Holding the pen over the parchment, I paused, unsure exactly what to say. A knock on the door lifted my head.

A servant I didn't know stood there in freshly pressed livery. "Yes?"

"Your Majesty, a messenger has come from—" he swallowed hard, "—Rubezahl, king of the wild fae."

King of the wild fae, huh.

Maybe Bres and Josef didn't need to go after all. "Empty the throne room and have them wait in there. Collect Bres for me too." I paused. "Cinth, Rowan, and Bracken also. Those three will stand in the shadows."

I didn't trust many of the people around me. Hyacinth was a given. Rowan and Bracken . . .well, they'd turned on me before, but I'd trained with them. I knew them better than most people, and if I didn't trust them entirely, then I trusted that I understood their *limitations*. That naturally made me more comfortable with them than others, and I knew that both of them saw things in a different way to myself, which was valuable.

I closed my eyes, wishing Lan was here with me. He was better at this leadership business. Already he had the Unseelie court in hand as my regent.

"I don't want this," I whispered to myself.

I'd never wanted a crown. I still didn't. I wanted . . . my family, my friends, and my freedom. No point feeling sorry for myself though—this was a step up from being on the run. Shaking off the moment of self-pity, I made my way to the massive throne room.

When I got there, Salli, the court administrator, was waiting. Her jaw dropped. "Your Majesty. You cannot go in there looking like—"

"Like I could slice them in half without breaking a sweat?" I brushed past her. "Yeah, I can."

The throne room wasn't empty the way I'd asked for it to be. Adair and Josef were present, and so was half the court. Bres stood on Adair's other side.

My blood began a slow boil at the blatant disrespect, the flaunting of a simple ask on my part. I didn't bother looking at the messenger who knelt waiting other than to note that their head was bowed, and a hood covered their hair and face.

There were two ways I could play this. Scream and get everyone out of here or talk to the messenger as if I'd *wanted* all these witnesses here...which would be letting Adair and Bres win. Because I had no doubt this was their doing.

Neither of those options would work in the long term.

"I see," I said softly, magically amplifying my words so that everyone in the room heard. A few of the fae looked at the ground, but Adair just smiled, her eyes like ice. She and Bres thought they'd backed me into a corner.

We would see about that.

"Rowan, step forward," I ordered.

My former classmate stepped up and knelt in front of me, one fist to the ground. "Your Majesty."

"It seems that our general, Bres, isn't able to retain even the simplest of orders." I locked eyes with my former trainer, daring him to gainsay me in public.

His entire body stiffened, his nostrils flaring.

"General Bres, you are released and given over fully for the training of the young fae. I know it brings you great joy to see the next generation rise in their abilities." My lips curved, and Bres gave a tight bow.

"Your Majesty."

It sounded as if he were being strangled.

Good.

I looked down at the person I'd once called friend. I'd even trusted Rowan for a time before his error in the final trial for the Untried. Thinking back though, what he'd done seemed. . .small when compared to what real evil looked like. And I could admit now that his comment had hit on festering wounds I'd carried. People deserved second chances. Not three. But two, I would do. "Rowan. Your oath."

He slammed a clenched fist over his heart. "I, Rowan of House Yellow, bind my sword to obey the orders of Queen Kallik. Should I ever fail in this, then I shall forfeit my place in this world."

I felt a magical warmth fill my fingertips at his pledge.

Rowan glanced up and lowered his voice. "And though an oath is made, I would have acted as such anyway. Because I don't make mistakes twice."

Good to know. Time would tell. I mean, I'd spent years training with this man. I'd seen him make hard choices out of kindness when an easier, unkind choice was possible. I also recalled that he was at the top of our class when it came to strategizing, so maybe he wouldn't be bad to keep around. I nodded. "Soldier, your first order of business is to clear this room. Immediately." I stood before the throne, waiting.

Rowan was up in a second, and he had the group moving with Bracken's help in a few seconds more. I tried not to show how impressed I was at his efficiency, but I was.

Adair stormed out, Bres and Josef hot on her heels. She was a growing concern, but I really didn't have time to deal with her shit right then. She knew it too. It was exactly why she'd mistakenly chosen to make a show of force.

Cinth snuck up behind me. "What about me?"

"Stay behind, please. Listen for things I might miss," I murmured.

She patted me on the shoulder and walked over to stand inconspicuously by the wall.

I took a few minutes to observe the messenger. Slight, very slight for a fae, and they hadn't moved, not once during the whole drama of Bres's demotion and Rowan's oath

The main door slammed shut.

"Bracken, seal the room," I ordered.

"Of course, Your Majesty."

"None of that shit when no one is around, thanks."

She grinned and moved from door to door, sealing them so that no one could listen in either with their ears or a spell. When she was done, I stepped off the dais to address Rubezahl's messenger.

"What word do you have for me from the giant?" *Look at me, almost sounding like a proper ruler.*

The messenger kept their head bowed and it muffled their words. "Rubezahl will not stop until he has all he desires. You must kill him."

Okay.

I tilted my head. "You aren't here on his behalf?"

A shudder rippled through the cloaked body. "I had a chance to slip away and seized it. He . . . he has hurt me for far too long, claiming he was doing what was best for me and for our people. But Rubezahl uses people for his own purposes. Just as he used you."

A chill rippled through me as I registered just who the cloaked figure was. I took hold of a single thought, repeating it in my head. *I think your hair is pretty.*

A laugh rolled from her, and she lifted pale hands from under the folds of her cloak to lift her hood. "I did not think I could fool you, Queen Kallik. I may be a mind reader, but *you* are the one who sees."

And see her I did.

The question now was, what the hell was I supposed to do with her?

CHAPTER 3

I stared at the white-haired mystica fae. "Whatever it is will have to wait. I literally have an army on my doorstep."

She burst to her feet. "No, you must hear this."

Narrowing my eyes, I said, "Which would be an ideal way to delay me if Rubezahl wanted to get a jump on me."

"Do what you need to do," she held up both hands, "But you would be foolish indeed not to take advantage of what I offer. I can read minds, Queen Kallik. *All* minds."

Even Rubezahl's? I thought, watching her closely.

"Even Rubezahl's," she said, nodding. "Which is why I can tell you that any missive you send with your underlings will be ignored. Rubezahl is not here for peace negotiations. He never was. If at one point, he might've taken such a path, it is now closed in his mind."

I resisted the urge to rub my temples. "Being privy to my thoughts, you would know exactly what to say to convince me, I suppose."

Her tone gained a bitter edge. "Yes, my kind has that reputation. Those of us who are left, anyway. We've been destroyed for it, and it made me vulnerable enough for the 'protector of the outcasts' to mold me into a weapon."

I lifted my head. Dammit. I did *not* have time for this. But she was right. If she'd turned against Ruby, then her information could prove invaluable. It could save fae lives. Human lives. If I spent twenty minutes speaking to her, it could prevent war.

The mystica fae bowed low. "And that is why I am here. Your heart is true."

"Damn right it is," Cinth said from her station at the wall.

"And," the fae's eyes slid to my friend, "the hearts of your nearest and dearest are also true. Not only do you possess goodness, but you also have the ability to recognize it in others. In my experience, that is rare indeed."

I clasped my hands behind my back. "Rowan." Glancing his way, I caught him tearing his focus from Cinth.

Another one caught in her net.

"Kallik," he said, bowing and shooting another quick look at my friend.

Goddess save me from penises and their inability to concentrate. Except for Lan's. "Put our army on standby. They must be ready to engage at a moment's notice. Send word to the Unseelie regent to do the same with our army there. Then take a few of the queen's guards to deliver a message to Rubezahl. Tell him that I feel the plight of the fae who have been outcast to the Triangle over the centuries. I would like to speak with him or other representatives of the children of the moon to work on establishing a united future. These spokespersons will not be harmed while in my courts. If contact is not made within twelve hours, I will consider his continued silence and presence here a declaration of war." I paused. "And thank him for sending his mystica fae as a goodwill gesture."

The white-haired fae before me jerked.

I shot her a look. *Just in case you planned to play both sides.*

A small sigh left her pink lips, but she dipped her head. "Rubezahl will be furious."

I'd expected as much.

Rowan snapped his booted heels together. "Yes, Your Majesty. Immediately."

Gross. The 'Your Majesty' thing was like a chunk of food stuck in my throat, but Rowan was still impressing me thus far. "Report back as soon as you can."

He bowed again and strode from the throne room, casting yet another look at Cinth before he flushed. Seriously? Rowan had stayed at the orphanage for a time, but he was one of the so-called lucky ones. He'd been taken in by a fae family after a few years. Clearly, he hadn't experienced *grown-up* Cinth.

I shook my head and peered at the throne. My ass would be numb after ten minutes on that. Crossing to the nearest table, where Uncle Josef usually sat with other royal relations, I lowered into a chair and started thrumming my fingers on the wooden surface. Rubezahl might ignore my message, but it was *something.* After twelve hours, I'd have my answer one way or another. I took a deep breath and focused on the mystica fae, then gestured to the seat next to me. "Okay, speak. I appreciate hearing about anything that will bring the disagreement with the strays to a swift and peaceful end."

In a movement so graceful I'd nearly classify it as floating, she did as I bade, interlocking her fingers on the table and studying me. "I was by no means a young and naïve fae when I first met Rubezahl. Even then, there weren't many like me, and it was rare to find other fae who were not wary of our presence.

We were hunted, enslaved and used by the wicked, and now there are even less of us. Only a handful." Her lips curved. "Rubezahl was not one who was wary. What was more, he had a heart such as yours."

I arched a brow. "Goodie."

She lifted a shoulder. "He still does."

Extra goodie.

Her smirk widened. "The problem with a villain is that they believe in their plight. Though I'd seen the world, I had not seen his particular brand of evil." Her sharp gaze found my eyes. "It is so much easier when people are openly vile. And, well, I must say that after he helped me recover from the mistreatment I'd faced, I overlooked many warning signs. I did not want him to be the villain. He was, at that time, far more like my hero."

Yup, I'd felt that way myself. "He made you drink his tea too."

To my surprise, she shook her head. "No, never the tea. That was a rather large warning sign that I regret ignoring. I . . . had a hand in that, so to speak."

"What do you mean?" I asked, my attention sharpening.

She closed her eyes briefly. "There was a time when Rubezahl needed to recruit certain members of the stray community. The wild fae were too content being wild. The law-breaking outcasts were too content with their law-breaking. The peaceful strays wanted to simply live their lives without conflict. And Rubezahl and I—at the time—strongly believed that the only way to change the rules and restrictions of fae society was for the strays to band together. We were gaining traction, but not at a viable rate. Each person we won to our side was a potential weakness. A potential spy for the courts. If the courts found out we were gathering before we became a force to be reckoned with, then they would simply crush us. Our growth had to be exponential. And it was not. Together, early into the wee hours of the morning, we would agonize over how to achieve the impossible.

Until Rubezahl reluctantly, or so I believed at the time, mentioned the properties of my blood."

I leaned back. "Which are?" Most people were completely unaware mystica fae still existed. Beyond the basics, I knew little of them.

She hesitated. "Please understand that I disclose this information at great risk to myself. To read minds is one thing, but if the general populace learns that mystica fae have the ability to alter thought and destroy other's minds, it will be another entirely. It is what the most power hungry fae once hunted us for. Our blood."

I tapped a finger on the table. "Tell me how, at this point, you weren't able to read Ruby's real intentions."

"The protector of the outcasts possesses no small amount of magic himself," she answered. "And though he doesn't inherently have the ability to block me as some fae do, he does wield an object, one he uses with great mastery and subtlety, that allows him to shield his thoughts or alter the way they're projected."

I blinked. "His harp."

"Yes. He used it against me for a long time. And while I will not deny that bringing the courts to their knees appealed to me greatly in those angry, hurt days, the harp was—shall we say—instrumental to my agreement to donate my blood to a brew that would help convince the Triangle leaders to join us."

The lines connected all at once. At the sanctuary, I'd asked whether she was injured. She'd been in pain and had been so fearful that I'd noticed. "The tea has your blood in it."

The mystica fae swallowed. "It does. I even helped Rubezahl find the specific charm needed to bend the properties of my blood to his will. It was lost and buried, but I managed to get hold of it." Her jaw clenched.

She was the one naturally capable of mind magic, but Rubezahl had sunk his tenterhooks in well and truly. "I'm sorry he did that to you."

Her eyes widened in surprise. "You are?"

"At least the others of your kind who were enslaved weren't taught to love their jailors beforehand. I assume you tried to stop giving blood at some point?"

"My concerns over some of his errant thoughts and actions had grown larger than I could avoid," the fae said. "He wasn't using the tea to *open* the minds of those he sought to convince. He wasn't using it to lessen their discomfort and fear. He was using our brew to override thoughts and beliefs, and to insert his agenda as fact in the brains of strays."

The truth sickened me, especially since I'd been the victim of the brew myself. "How much of your blood does he have?"

"He took more from me recently. By force. He has enough to win, if that is what you are asking. Those under him have consumed the tea for so long now that they only require very occasional top ups. Only once every five to ten years. He could hold them captive for centuries."

Dammit. "It is important that he gets no more." Both for her sake and ours. For everyone's sakes really. Who knew what the strays would have chosen if not for that tea and Ruby's harp? His army was also brainwashed. Utterly. Trapped and forced to bear the consequences of the actions someone else had chosen for them.

I drew a hand over my face.

Fuck. How could I send our armies to kill them?

"You know," the woman said quietly. "If I learned one thing when by Rubezahl's side, it's not the *person's* thoughts to watch but how they treat others. That is the real clue. And that is the difference between you and the giant who seeks to dethrone you."

He could have the throne and the numb ass that went with it.

But I wouldn't allow him to hurt the court fae—no matter how much I agreed with him about the need to fix the crueler aspects of our age-old society. Now, I was faced with the task of saving *his* army from their leader.

Standing abruptly, I paced beside the round table for a time. Stopping before her, I tilted my chin. "I need everything you have on Rubezahl. What is he planning? When will he strike? What is his weakness?"

Her face hardened. "I'll give you all that and more. With pleasure."

After hearing her story, I was certain she would.

The throne room doors burst open, and my heart leaped as Faolan entered, sword swinging at his hip. I hadn't seen him in a week, and he wore a different version of the light armor I wore, but that was where the resemblances stopped. Sensual charm pulsed out of him with every coiled step. The rampant hints of bad boy and the tinge of darkness visible in his tall, lean-muscled frame had the power to set hearts racing from half a mile away. *My* heart was racing, I wanted to hold him tight and never let him go. It killed me that we were having to keep how we felt under wraps. The courts wouldn't understand that me being half Unseelie negated the strict laws that kept fae of each court separated. A sick churning in my gut told me they may *never* understand, and in all honesty, I had no idea what to do if that happened. I was sure Lan must be wondering the exact same thing, yet our ability to talk about it while in opposite courts was nearly impossible. Maybe soon we'd find our chance to just be us for an hour or two.

Dark eyes scanned the room until, as though drawn, they snapped to me.

"An outcast army," he said, kicking the doors shut.

I waited for him to reach me, drinking in the surety of his walk and the intense focus of his expression. This was who I needed at my side. "Yes. A missive has been sent." I gestured to the mystica fae. "And you're just in time to hear more."

Faolan stopped short, scowling at her. "You."

"Me," the woman said dryly. "And you are the Unseelie regent now, I hear."

He ignored her, looking back at me. "She can read minds, Alli."

That wasn't all she could do, but I'd keep that to myself for now. "Yes, which puts her in an excellent position to help us since she spent years at Ruby's side, don't you think?"

Lan crossed his arms. "We'll find out."

"Yes," I said to him, an edge to my voice. "I will. And you are welcome to join the discussion. I'd value your input."

Some of the darkness leached from his gaze. He lowered his arms. "My apologies. The messenger only knew there was an attempted assassination outside of your quarters and an army was setting up camp on Unimak."

Ah, he was worried.

"Forgiven. And I'm fine, as you see. I heard the clatter of swords, nothing more."

Which made me wonder what, exactly, I'd heard—a warning from the spirits or my sister, perhaps?

We both sat, and I leaned forward. "Tell us everything."

The mystica fae glanced at Lan, and I was never more envious of her ability to read thoughts. How often I'd wished to know his mind in the past. I'd stopped caring about his walls in Underhill—he'd seemed to lose so many of them—but my senses told me that the walls between us were building again. No surprise with him being back in the Unseelie Court and faced again with the horrors and pains of his past.

"I was not on Unimak when the outcast army was last here," she said slowly. "But I heard a detailed account of it from those whom you were unable to round up. Rubezahl transported you from the fight after baiting you with his children to drain your reserves."

That was about the size of it. "I admit that I have no idea how to defeat him. His power is greater than mine." He was centuries older than me and had true mastery over his gifts.

"Of his own right," she murmured. "No. But there is one thing that would help you defeat him. Securing it will be almost as difficult as battling him, however."

I lifted a brow. "Difficult is my middle name. What's this thing you speak of." The answer dawned on me even as the words left my lips, but she beat me to the punch.

"The thing that helped him make the tea in the first place. Rubezahl's harp." Her face clouded. "Secure his harp and half his power."

CHAPTER 4

I stood alone in the throne room with Faolan. *At last.* I'd sent the mystica fae—Ailbhe, her name turned out to be—with Cinth to get cleaned up and settled in. With two guards at her door to be on the safe side.

"You're willing to trust a fae who was in Rubezahl's pocket until a few minutes ago?" Faolan said. "That isn't smart, Orphan, and last time I checked, you were anything but stupid."

"Backhanded compliments already? Trying to make me swoon, are you?" I leveled him with a look.

"Not in the least," He bowed stiffly from the waist.

I reached over and grabbed him by the ear, dragging him upright. "Knock it off, Lan."

He grimaced as I twisted his ear for good measure, but he didn't fight back. Not like he would have even a week ago. He didn't throw me up against the wall, pin me there and press his body hard against mine, leaving me breathless and wanting.

Walls. I'd forgotten how much I hated his walls. I'd thought once they were down, that was it. That me and him would always be okay.

"Your Majesty," he murmured, confirming my fears.

A deep ache opened in my middle, erasing the excitement I'd felt upon seeing him in the throne room. We were alone for the first time since the battle, but he was falling into old habits. Habits he'd formed to survive pain from his parents and the other fae. Pain caused by mostly everyone *but* me. He was hiding behind the role I'd given him, trying to restore order in that damn head of his.

Queen and regent.

Seelie and Unseelie.

Forbidden.

All of that meant something huge to him. To be fair, it meant a lot to me too. I'd already wondered if the courts could ever understand what we were; *how* we were different. I knew that the timing of any 'coming out' would need to be thought through. But it wasn't this enormous mind-block for me in the way it was for Lan.

Foolish girl. Why did you think it would be different for him this time?

And the thing was. . . his walls only ever came down in his own time. Even I didn't hold that power to help him.

I released Faolan, feeling the deep chasm between us—one of *his* making—and it hurt so much worse than the first time because everything had been so open between us in Underhill.

My voice was hoarse and tight as I forced out the words that needed to be spoken. The plan I would tell no one else. "We need to secure a small force that we can trust and have them infiltrate Rubezahl's camp. Despite whatever trust issues I may have with Ailbhe, I agree with her that the harp is key. We need to secure it." I stepped away from him and walked to the closest window.

The more people we took on the infiltration mission, the better chance we had of getting caught . . . and being forced to drink Rubezahl's tea. Because I was sure he wouldn't kill my people. Why do that when he could convert them to his side and increase his numbers?

He'd steal them over like a thief in the garden, plucking out his favorite flowers. How could I stop that from happening?

I walked over to the eastern lookout, which provided a view across the rough ocean waves. Somewhere beyond was the mainland of Alaska. Part of me wanted to run away from this landslide and let someone else deal with the threat of Rubezahl.

What a pretty thought.

"Did you have any soldiers in mind?" Faolan asked eventually. "There are several I trust from the Unseelie army."

I held my hand out over an unsprouted plant on the windowsill and gently pulled energy from it. My deep indigo magic curled around me—it still tended to show as that color instead of white lightning until I truly submitted to my essence. The deep green vine burst into bloom, vibrant red petals unfolding in a matter of seconds. I brushed a finger over the velvet petals, the floral scent spilling around my face and filling my senses.

I put Lan's question aside because the *real* question was...how did one steal from a thief? And did that thief know me well enough to anticipate my plan?

Should I instead do the unpredictable?

"Your Majesty?"

I closed my eyes; glad my back was to Faolan. "Send me two of your most trusted Unseelie soldiers. I'll send them with two of my Seelie guards."

His armor clinked as he bowed again. "Your Majesty, I will have them to you within the hour."

His boots pounded on the marbled floor as he headed for the door.

"Wait." I still didn't leave my lookout point, but he stopped.

My heart hurt, and he . . . *he* was the one cutting it out a piece at a time. Why was he doing this *again*? I had an army on my doorstep, a giant after my life and people, and a pain in the ass for a stepmother. Right now, I needed support, not this...this extra distraction and heart ache. This wasn't a game. Peoples' lives depended on my ability to keep my head clear and my decisions objective.

Lan was, and had always been, the exception when it came to my ability to control my emotions.

My lower lip trembled, but my words were firm. "It will be hard to meet each night while this is going on. Let's stop that for a while."

He sucked in a sharp breath that echoed through the room, but he said nothing.

The silence was terrible. Too much. My resolve began to slide. I couldn't bear this.

He finally spoke, though his voice was tight and thick with emotion. "Yes, Your Majesty." The door shut behind him, and I almost slid to the floor, gripping the flower and vines so hard that the pain drew a gasp from my lips.

I opened my hand.

Tiny thorns that couldn't be seen by the naked eye had driven deep into my fingers and palm. My skin was slick with blood, which coated the petals with an even darker red.

A throat cleared behind me. "Alli?" Cinth's voice was a gentle balm to my breaking heart.

I whispered, "Are we just dragging out the inevitable? Do I need to let him go?"

Her arms wrapped around me, and she rocked me, stroking my hair like she'd done when I was little. "Oh, my friend. What's happened?"

For just this moment, I'd let someone hold me, and stop pretending to know anything about being a queen, a politician, or anything but a woman who had a heavy, breaking, heart. I started talking.

By the time the worst of my grief had poured out and Cinth had helped me clean my tear-stained face, two Unseelie guards sought entrance to the throne room.

I pulled myself together as they entered. Dressed in dark leather from head to toe, they had familiar red crescent moon patches over their hearts.

"Your Majesty?" An advisor lingered in the entrance. "The soldier has returned."

Rowan? I nodded, ignoring the Unseelie for now. "Please instruct him to report to me, and to bring his two most trusted Seelie guards with him." How would Rowan go with a little challenge?

No one spoke until he arrived with two soldiers in dark leather, a sunburst patch over their hearts. The guards had their faces concealed, as was typical with assassins of the realm, but I could tell one was male. One was female.

Rowan bowed low. "Your Majesty. Your message was delivered successfully and without incident."

"Rubezahl did not respond?" I asked, already knowing the answer.

"He did not."

The giant had twelve hours then. We'd have our answer in the morning. And if I were Rubezahl, then I would assume the queen would not try anything during that time, that she'd keep her word, and I intended to make the most of that. In truth, my plan did grate somewhat at my sense of honor.

But my gut told me unpredictability was the best option to outsmart the thief in the garden.

I took a breath. I had another challenge for Rowan. "The four of you will depart on a mission immediately. You are to retrieve a magical object from the leader of the outcasts. Getting in may not be the issue. Getting *out* with the object could prove harder. I'm assuming that I don't need to outline all the dangers of entering the enemy camp?"

Each of them shook their heads.

"One danger you must be made aware of. The giant brews a special tea. If you are caught, it is likely that he will make you drink it. This tea will scramble your thoughts and slowly turn your allegiance toward him. If you can, refuse to drink any. I tell you this in the hopes that knowledge of its effects may lend you some resistance."

Rowan made a movement to my left. "That's how he controls people?"

My answer was grim. "Possibly how he controls his entire army. The longer someone has consumed the tea, the longer it takes for the effects to wear off. Some have drunk it for decades and centuries."

Cinth, who'd returned to her position by the wall, spoke up, "Will those fae ever regain their true minds?"

"I have no idea," I said quietly, then louder, "Rowan, can you give any insight about Rubezahl's current position?"

He straightened. "The children of the moon have disembarked their boats on the far southern tip of Unimak. The largest tent was near the center of their camp. We believe the outcast leader is there."

Doubt it. I tilted my chin. "We have a chance to recover an item of great power from Rubezahl. But what I tell you now must not leave this room."

The four fae didn't so much as flinch. Each of the guards put a fist to their chest and quickly swore a magical oath, one after the other.

"On my honor and on my bindings to you as queen, I swear to take this knowledge to my grave."

Good enough.

"The giant carries with him a harp, usually slung under his cloak. A harp that once belonged to Lugh." The Oracle had told me as much while we were in Underhill. I paused and let those words sink in. Anything from Lugh was powerful, dangerous, and more than a little coveted. I mean, I even coveted his damn grandson.

I crossed to a table and leaned over a map that Ailbhe had sketched for me after our chat. "This is the camp. Rubezahl is not at the center, though he has clearly taken pains to make us believe that is the case. He was last located at the very southern tip closest to the water." I looked up. "I want you to go through the camp, north to south, to get to him."

Each of the fae nodded again, their eyes locked on the map.

"Why not go through the water?" the female Seelie guard asked.

"We'll have a second team coming from the water as back up." I answered. "I have no doubt that Rubezahl will be expecting company."

"You want us as a distraction?" an Unseelie grunted.

I shook my head. "No, I have every hope that the four of you will complete this task. The water team will be your extraction point. Should you fail, the second team will step in."

Should you fail meant 'should you be captured and brainwashed'. Then there was the obvious risk that Rubezahl could simply kill them and keep his tea for those he truly needed.

They knew it, and so did I.

"Aim to be at the outskirts of the camp near the witching hour," I said. "I will make sure Rubezahl leaves the harp behind in his tent. Wherever that may be. I wouldn't be surprised if the tent in the center of camp is a decoy."

One of the Unseelie turned his head my way but didn't question me.

Yeah, I had a part to play in all of this too.

"Go with speed and the Goddess at your backs." I touched each of them on the shoulder, an old blessing not often invoked. But it felt right.

The fae saluted me and filed out.

Rowan was the first to speak. "Queen Kallik, what are you planning?"

"The giant wants me, regardless of his silence. Let's give him what he wants." I glanced at who I hoped would be my new general.

"But the harp—"

I held up a hand. "You are in charge of coordinating the two teams, Soldier, and I will create the situation that gives them a chance at success."

"I trust your judgement, Queen Kallik." He saluted and turned. Catching sight of Cinth, Rowan stumbled as he strode toward the door. Walking was generally better when both eyes were used. He bounced off the edge of the door frame before hurrying away, red-faced.

I glanced at Cinth. "Could you tone down the brain scrambling until after we win this fight?"

Cinth watched him go, a hand on her ample hip. "I'm not doing anything. Just standing here. You know me. But he has changed, don't you think? I don't remember him being so handsome. Hard to think of anyone who continually pulled your hair as anything good, I suppose."

He'd done that? I couldn't recall. "Guess so. I—"

"I liked what he said just then. That he trusts your judgment. It's not every man that will accept the authority of a woman."

True that. "I trained with him for years."

"Oh yeah. Anything I should know about?"

I blinked. Cinth was asking a ton of questions. Was it the personal tie to Rowan or something more? "Nothing happened between us, if that's what you're asking."

Her lips curved. "Good to know."

When it came to romance, Cinth liked to play with her food. I rolled my eyes. "Take it easy on him, would ya? I'm thinking he may be good to keep around."

Cinth hurried forward and grabbed my hand. "Witching hour is a good six hours away. Come with me."

"I need to prepare—"

"Yes, I know. But you also need this," she said.

Was it a beetroot and cherry tickle? Because I always needed one of those. "This? What?"

She led me through the castle, all the way down to the kitchens. The last time I'd been there I was on the run for my life. This time, though, she drew me through a side door that led to a small storage room and smelled of disuse and old spices. "Sit."

I lifted my eyebrows. "On the floor? A queen does not sit on the floor."

"Get your ass on the ground." Cinth was grinning. "You need love, my friend. And I don't care if you're a queen."

Thank the goddess for that. If only more people felt that way. "What kind of love? I'm not into one-hour flings the way you are—" I tried to push past, but she gave me a good shove, caught my ankle with her toe, and landed me on my ass.

I stared up at her, shocked. "Where the hell did you learn how to do that?"

"My best friend is a kickass fighter, and I've been watching."

Respect.

She pointed at me. "Now just wait here. And close your eyes."

Lugh's left nut, what was she up to? I kept my eyes closed and breathed in the smells, a hint of nutmeg, cardamom, and lava jasmine floating in the air.

The door opened. “No peeking,” Cinth admonished. “Hold out your hands. No, not like that—do it together with your arms, like you were trying to push your boobs up.”

What boobs?

“Cinth, this isn’t the time—” A silky soft fur ball was dropped into my arms. Then another and another. I blinked open my eyes to see a pile of spotted snowcat kittens, their wings not yet budded on their backs, cradled in my arms.

My jaw dropped.

The padding steps of a much larger cat caught my attention.

“Greetings, Queen Kallik.” The mother of the cubs stepped into the room, plunked herself down on the ground next to me, and started to purr.

I smiled at the mother. “Greetings. Your children are beautiful.” The kittens mewed and wrestled over one another to attack the ends of my hair. Their bright blue and green eyes blinked up at me in complete trust.

Oh no.

“Cinth...”

“A pile of kittens is no Faolan, but they’re sweet. And beautiful. And you’re fighting for them too. For all fae creations.” Cinth sat down and laid a hand on the mother, scratching her gently. “Rubezahl won’t be kind to any fae that refuses to believe or act as he wishes.”

“Like the land kelpie that got me and Lan to Underhill,” I said softly. We’d found him chained and contained in the outcasts’ sanctuary. Who knew how long he’d been the giant’s prisoner?

Cinth nodded. “Others too. Like the mystica fae. And how many more that we don’t know about?”

One of the kittens climbed up my front to balance on my shoulder, then tried to nurse on my ear. I laughed and pulled the little monster off. “But kittens, Cinth? Really?”

"It was this or another beetroot tickle, and if I slip you too many more of those you aren't going to fit into your pants anymore." Cinth reached over and gently tugged on the long ends of my hair. "Don't break, Alli. Not under this strain. Don't let the weight of your position take over. You'll survive giving up Lan. I promise."

I wasn't so sure.

I picked up two of the kittens and brought them close to my face. They smelled like snow and tree sap. The pair of them batted at my face with their tiny toe beans.

The female snowcat rolled onto her side and flipped one of her pristine white wings up and over my face, stroking me with the feathers. "Listen to your friend. All hope is not lost, young queen. Not until the last fae heart stops beating, not until magic no longer courses through this world, and Underhill is truly gone from living memory." She tipped her head up, and I swear for a moment she grinned. "I should know. Hope is a thing I have learned a great deal about in my many lifetimes."

I rested a hand on her head. I heard the message behind her words. Life went on. "Thank you. I'll try to remember that."

The kittens wrestled across my lap, nipping and swatting at one another. Free from fear and oblivious to the danger around them waiting to gobble them whole.

Cinth was right. I wasn't just fighting for the fae or the humans. Every creature Underhill had ever birthed was in danger.

My heart still hurt, but this was exactly why I'd drawn a line with Lan. I had to protect these creatures with every part of me. I couldn't let anything, or anyone stand in the way of that.

I looked at Cinth. "I *am* going to stop him."

She smiled. "I know. Just do me a favor and don't die along the way, okay?"

She'd meant the comment lightly, so I returned her smile, but the thing was . . . I was almost certain this wasn't a joking matter. My sister had died trying to accomplish the same task. Had there been others before *her*? Regardless, she'd told me that I was the fae's last hope. If I failed, no one would come after me. And I was pretty sure I knew what it would take. Maybe I'd known from the moment Queen Elisavanna's death had been confirmed by the Oracle. Maybe even before that.

Rubezahl's death would cost me my own life.

CHAPTER 5

"Thanks for the lift," I muttered to the land kelpie who'd accompanied our group from Underhill not so long ago.

He stamped his right foreleg, tossing his icicle mane. "Quiet yourself, imbecile. It's not for you that I came. If I get a shot at that motherfucker, I'm going to shank him right up his oversized asshole."

I grimaced, part of me curious as to how the land kelpie would accomplish a shanking when he had no horn. But I wouldn't put it past the oldest land kelpie in existence to answer my question with a physical demonstration. On me.

When it came to fighting Rubezahl, however, the kelpie could be depended upon as an ally. Actually . . . he'd never let me down despite how he spoke—

"Stop moving your masculine thighs. No wonder you keep failing when you fuck around so much."

Nope, no trying to justify his behavior. Guy was a four-legged dick.

I scanned the camp below. The outcasts were still very much in the set-up phase. Fae of all shapes and sizes raced around at the bottom of the slope I stood at the top of. It didn't take long to locate the huge tent at the center.

I'd voiced my suspicions to Ailbhe before leaving, and she'd confirmed the tent was a decoy.

And yet . . . I'd made a point of publicizing her defection, so Rubezahl would know she'd shared his secrets.

My gaze drifted back to the massive tent at the center, a literal beacon.

Only an idiot would choose such a place to keep out of sight.

Or a genius.

"Dammit. I'm going straight into the guts." Closing my eyes, I opened to my magic and cloaked myself in white lightning. A few experiments had proven it a much easier and more reliable way of cloaking myself than the method favored by Lan and other Unseelie.

I started down the hill, ignoring the hissed "Imbecile" aimed at my back.

Silver puffs and trails in the air alerted me to the presence of pixies bolting and twisting through the remaining wildflowers dotting the long, steady slope I walked upon. The tiniest fae creatures didn't have much magic, but what they lacked there, they made up for in speed. My eyes couldn't track them at all, and if not for the silver trails left by the females and the golden ones left by the males, pixies would make excellent spies.

I'd nearly made it to the bottom when a tiny form bounced off my thigh and emitted a furious squeak. The pixie rolled head over heels across the ground, then sat to rub her head. The moment her expression turned suspicious, I dropped my disguise.

Pixies were quick and highly intelligent.

Her silver eyes widened at the sight of me, and I stood tall. "You may inform Rubezahl that the Queen of All Fae is here and desires an audience."

Squeaking up a storm, she bolted, a horde of other pixies swarming to join her. They disappeared into the camp, and I trailed after them, mentally checking off the various weapons strapped to my body.

I'd spent my life training with them because I'd given up hope that my magic would ever become stronger. And now the lives of so many depended on my mastery of my power and not my swords.

Upon seeing me the outcasts paused in their tasks, but they did not attack.

I continued through the camp as though I had every right to be there, which I did. This was my island now, and they were the invaders.

Eventually the tip of the massive tent came into view, and I paused in a clearing expansive enough that no one could sneak up without me noticing. The first fallen leaves of the season would provide further protection against sneak attacks by cloaked Unseelie.

I pushed indigo magic into my throat and chose my words, trying to sound more like my advisors and less like an inexperienced queen. "Rubezahl, come now. The time has arrived for us to speak of a peaceful way forward for our peoples. You know that I am unlike the rulers before me. I have lived amongst you and the wild fae. I understand your struggles and your wants. We can come to a truce, I am certain, if you will but speak with me. The lives of many depend on your ability to set aside personal prejudices. Will you do it?" *Ha*, not bad. They might've been proud of me for that one.

After waiting a beat, I added, “As a gesture of goodwill, I’ll require you to leave the tool you use to manipulate behind. I’m sure you can fathom why.”

Nothing.

Then.

“An honor,” said a great voice that shook the very ground. “A visit from the so-called queen herself.”

I extended my arms wide, choosing to ignore the shot at my title. “As you see, I am here alone. Will you stand by your message of finding a better life for the children of the moon, old friend? Or will you unnecessarily put fae lives at risk?”

At the fringes of my vision, I noticed some of the outcasts exchanging looks as Ruby’s silence extended. Although the tea influenced those who drank it and compelled them to gloss over certain inconsistencies, doubt could be introduced. The Oracle had done so with me not long ago.

Rubezahl had no choice but to speak with me—unless he wanted to force feed his army to drink gallons of tea to forget the way he’d ignored everything he’d said he wanted when I offered it to him.

The great voice burst through the camp again, and I knew both of the groups I’d sent ahead of me to collect the harp would be listening hard. “I will speak with you, Kallik of No House. I will even grant you the boon of leaving my harp behind.”

Please be listening.

He *always* had Lugh’s harp attached to his belt. Wherever he exited from would be where the harp remained for the duration of our conversation.

The ground shook for another reason all together, and I strained my ears to pinpoint the giant’s approach.

I’d been right.

The giant who’d fooled so many came from the direction of the central tent. And just like the first time I set eyes upon the protector of the outcasts, I took in his long gray beard and age-enlarged knee joints. The layered tunics, the twinkling blue eyes, and the mild expression.

How evil could appear so innocuous was anyone's guess.

I dipped my head when he stopped opposite me in the clearing. "My thanks." *For the boon,* I refrained from adding. My ego could take a few hits if it meant the courts gained possession of the harp.

"Young one," Rubezahl said, also dipping his head.

"Your disrespect makes your true sentiments obvious, friend," I replied. "You claim you're here to negotiate for a better future, are you not?"

His expression didn't change at all, yet the fingers that usually lingered near his harp twitched. "Peace has always been my aim."

I smiled. "I am relieved to hear it. There's a nice slope just beyond the confines of your camp. Shall we walk there to—"

"Here shall suffice."

Damn. "Of course." I glanced at the surrounding outcasts. "First and foremost, I wanted to discuss the special tea you've brewed for your friends and guests over the decades and how it affects them."

This time his nostrils flared. He slowly crossed to me, and one of the sincerest smiles I'd ever received spread on his lips. "On second thought, the wildflowers there looked particularly lovely. Perhaps, for old times' sake, we can sit amongst nature and talk as friends. There is time yet for war tents, hard chairs, and harder conversations."

Funny how he'd changed his mind. Then again, he couldn't allow his people to learn about the tea. I half-turned, and then we walked side by side back the way I'd come.

My heart pounded against my ribs at the thought of the two small forces of Unseelie and Seelie closing in on the central tent. Ruby would have left protections on the harp, but I had to trust in my assassins and their abilities.

"Leadership suits you," the giant murmured as we left the last of the tents behind.

It did? "Leadership is an ill-fitting jacket," I answered. "Maybe I'll find a good tailor in time to make adjustments."

He laughed lightly. "I know the feeling well."

I glanced up at him, but a sliver of my mind remained fixed on my weapons—and how to draw them in the blink of an eye. "And yet you have led the strays for so long. I think perhaps it has grown on you. King of the wild fae, isn't that your title now?"

"What is a leader but someone who sees a problem and eventually succumbs to frustration that nothing is done about it? I am where I am because no one else would take action."

That wasn't my story. "Can't relate."

He stopped and lowered himself to a jutting boulder. I remained standing and faced him, firming my expression.

His lips twitched. "Is this the part where we . . . how do the humans say it . . . cut the crap?"

"Sounds good to me. You're not here for peace."

"No, young one. We are beyond that."

"*You* are beyond that." I pointed out.

He lifted a shoulder. "Perhaps. I am old. My mind is not as flexible as it once was. I admit this."

I gritted my teeth. "The things you've done, Ruby. Why? You could work with me, instead of against me all along."

The giant smiled, displaying the square teeth typical of his kind. "And what of the other suppressors of our kind? You do not represent humans, and you will not take up the outcasts' cause against humans."

"Incorrect," I was swift to say. "I will not represent the outcasts with you whispering in my ear. There is a difference."

"One that renders any negotiations pointless."

I had to keep him talking. "Control means so much to you?" It had cost him the life of the woman he'd loved for so long. Yet there was no trace of any grief or remorse upon his features. It was as if he simply detached himself from the horrific consequences of everything he did. Like he reasoned the death and pain away as a justifiable means to an end. To all appearances, Rubezahl seemed absolutely content with what he'd done and what he was still doing.

He kept smiling, staring at the sea on the opposite side of the camp.

That was obviously the only answer he intended to give, so I pressed him, "The humans. Tell me what your issue is with them. Beyond the obvious." The fae were confined to previously barren areas of land all over the world. Yes, we had riches and freedom within those patches. Yes, we could travel between the courts and, pending approval from human governments to other areas of the world. But none of that changed the fact that we were tolerated guests in a foreign realm despite having roamed this earth for as long or longer than humans. Most fae had a slight prejudice against humans. And, in many cases, the prejudice was far more than *slight.*

"It is different for those who grew up in the courts," the giant deigned to answer. "In the Triangle, my fae encounter humans far more often. Their . . . lack of respect for nature. Their tendency to view us as zoo animals. The *filth* they leave behind." He pressed his lips together. "Their very stench is beyond the pale."

Phew. He hadn't smelled any of the wild fae recently. They took the prize in the smell department. "Their culture is not our own."

His blue eyes lit up, and he met my gaze for the first time. "Exactly. Their culture does not allow for tolerance of *other* cultures. Their herd mentality is like that of bison—they close in at any hint of difference. Before they knew of us, they fought humans from other countries and races. Then we appeared and gave them a common scapegoat. Humans will never accept us.

One, we have something they do not—our magic. Two, their brains simply cannot sustain long-term peace. After a war concludes, they forget the hardships of battle. And it takes more adversity to restore their gratitude for the small things."

I pondered that, then replied with a guess that had been brewing since my time in Underhill, "Is that why you've killed so many humans in the Triangle?"

His smile gained an amused twist. "In the days prior to technology, we managed many deaths without notice. But Alaska has changed as surely as the rest of the world despite being considered the end of it."

"Thirty thousand," I said quietly, my insides quaking at such a number. "So many lives lost."

Rubezahl shook his head. "My children can hardly be blamed for all of them. The Triangle is still a danger for humans who persist in venturing from the path. There are still rivers, freezing conditions, and animal attacks. But we did what we could to even the odds, in anticipation of the day we met them in battle."

He spoke of humans as if they were flies to be swatted away.

And maybe I could agree with human's lack of tolerance for those they perceived as different, but that was where the similarities between me and Rubezahl came to an end.

The urge to glance back at the camp and the sea where my assassins would make their escape was nearly impossible to deny. Just a little longer. "I would never condone the mass murder of humans."

"You will not carve out enough space for our kind if you do not," he said with a bite. "They've infested this land like termites."

I sighed. "It's *their* world, Rubezahl. They don't welcome us, perhaps, but we have our own realm. We just chose to live with a foot in both because of Underhill's unpredictability. Though they distrust us and make things harder for us than is needed, they didn't need to give us parcels of land to live on. They could just as easily have turned their weapons and iron on us instead." They still could. *That* was the greater concern for me—rather than occupying myself with expanding our territory on Earth. I couldn't think of a more idiotic thing to do.

"Indeed?" His tone was off. "Perhaps before the end, I shall tell you what I have seen during my long life. Perhaps we shall meet and discuss this once more."

I gestured to the camp. "There's no time like the present."

He focused on me for the second time. "No, I think not. However, I will say that considering the humans' numbers, they must be dealt with in a subtle manner. That's why we've taken lives here and there over the decades. If we wage fae war here, then they will be on their guard. They will be on the defensive, and a human who fears for their survival is a vicious creature indeed."

It was almost a compliment to their race, although I knew he didn't intend it that way. "You wish to war in secret. In Underhill."

The idea had merit. Regardless of my sentiments, it was my *job* to consider political implications now. If I won a battle on Unimak, I'd still have to clean up a shitstorm with our realm's hosts.

And getting Ruby and the outcasts back into Underhill would give me more time. Time I sorely needed.

"Correct. For that to happen though," he interrupted my train of thought. "I would require my harp."

My head snapped up. *Huh?*

Rubezahl got to his feet, soon towering over me, rage etched in every wrinkle of his weathered face. "Nothing happens in my camp without my notice. Did you expect I would somehow miss the four assassins you sent in to steal my instrument? You fool of a child. Did you never wonder if I had another purpose for being out here with you?"

His eyes flashed black, and I glanced toward camp, stomach clenching at the sight of my four fae on their knees in front of the tents, hoods over their heads.

The outcasts behind them held wicked curved blades, and I sucked in a sharp breath, unprepared as a blade was drawn through the throat of the first of my fae, a Seelie.

"Stop," I ordered.

Rubezahl turned his back on me, walking back toward camp.

As the second outcast lifted his blade, I cast white lightning his way. Ruby batted it aside as if it were a mosquito.

And the second of my assassins, an Unseelie, went gurgling to his end.

The female Seelie was next.

I ran after Rubezahl. "Leave this place and take your army with you. We will meet in Underhill." *Hopefully no time soon.* I'd made a portal once, and I was confident I could make one again, but I needed time to figure out how to battle the giant and win.

His steps rather larger than mine, the giant had approached the remaining Unseelie assassin, who still clutched the golden harp we'd come for.

They'd gotten to it, but I knew it wasn't by their skill. The path had been left open for them. I'd sent the guards to their death, unable to outthink the thief in the garden after all.

My fists clenched as Rubezahl turned, a cruel smirk on his face. "I shall, Kallik of No House. I have what I came for."

He ripped off the hood of the Unseelie, and the very ground beneath my feet might as well have disappeared.

"No." The single despairing word toppled from my numb lips.

Lan looked across the divide at me, dark eyes unfathomable.

My last word rang between us as surely as the harp did when Rubezahl extracted it from Faolan's grip.

"Time to relocate to Underhill once more, don't you think?" the giant said, holding up the harp to the level of his smirk.

Confusion wrapped around my mind before my focus slammed to the harp all over again. *Relocate?* The *harp* was how Rubezahl was moving between realms?

Elisavanna couldn't have known, surely, or she never would have given her life in the belief she was trapping Rubezahl in the fae realm.

The giant strummed a series of notes.

And in a blink, as though they'd never been here at all, the army of outcasts disappeared.

Chapter 6

I stood staring at the empty space where the entire outcast army had been, where Lan had knelt at Rubezahl's feet.

They were gone as if they'd never been there.

Pixies flitted around me in a shower of silver and gold dust, their high-pitched voices gathering in a whirlwind as they likely questioned what I would do now.

But I could barely fathom what had just happened, let alone what should happen next.

"Pull it together." I spun, admonishing myself, and bolted toward the castle.

The pixies tried to keep up with me, but I left them behind as I drew on the power of the earth and fed it through my body, my indigo magic swirling around and through me. I sprinted up the slope as if it were nothing, leaving behind a slipstream of flower petals and windblown grasses. As I ran, anger surged through me, and the power within me shifted, a swath of death roiling from me as my Unseelie side roared to the surface shriveling the hill of beautiful wildflowers in a fierce wave of death.

I didn't even try to check myself. I didn't care that I was killing nature.

Rubezahl had Lan.

Lan was the one he'd come for.

My Lan.

The Lan I'd turned my back on . . .

Shaking my head, I focused on the real question. *Why?*

Rubezahl had wanted Lan dead before now. He'd asked me to kill him, when I was under his influence, although nothing could have influenced me to do *that*. Anger and fear wove through my chest, choking me as I stumbled through the castle gates. The guards let out an alarm, running to help as I dropped to my knees. I didn't care. I just needed answers, and there was one person who potentially had them. "Get Ailbhe. Send her to the war room immediately."

The fae on my left saluted and took off in a clatter of armor. The other—a young pureblood I didn't recognize—offered me his hand.

I shook him off. "Go with him, soldier."

He saluted also and took off at a run. I stayed on my knees a moment, ignoring the looks cast my way.

"Look at this. This is not how a queen behaves." Adair's razor-sharp voice cut through my shock.

I glanced up from my kneeling position to see her glaring down at me.

"Not the time." I growled as I pushed to my feet. I took a step forward, and she held her ground.

So be it.

I kept moving, using my shoulder to knock her out of my way. Not hard. But she threw her hands into the air, screamed, and fell daintily to the ground. Screeching, she rolled around clutching at her belly. "Goddess save me!"

"Adair," I snapped her name, not bothering with titles. "This is not the time for your stupid games." Not queenly, not in the least, but I didn't have time for her bullshit.

"Oh, the baby, let the baby be okay," she cried out, and then lay still on the ground, pretending she'd passed out. Her breathing was too hitched. Her eyelids weren't closed. She was watching me.

And then her words sunk in.

Because I didn't have enough going on . . .

"Baby?" I repeated.

The crowd that had gathered surged, and fae coming forward to help her to her feet. A woman cooed and patted her belly, wiping tears from Adair's face.

I stepped toward her, and she cringed away.

The woman stepped between me and her—as if *I* were the monster. Please.

My jaw ticked, and Adair gave me a sweet smile as she cupped her belly. "I'd only just found out I was pregnant when . . . w-when Aleksandr was killed." She lowered her lashes demurely.

"I didn't know you were pregnant, Adair," I said. "Of course, go to the infirmary. I suggest you stay there for at least the next month. Just to be sure that you are well cared for and have no further accidents."

Her eyes flashed.

The infirmary was outside the castle, to avoid the spread of contagion.

"I can't—" she started.

"I insist." I said softly and bowed from the waist. "I would hate for anything to happen to a sibling of mine."

She had no choice but to take the offer. "Of course."

"Take Josef with you for company maybe," I threw over my shoulder, already hurrying toward the war room.

Kid was probably his anyway.

I had to put Adair and . . . well, whatever game she was playing—because I highly doubted she was actually pregnant—out of my mind. Goddess above and below, though, it would be just my luck to have to add a miserable, pregnant, moody-ass Adair to my list of woes.

Yet I would rather deal with her shit than dwell on what might be happening to Lan.

Lan.

I could see his dark eyes as he stared across the clearing at me, flecks of gem-like color swirling within them.

The way they only did in my presence.

A sob caught in my throat as I rushed up the lobby stairwell. At the top, I leaned against the stone wall to compose myself. I couldn't break down. Not now.

Picking up speed, I took the remaining stairs two and three at a time until I hit the fourth floor.

I flung the war room door open to find Bracken, Cinth, and the Unseelie General Stryk.

"We have a problem of gigantic proportions." I said without preamble, not caring that the pun was horrible. "Rubezahl figured out the ruse, and he killed three of the assassins and took the fourth as prisoner. He took Faolan and the army back to Underhill." I watched General Stryk and caught the slight tightening of his jaw. "You knew Lan was going in."

He nodded. "As the grandson of Lugh, he had the best chance of actually taking the harp without detection. He discussed it with me, and I agreed."

They agreed.

I already carried a strong strain of dislike for the General from when he'd whipped Lan, despite Lan's assurances that he'd agreed with the disciplinary measure. They'd now undermined me by leaving me out of the loop, and since Lan wasn't here for me to yell at, General Stryk was about to feel every ounce of my anger.

I softened my voice, fury rising within like lava from the center of the earth, hot and molten and so *very* deadly. "And neither of you chose to tell me?"

He didn't look away, though a small bead of sweat started at the edge of his hairline. "Would you have allowed him to go in, Your Majesty? I think we both know the answer to that. We did what we believed was best."

I placed my hands flat on the table and leaned into it. "That's *my* choice to make as queen. *Not* yours." Magic swelled from me, deepening in color as the wood below my hands cracked and aged, rotting. "And now, because of your stupidity and his fucking ego, he has become not only bait, but a fucking liability to both courts!"

The general blinked. "He would never turn on you."

"He won't have a choice!" I roared the words. The walls shuddered, and the general paled. My breath came in pants as Unseelie magic rocketed through me in a way I'd never experienced before.

This was power. Raw, dangerous power. My magic swirled harder and darker until it was almost black with the barest hint of indigo to mark it as mine. I lowered my voice, though my rage was far from subsided. "Rubezahl can force-feed him the tea that comes from Ailbhe's blood, you fool. He can turn Lan against us. As the grandson of Lugh, his words carry weight with all the fae."

On cue, the door opened. A bloody and limping Ailbhe entered the room helped by Rowan.

"What happened to her?" I growled.

She winced as Rowan helped her onto a chair. "They found out what I was."

Who? My gaze snapped to Rowan. "Report."

"Two soldiers were beating her when I came upon them. They were shouting about her being a mind reader. I dealt with the soldiers and took the liberty of seeing them to the dungeon to await your decision on their punishment, Your Majesty."

I rubbed my temples. The two soldiers I'd sent took things into their own hands. *Bastards.* "Ailbhe, my sincere apologies. Such treatment will not be tolerated."

Her long, silvery-white hair—stained red in places—was braided into a crown, and her dress was a simple pale pink gown. She lifted her chin. "You speak truth, and I thank you. Tolerance for those who are different is rare to find." She glanced around the room. "But I see that in this room it is not so rare." Her attention landed on Rowan, then Cinth—who was watching Rowan, a slight wrinkle between her brows—then Bracken. Finally, they settled on General Stryk.

"Please, let me send for someone to heal you," I said.

She didn't look away from the general. "My injuries are not severe, and I would rather wait to receive treatment until after this meeting." She blinked. "Forgive my interference on the matter we walked in on, Your Majesty, but the general is loyal to you. For the first time, he sees you as a queen to be reckoned with."

She'd answered the thought buzzing in my mind, but General Stryk glanced at her and, blanching, stumbled away a step as he put his hand to his sword hilt.

"Do. Not. Dare." I growled. Inhaling through my nose, I pulled myself together—slowly and with effort. To my left, Cinth sniffed. "Men can be stupid, Alli. You know this."

Another time I might have laughed it off. I might have winked and agreed. But my heart had started breaking in the throne room earlier, and it had broken a little more when I'd pulled off Lan's hood. I couldn't quite contain the pain inside my body.

Rowan cleared his throat and touched a hand over his heart. "Your Majesty, do you have an order for me to take to the dungeons now, or should I return for one later?"

I pulled my thoughts together with effort. Why? Because by helping Ailbhe, Rowan had just proven himself. He'd taken a couple of challenges in his stride already, and his reports were efficient. And he really had been top of the Tried in strategy. "Soldier, how would you punish them?"

His eyes widened as he snapped his heels together and straightened. "Queen Kallik, I would strip them of their rank and give their families the choice to champion them."

If they'd come from riches, their families may choose to champion them, which pretty much meant paying for their living costs and employing them to carry out family business. "And if the families choose not to champion them?"

"I would reassign them to jobs befitting of their moral caliber."

I smiled. "That is the order you are to give then."

Rowan saluted. "Right away, Queen Kallik."

"*After* you sit in on this meeting."

He frowned. "I'm afraid I don't—"

Walking to stand before him, I said, "I hereby call you to the position of General of the Seelie Army."

Rowan's gaze snapped to mine, a mixture of shock and gratitude shining in them. "General?"

"General." I tilted my head. "Unless. . .you're not up to it?"

His expression firmed. "I will do my absolute best to learn and meet your expectations."

I had a strong feeling he would. But that was all the energy I could expend on this subject for now. I turned back to the table.

Cinth moved closer to me, smiling at Rowan as she did, and her presence helped calm me better than anything else. I had to keep myself from leaning into her for comfort. "Rubezahl took the entire army of outcasts into Underhill, along with Faolan. I imagine that he expects us to meet him there to battle for the right to rule Unimak."

General Stryk cursed. "Does he truly think he can beat us? His ragtag wild fae do not outnumber us."

I forced myself to take hold of my Seelie magic and pull it through the room to put the strategy table back together. I made the four corner posts into four saplings and bound them together into a flat surface. The act of using my seelie magic calmed me slightly.

I rested my hands on it once more. "We have to assume Rubezahl is stronger in Underhill. Otherwise, why would he leave Unimak? It would be foolish to assume he doesn't have the other fae creatures there on his side." My words were met with complete silence.

"Then we'll face them too," General Stryk said softly. "That is how it is done."

He was right. We'd have no option to. But every fae swore an oath to Underhill and to me that included her innocent creatures. I looked at Rowan. "Any thoughts?"

His eyes locked on one of the floating orbs at the periphery of the room. He touched it and brought it forward. "You are certain that we must go into Underhill? There is no drawing him out?"

I dipped my head. "In that regard, I hate that I must agree with the giant. We cannot war where the humans can see. If we add more fuel to their fear, it will put us in a precarious position with them, even more so than we are now."

Rowan frowned at the orb, spinning it down onto the new tabletop. He pressed it downward, magically flattening it until it covered the entire table. A sweep of his fingers turned the tabletop into a map.

I didn't want to appear impressed...but I was. The guy had been on the job for five seconds.

"Underhill, as accurately as it can be portrayed, seeing as it changes on a whim," Rowan said. "This map gives you an idea of the sections in the fae realm. It's old..."

The table was separated into two dozen labeled areas, and showed some of the more permanent dangers, including a few of the creatures. "Dragons to the left, giants to the right," I whispered.

"'And here I am, stuck in the middle with you,'" Cinth whispered back. She put her hand on top of mine, and I took a deep breath.

The group of us stared at the map.

Ailbhe pointed to the northern tip of Underhill, tapping it with her finger and zooming in the image. "This is where I think he will wait for you. It is one of the few areas of Underhill that is unchanging. Dragonsmount."

I stared at the deep valley. Only one way in and out. The mountain was shaped like a dragon's head reaching for the sky above. A perfect place to make your last stand or set a trap.

"I could make my tickles and fill them with a sleeping draught." Cinth offered. "None of the wild fae would turn them down."

Rowan eyes glowed as he looked at her. "I hear that no one turns your food down, Hyacinth."

"Just Cinth, please. And how about you come find me to sample a few things?" She blushed, and my jaw almost clanked to the floor. Cinth never blushed. And what kind of samples was she offering up?

Only a matter of hours had passed since she first made gooey eyes back at him. That had to be a record. And to my knowledge they hadn't interacted since the orphanage days.

I stared at the map, Dragonsmount rearing its ugly head in front of me. Lan was being kept there, and I had to find him. Sooner rather than later. Maybe we could never be together, but I couldn't live in a world where he wasn't at least breathing the same air as me.

I turned from the table and let them strategize.

Ailbhe made her way to my side. "You love him."

No point denying it. "Yeah."

"There won't be another like him for your heart," she told me. "I don't need mind reading for that. I can see it clear as day."

"You aren't really helping." I wiped a hand over my face.

She sighed. "Sometimes . . . we have to give up everything to get everything."

I peered into her eyes. "What are you saying?" The Oracle had pretty much filled my lifetime quota for cryptic comments

Ailbhe shrugged. "Just something my mother used to say."

I thought about facing Rubezahl.

I thought about what it would cost. Probably my life.

Our confrontation was coming, and if it went the way I thought it would, I'd have to say goodbye to Lan anyway.

"Your Majesty," Rowan interrupted my rather morbid thoughts, "I think . . . I have an idea that could work. Based on what Hyacinth suggested."

I walked back over to the table as General Stryk shifted his focus to Rowan. "What are you thinking, boy?"

Kudos to Rowan, he didn't take the bait.

Rowan swept his hand over the map. "The winds sweep over Underhill from southwest to northeast. If we can come in here," he plonked his finger down on the southwest corner, "and release a sleeping draught in the wind using the pixies, then use a little air flow to push it along, we may be able to give ourselves an edge. It would sweep through the valley, and a lot of the creatures would pass out. Of course. it will just piss off the stronger ones, so there would be a downside." He fidgeted under my heavy regard. "Perhaps there's no way to know which creatures it will take—"

I pursed my lips. "How long would it take to make enough draught?"

"Around a week." Ailbhe said. "A few days less if the Unseelie poisoners help."

A week. I didn't want to wait a single *day*. But the odds of me opening a portal between the realms before fall solstice in several months without Lan was next to none. I needed time to figure out how to hell to get the court armies to Underhill without killing myself in the doing.

If only we'd managed to secure the damn harp, then Rubezahl would still be here on Unimak. Lan would be too. We could be fighting to get Lan back *right now*. I curled my hands to fists, resisting the urge to rub my temples in the present company.

"Queen Kallik," Ailbhe murmured. "I was unaware that the harp had this ability."

She was? At least I wasn't the only one.

"It brings something to mind," she said. "Do you ever recall being in one place with Rubezahl then quite suddenly in another?"

A wrinkle formed between my brows as I looked at her. A memory surged to the forefront of my mind.

Bowl of too-hot stew in hand, I made my way to sit next to Rubezahl.

He glanced down as he smoked his pipe. "Young one, I can tell you wish to speak with me. Please, be at ease." He waved his hand, and I gaped as the wilderness disappeared, replaced by the interior of his office.

"An illusion?" I sat on the bench across from him. Felt pretty real to me, but then again, so did Underhill for eight years.

"Yes and no." He smiled. "But this will give us privacy. None will hear us speak."

It hadn't been an illusion at all. He'd really moved us back to his office.

She nodded, hearing the memory as I had it. "He has always, to my knowledge, been able to transport small numbers of fae."

Small numbers.

She was right. If he'd been able to move his army, then he would have—to attack the courts on Unimak—but instead he'd marched through the Triangle to get here. "But he moved the outcast army and Lan to Underhill today."

"He did," she said. "Which might help to decode something else I overheard in his thoughts recently. He was laughing that Underhill was too lazy to fix the damage after Elisavanna's move."

"Elisavanna's move to force a portal between realms?" I said. Then immediately followed it with, "She damaged the barrier." My eyes rounded. "She weakened it." If that was true, then I would likely be able to transport more people. And possibly open a portal without the help of a solstice or Lan.

I'd need to test the theory, but there was little point taking my army to Underhill without a strategy to defeat the oversized bastard.

I dipped my head in the mystica fae's direction, allowing her to read my silent appreciation, then looked to General Stryk. "The poisoners?"

His eyes darted between me and Ailbhe. "Queen Elisavanna kept a team of them on hand. They can be at your beck and call in a matter of hours." He bowed from the waist. "I must say this is a dangerous plan, Your Majesty. A single shift in the wind, magical or otherwise, and that same draught will wipe out our army. Underhill is ever unpredictable"

Didn't I fucking know it.

I hummed, then glanced up. "Perhaps we can turn to the humans for help."

Several sets of eyebrows climbed, and I smiled without a speck of humor. "Bracken, get me a phone. I need to make a call."

"To *humans*?" General Stryk said incredulously.

Well, kind of. "To supernaturals, actually. *And* humans." *And fae.* Maybe I shouldn't have complained so much about all the political calls since I took up the throne. Those calls were how I knew about a war that had ended just a few weeks ago. "I need to talk to a werewolf in Deception Valley."

I knelt in front of a grave. I'd felt drawn to the human side of Unimak, and although I'd told myself I was going there to practice my magic in a safe setting, deep down I'd known the truth. I'd come to see her grave.

But why? There were better places to get answers.

The last time I'd knelt here, I'd wept. Back then, I'd believed this to be my mother's burial site. Now I knew the truth—she may have carried me in her womb, but she was not my biological mother.

Encouraged by summer, weeds covered the space below the inuksuk, but I possessed none of the usual urge to pluck them from the ground.

She'd lied to me as surely as the rest of them.

Maybe that wasn't fair. I mean, who knew what she might have divulged had she not died when I was five. And yet . . . she'd chased away the nightmares and kissed the bruises on my knees. I'd believed every word she'd ever told me. Remembered it. Revered it.

The betrayal . . . the loss . . . was a dagger in my heart.

"Did I ever know you?" I asked the ground, cold in the weak heat of dawn. No one answered, of course. Despite my earlier sentiment, I cleared away the weeds before standing.

There was much to do in the week it would take to ready the sleeping draught for our initial attack on Rubezahl's army. The worst of it was that I didn't know if Lan was still alive. And since there was a time differential between Earth and Underhill, Rubezahl would have exponentially longer than we did to prepare for our confrontation. Time was too short, because even if I did manage to get that damn harp from Ruby, I still didn't know whether I was strong enough to destroy him. Then there was the issue of getting my army there in the first place.

I really hoped Ailbhe was right. Because if not, then I was fresh out of ideas on how to open a portal without waiting for the fall solstice.

Inhaling, I opened myself to the magical forces that had deigned to use me as their conduit. Submission to the magic was key. That was what transformed the indigo to formidable white lightning. Something no one else could match.

In theory.

Visualizing two translucent layers sliding against each other like the membranes of dragon wings, I then imagined the barrier between them dissolving away until they were one.

Lightning danced between my fingertips, akin to a coin in a thief's nimble hand.

I let the power build as I'd done before.

Build.

Build.

But not as much as when I'd opened one from Underhill to Unimak. I had to hold this long enough for far more people to pass through. I released the lightning I'd summoned, holding on to the image of those fused layers in my mind's eye, and was rewarded when a portal—far smaller than my last—yawned before me.

Large enough for fae to march through three astride, though the taller ones would need to duck.

I held the portal until my body began to shake. Until the lightning began to burn me from within. At least that's how it felt.

Cutting off the magic, I dropped to one knee, breathing hard, and the opening between the realms disappeared.

I checked the position of the sun. I'd been able to maintain the portal for longer. Far better than the first time, but we had thousands of fae to transport, and I was exhausted from today's effort after a measly ten minutes. If Rubezahl chose to attack the moment I entered Underhill, then we were screwed.

How the hell did this all land on me again?

Shoving to my feet, I drew from the earth underfoot to replenish my body. There was only so much that could be done to counter *magical* fatigue, however, which was a massive part of the problem. Rubezahl had lived for centuries, flexing his magical muscles all the while, growing stronger and stronger, while I'd only just unlocked the secret to my magic.

I settled into a run back to the courts, although it took time for my strides to lengthen and for me to find the inherent easiness I'd always experienced when running.

I had to see the Oracle when I entered Underhill again.

And the blooded fae, Devon—the fae realm's mouthpiece.

Maybe they'd be more open with me now that I knew the truth about Rubezahl. Now that I was queen.

Running alongside the dividing river, I soon reached the bridge where Adair had first tried, via her guard, to drown me.

Where Lan had saved me.

A lump rose in my throat. What fate had befallen him in the last three days? If only I could have stepped through the portal I'd just made and gone AWOL to find him again . . .

Instead, I was stuck on Unimak receiving damn letters from Adair about her pregnancy. She'd sent a confirmation from the infirmary that she was indeed knocked up. The soul signature of the growing baby in her womb was consistent with my father's magic.

Looked like I'd have a sibling in another six months.

At this rate, I'd probably never meet the child, not that I wanted to if the baby took after Adair.

And that enormous list of things to do just reminded me that I had to loop General Stryk into my plan. May as well stop there and show my face to the other half of my people while I got the chance.

Crossing the bridge, I wound through the dark and thorny brambles of the Unseelie territory. It didn't inspire wariness today. Rather, the surroundings reflected my dark mood and gave me a kind of forlorn comfort.

I slowed to a walk after striding through the gates, ignoring the side-long looks of the Unseelie up early enough to catch a glimpse of me.

"Open the gates for the queen," the guards called ahead.

I didn't break stride as I slipped inside the courtyard and proceeded to enter the castle.

A male servant scurried to the left, a bucket of water in his arms.

"You," I barked.

The Unseelie blanched but skidded to a halt, water sloshing. "Your Majesty!"

That's me. "Send word for General Stryk to attend me." There, that sounded haughty enough.

The Unseelie appeared appropriately awed by it. "Yes, ma'am. Where you want him then, please?"

I deciphered his strange way of speaking, then said, "Show me to Queen Elisavanna's personal chambers and then collect the general. He will attend me there."

The servant bowed, sloshing more water onto the floor. He didn't pay it a second glance as he moved ahead, leading me deeper into the Unseelie palace.

In comparison to the expansive, golden halls of the Seelie castle, this place was broody and foreboding. Candlelit and full of shadows, the air redolent with a hint of musty moisture that seemed a purposeful reminder of the existence of dungeons.

Maybe Adair's supporters could do with a little tour through this court. Might do them good.

"This you moving in then, ma'am?" the man panted over his shoulder.

"Why do you ask?" I responded vaguely.

"Ain't nice to play second flute to the Seelie is all."

My brows climbed. Is that what the Unseelie thought? That I'd chosen the other court over them? "I have no immediate plans to relocate here. The combining of the two courts requires some planning and—"

"*Combining* the courts?" he said, aghast. "That's a surely shit idea." The servant shot me a wide-eyed look. "I mean, uh . . . f-forgive me, Your Majesty. Don't blast me with your lightning magic like you did them giants."

I sighed. "I won't. But rest assured, everything I do will be with the good of all fae in mind. I am, after all, queen of *all* fae. Not just half. The Unseelie will never be forgotten."

And I felt a hell of a lot more at home here than I had upon waking in the Seelie castle this morning.

I scaled two flights of stairs after the servant before, out of breath, he gestured to the rooms. "Right in there, ma'am. Dead queen's bed and all."

His description made me grimace, but I concealed it. "Thank you. The general. With haste, if you please."

If you please. Snort. Did I sound ridiculous to him, or just to my own ears?

Without waiting for an answer, I entered the chamber, immediately noting that not a speck of dust rested upon a single surface. It confirmed what I knew—most Unseelie wouldn't take kindly to me being in their beloved queen's personal space.

Which meant I should hurry.

Leaving the four-poster canopied bed, I beelined for the elegant dark wood desk against the far wall. Papers were stacked neatly in the drawers, along with a few letters, which I shoved under my belted tunic to devour later. I was queen now, and I needed all the help I could get. Plus, if they remained here, then there was a risk someone *else* would take them.

Nothing else seemed wildly important—an array of quills and ink pots and a few different wax seals. Something glinted in the back of the drawer, and I reached for it, yelping when something pricked my finger.

Scowling, I snatched the thing out and stared at it.

A straight rod ran through small columns, and I'd pricked my finger on a sharp, pointed bit. In all honesty, this looked like one of the small puzzle games given to toddlers. I remembered being envious of the children playing with them but had never personally had one.

"Why keep such a thing in your top desk drawer?"

A knock sounded at the door, and I quickly pocketed the small puzzle toy bumping the drawer with my hip to close it. Moving to the center of the chamber, I called, "Enter."

General Stryk seemed alert despite the hour. "Your Majesty." He scanned the room. "An unusual meeting place."

"Is it?" I said vaguely. "You heard the news?"

"The werewolves in Deception Valley have something for us?"

Well, not the werewolves as such—wait, I had to remember that they called themselves *Luthers*. The tribe they'd just warred against and now had a truce with had something for us though. "Yes, gas masks. One thousand of them. We managed to import a prototype yesterday. The poisoners here have found the masks to be effective. We won't have enough for our entire army. But the front lines will have protection."

He nodded. "It's good to have friends in different corners."

Friends . . .

The woman I'd spoken with, a werewolf named Andie Thana who was also a representative of the tribe, had been ruthless in her negotiations despite being sympathetic to our cause given her own recent predicament. Let's just say it was a lucky thing the courts were filthy rich, and Thana was obviously happy to take advantage of that fact. "I need you to run a few maneuvers with the Unseelie army."

"Such as?" the general asked, standing at ease.

"Standing in rows three astride and sprinting through a space just large enough to accommodate them as fast as they possibly can."

The general blinked twice. "And this is to accomplish what exactly?"

"I can open portals between this realm and the fae realm," I announced.

He blinked another two times. "I see."

"But I can only hold them open for so long. I'm sure you can see the obvious disadvantages should only a small portion of my combined army make it through."

The general's expression tightened. "Easy pickings."

"Exactly. I will be directing the Seelie army to do the same training."

He bowed. "Is it likely that we'll all get through?"

"No. And we must prepare for that separately. I will expect you at the war chamber in the Seelie castle five hours from now to strategize on that count."

"Yes, Your Majesty."

My display of Unseelie power the other day had seemingly convinced the general of my worthiness. The fae glanced around the chamber. "The queen never spent much time here. She wasn't prone to sleeping for more than a few hours each night. But she did spend a lot of time in her study on the third level." The general displayed a broken tooth with his smile. "Just a thought if you're considering another dawn visit."

My lips twitched. "I'll take it under advisement."

The general left, and after another cursory and curious sweep of the chamber, I did the same.

The room had told me nothing about my biological mother. I only knew her as a mysterious figure, powerful and intelligent beyond the norm.

She'd given her life to save me from Rubezahl.

Through Lan, she'd guided me, and out of the three figures who'd conspired to bring me into this world, she was the one I found it easiest to forgive. She'd tried, in the end. The swords, the protector, and the information.

Perhaps that didn't forgive a childhood of absence.

When I reached the river bridge again, I drew out the puzzle game I'd taken from her desk. I couldn't make sense of the curves, which were thick in some places and thin in others. The children I used to watch had used their magic to somehow figure out the puzzle. I recalled that much.

I opened my magical sight and sucked in a breath at the sight of the interwoven bands of Unseelie and Seelie power wrapping around and through the small trinket.

"Like me," I whispered. It wasn't the white lightning, but it was clearly a mix of both fae essences.

And I'd found it in her desk drawer.

It had to mean something. Had she intended this for me to find? Was she helping me from the grave?

I pocketed the toy and ran on, not slowing to a walk until the castle was near.

An airy voice floated to me as soon as I did, making my skin crawl and my ire rise.

"Queen Kallik, a moment of your time."

Fuck my life. I glared at the infirmary sign overhead, cursing myself for not having taken the street behind to avoid any chance of seeing my stepmother.

Because of course Adair was up at the butt crack of dawn too. I forced a smile. "Adair, how nice to see you looking well."

Her gaze narrowed, but she seemed to collect herself—for once—and slowly exhaled. "You received my message?"

"Which one? There were several."

"The one confirming the pregnancy and the identity of the father."

I pretended to think, and she lowered her gaze. For the first time, the practiced gesture almost convinced me. "I know what you think of me."

I resumed walking, and she fell into step beside me. "And what's that?"

"That I'm willing to sleep my way to the top."

That was pretty much spot on. "I find it hard to think much of a person who has treated me the way you always have. I would be dead right now if not for other people saving me from your . . . kindness. And my spirit would be crushed if not for those near and dear to me." *And myself.*

She pressed her lips together. "It is not easy to believe you are about to embark on a romantic journey with your new husband, only to discover he has a child."

I glanced at her. "That evening at the solstice?"

That was the night my father's magic had wrapped around my hands. It had *known* me. Now, I knew the phenomenon was a regular occurrence for fae parents and their children. Back then . . .

"Yes," she said quietly.

A tiny wisp of empathy rose within me. I quashed it. "And you chose to stamp on the child instead of the one who deserved it."

"A *king*," she defended herself. "Aleksandr was many things, and I loved him in my way, but he was not a man to argue with."

"Did he hurt you?" I shot her a quick look.

"I know when I meet a person whom I cannot outsmart," she declared without anger. "It does not happen often, but Aleksandr was such a person." Adair glowered at me. "And you are proving to be a pain in a similar way."

Was that an almost compliment? "You have until I reach the castle gates to get out whatever you want to say. I have bigger things to focus on than your pregnancy and continued access to nice things."

Adair picked up her skirts to keep up with me. "You think that I killed Aleksandr. The rumor is spreading through the Seelie court."

A laugh burst from my lips. "And let me guess . . . your reputation is suffering. Adair, you spent the last several months spreading that rumor about *me*. Something you knew couldn't possibly be true since I was standing right beside him. And if you thought I was in with the outcasts, the fact that I'm currently at war with them tosses that notion into the trash."

Pink tinged her cheeks. "I did not kill my husband."

"So you say. And yet you've been after the throne ever since."

She gripped my arm, breathing hard. "*Why* would I do it? My monthlies hadn't shown. I was pregnant—finally—at *last*. With the knowledge of your existence buried, *my* child was to sit upon the throne one day. The second that arrow pierced Aleksandr's throat, that future was obsolete."

I'd say a little before that actually—when he announced I was his heir. But whatever. "You expect me to believe you?"

"I think your hatred of me—" she swallowed, "—which I did much to deserve, I admit, won't allow you to believe me."

And yet . . . I found myself doing just that. And she didn't have to know that. "Do you know what all the bullshit you pulled during my childhood taught me, Adair?"

Her expression was guarded.

I gripped her wrist tightly and squeezed until she was forced to release her hold on my arm. A whimper escaped her lips. "It doesn't matter what others think of you. It only matters what you think of yourself. Only the weak can be formed and torn down by the words and actions of others." I tilted my chin. "I am worthy to be where I am. My failures and the things you put me through have only made me stronger. I stand by who I am." I released her wrist. "Can you say the same?"

My insides quaked as I finally gave voice to the words I'd longed to say to her for so long. All my hurt was contained within them, and now they were out.

What was more . . .

I damn-well believed it.

Done with her, I continued toward the castle, only pausing at her soft call.

"I will never stop doing what is best for my child."

Given my past, that was the first comment out of her mouth that I could actually respect . . . no matter what it boded for me.

CHAPTER 8

I stood in the assigned room, unable to sleep, my thoughts consumed with Lan as I stared at the balcony of the Unseelie castle...right where he'd stood on the night before I told him that we were done.

He'd gone and put himself on a suicide mission in response.

My legs shook and here, in the privacy of my room, I let myself buckle. I let my knees smack the marble as I clung to the balcony railing for support.

General Stryk had claimed that Lan should be the one to grab the harp off Rubezahl seeing as the harp had been created by Lan's grandfather, but I knew that wasn't the only reason he'd gone.

I'd pushed him away, and now . . . I'd lost him.

My hands numbed on the copper railing, palms tingling as I tried to let out the pain. But it clung to me. No matter how I looked at it, he was in danger because of me. Assuming Rubezahl didn't just kill him outright—which he might do just to break me—then at the very least the giant would use Lan to control me.

In a strong moment, I'd decided to put the courts before my feelings for Lan.

I wasn't strong anymore.

A moan slipped past my lips.

Eyes closed, I struggled to breathe through the tightness in my chest, not sure I could do what was needed to save so many lives. Because I was struggling to care about anything but Lan. And that didn't bode well.

A soft hand pressed against my low back, and Hyacinth's voice wrapped around me. "Breathe, Alli."

A sob tangled in my chest. "Cinth. It's my fault."

She snorted. "He's an idiot who was trying to prove himself to the girl he loves. Men are dumb like that. Trust me."

When it came to men, I did. Her tone caught my ear though. "Did something happen?"

Her lips twitched. "Rowan just tried to give me a bouquet of flowers when he came to try my cooking. Half of them were poisonous. He was mortified, and I think his apology was sweeter than the thought of bringing me flowers—so maybe *he* isn't an idiot, but don't get me started on all the stories of guys doing crazy things for me over the years."

A wet laugh left my lips even as my heart squeezed. I *wished* that was all Lan had done. I couldn't help but feel my comment to him about not meeting on the balconies every evening may have spurred him to such measures.

Gently, she helped me to my feet.

I blinked up at her through the tears gathered behind my dark lashes. Her smile was as soft as her hands as she brushed the tears away. "Let's get you into bed. You need to sleep more than anything else. Okay?"

"I should be helping the generals train the guard. I should practice opening the portal—"

"Shush." She clamped a hand over my mouth. "Strip, and into bed with you. You can't do anything if you're asleep on your feet, and you know it." And just like when we were younger and she seemed so much older and wiser, she helped me undress and brushed my hair, braiding it.

Afterward, she released tendrils of her magic toward a cup, and soon it was steaming. "Drink."

A waft of steam slid up my nose, and I looked over at her sitting beside me. "You trying to poison me with those flowers Rowan gave you? It smells like chocolate, but there's a sharp undertone."

"You and your nose." She tapped the rim of the cup. "Something I've been working on since we were in Underhill. Devon thought you might need it at some point."

"That doesn't actually make me feel better," I muttered, but dutifully took a sip of the hot chocolate. The coffee tones melted across my mouth, coating it in a pleasant way despite the slight bitterness. Another sip and my muscles began to unwind from a deep-rooted tension that hadn't left me for the longest time—maybe ever.

It was enough for me to admit a truth I hadn't wanted to admit since this all began. I was scared. While I'd begun to believe in myself for the first time, I was fucking terrified. Thousands of lives depended on me, and the higher I climbed, the farther there was to fall.

"Drink the whole damn cup," Cinth ordered, her tone soft even though the words were firm. "It'll help you sleep and replenish your magical reserves."

It would? Count me in.

I lifted the cup to my lips and tipped it back, downing the concoction like a beer bomb. Eyes still closed, I handed her the cup. She took it, shoved me under the covers, and tucked them to my chin.

My eyelids already felt heavy, but I managed to open them a sliver. My heart stuttered at the sight of Ailbhe looked down at me.

"You'll thank me later," she said.

There was no fighting the drink I'd gulped down, no fighting the sleep that rolled over me and dragged me deep under its spell, but my mind was wide awake even as I fell into dreamland.

One blink and I stood in the middle of what appeared to be a field of sparkling bubbles. They spread out around me in a mist so thick I could see nothing else. I looked down at my hands and wiggled my fingers.

At least I could see myself. "Hello?"

I swayed and the bubbles around me whooshed and bumped into one another, the sound like the tinkling of high-pitched bells. They didn't pop as I ran fingers through them, instead bouncing away from my touch with more tinkling.

Where the hell was I?

Or, more importantly, what did Ailbhe do to me? I'd been so sure I could trust her. I'd been a fool to believe in one of Rubezahl's castaways.

I took one step, then another, and another. There was no sense of danger -no eyes watching me from the strangely lit bubble mist. Unless Ailbhe's plan was to keep me here indefinitely . . . in which case I was royally—no pun intended—screwed. Because her powers of the mind went far beyond anything I was capable of.

My gut clenched at that thought. As if in response, the sparkling bubbles around us darkened.

"Only one thing to do," I whispered to myself.

I stepped out, looking for a clue. Something. *Anything* that would lead me—

My body stilled, reacting to a sound on the edge of my hearing. There it came again, the barest breath of air, like someone sighing.

I turned right and shuffled forward, grateful that my feet were at least quiet, and there was no scuttling of stones or crunching of grass.

The bubbles thickened, sticking together, and I had to push harder to get through them, but there was something—or more accurately some*one*—on the other side of this sudden wall.

Pushing a hand between orbs, which had surprisingly thick shells, I reached blindly. Who would be beyond them?

My mother?

Devon?

I'd even take my sibling spirit guide.

"Please don't be Adair," I muttered.

"Gods," *he* growled, "If I turn into her, just kill me."

That voice...

I clamped down on a strong wrist and bent my legs, pulling for all I was worth. Because if there was any chance at all this moment was real, I was making the most of it.

Lan's hand came through the shimmering wall first, then his chest and face. Eventually, his gloriously naked body was revealed.

"Holy shit," I swallowed hard, "you know how to make an entrance." The words popped out of me, and then I was crying as I threw myself at him.

For half a second, I thought he wouldn't touch me back, but then his arms wrapped around my body. Tight. Familiar. So necessary.

"Orphan," he said in wonder. "I don't know how you're here —"

"Shut up." I grabbed his face and kissed him. I molded against his body, a body I knew. A body that had filled my dreams, only not like this. My hands swept the ridged planes of his torso and chest. It didn't matter how I was here, or even that this might only be some sort of a drug-induced hallucination. Lan was with me.

For this blip in time, all was right in my world.

A low growl slipped from his mouth, reverberating through me, setting off fireworks in my belly.

He slid his hands under the edge of my shirt, brushing against my ribs, belly, and lower back before he slid them upward and yanked off my shirt.

"I *am* dreaming," he spoke against my mouth. "I know you, Orphan. You'd never give yourself over to me, not like this. You chose a hero's path, the right path. But I don't care. I'll take you however you're offered to me. Because I fucking need you."

I blinked up at him, realizing that most of my clothes had been removed. I couldn't recall if his hands had done the honors or mine, or some sort of magic had made them dissolve because...weirdly...I didn't see them anywhere.

A naked dreamland with Lan? I could get behind that.

I cupped his face and stared into those dark rainbow eyes that had always, *always* undone me. I didn't want to live without them. Even if following the hero's path would mean doing exactly that.

"Is this real?" I asked in a hushed tone.

One of his hands slid into my hair and tangled in the long strands. "I don't care."

He rained hot kisses over my face, working his way down to my lips and then lower, nipping along my neck before brushing soft kisses across my collarbone.

His touch made it nearly impossible to think, to wonder if this was more than just a very, very good dream.

The best of dreams.

I sucked in a breath, choking slightly on a moan. "More."

His mouth was weaving its own kind of magic as he left a trail of heat over every inch of my body, leisurely moving toward the apex of my thighs. Too leisurely. As if he had all the time in the world.

His hands were at my hips, fingers sliding across my ass as he followed my curves. If this was just a dream, I could enjoy this fully, then I could let my mind go.

I could await the delicious moment his mouth moved to where I *really* wanted it.

But . . .what if Ailbhe had intentionally sent me here and this wasn't a private dream? What if we were being watched? Almost as if I'd called her, the mystica fae's voice rippled through the air.

You only have so much time with him before I must pull you back. Find out all you can about Rubezahl's camp.

For fucking *real?*

I groaned, and Lan chuckled, misinterpreting the noise.

"Where does Rubezahl have you camped?" I asked, though it was hard to speak through the sensations rocketing through my lower stomach. I had to pull my shit together, yet every touch of Lan's mouth and hands against my bare skin had my mind flying apart.

"Hmm?" He nipped at my inner thigh, and my knees buckled.

Lan gripped my thighs as he slowly lifted me until I was pressed against his face. One swipe of his tongue against my center wiped my mind blank. The bubbles around me shivered, bursting with fireworks as they reacted to my emotions.

His tongue moved upward again, firm and slow.

I choked, and as he retreated in preparation for another onslaught, my thoughts broke through the sensations. "Where are you, Lan?"

"Bound and blindfolded," he whispered, rubbing his face against my leg, as if marking me. "The giant will use me against you, Orphan. I can't let him do that. So I'll say goodbye now."

My eyes widened. *No.*

He pulled me down under him, pressing his body into mine.

Once more, I cupped his face. “Lan, I am really here. I need you to tell me where you are. I need you to help me find you.”

His smile was soft and so very, very sad.

I’d move entire realms to see that sadness replaced with joy.

“I can’t do that, Orphan. I love you too much to let him use me against you.”

I shook my head, but his body was already beginning to fade. “Lan! No, not yet!”

He was gone before I took my next breath. Scrambling to my feet, I spun in a complete circle, listening for another sigh or a moan, or *anything* that would lead me back to him.

“Faolan.” Not a shout, not even a whisper. More like a prayer. “Lugh, if you have any love for your grandson, let me find him. He can’t . . . I can’t lose him. Not even to do what I must.”

The air in this strange space suddenly charged with electricity. The floating bubbles popped in a pattern, one by one, creating a gap for a figure to approach.

Ghostly.

Male.

I swallowed hard. Kallik of No House might have dropped to her knees in pure shock. But not this Kallik. No, this Kallik was the queen of all fae.

As naked as the day I was born, I stood as the infamous Lugh approached me. Also naked.

It was just a naked kind of evening.

His smile was very much like his grandson’s, but the resemblance ended there. Where Faolan was dark, his grandfather was light. Blond hair, pale silver eyes, and pale skin. Leaner than Faolan too.

“It is not so simple as finding him, Queen of All Fae. He is on the verge of death. The torture he faces is . . .” Lugh’s eyes fluttered as if he felt the pain too. “Terrible. As it always is. Tell me, why shouldn’t I let him die and find peace?”

My heart cracked at his words. Lan was being tortured? "You can stop it."

"I cannot." Lugh sighed. "I have no more power in the fae world. Let him die. If you love him, then you would not ask him to suffer more for you."

His words crushed my heart to a powder. "I saw him here. He seemed well."

"This is a place of death." He swept his hand outward. "Or, more accurately, a place between life and death."

My legs folded. That couldn't be. No. I'd just seen him, and . . . "Please—"

"He is my grandson, but that means little to those around him," Lugh said. "Pity, the boy has more of my ability and heart than my own child."

"Then save him!" I yelled, forgetting myself.

Lugh arched a pale brow. "You would make a demand of me?"

"I would beg," I said brokenly.

"They believe him to be dying." He tipped his head. "I suppose, seeing as I do remember what love feels like, and yours is a love that rarely comes to this world. . . ," His face softened. "I can hold his soul from death. But you need to hurry. You will have to forfeit much of your planning. The training of your armies too."

I was on my feet in an instant. "We leave tonight."

My fingers began to fade, and Ailbhe's voice screeched into my consciousness.

"I'm trying to help her! Trust me, Cinth, I am trying to help her!"

"You stole my clothes and impersonated me, you bitch! Is that why you asked me how things went with Rowan? What did you do to her?"

A hand descended onto my translucent shoulder, pulling me back, but Lugh spoke my name. "The object from Elisavanna's desk. Take it with you when you open the portal to Underhill."

I nodded. I'd planned to after seeing the trinket was infused with Seelie and Unseelie magic. Oh what I wouldn't give for a few hours to figure it out. "Thank you."

Lugh removed his hand from my shoulder and faded, but his voice echoed after me. "I can keep him alive for one day only. You must hurry, Queen of All Fae."

Another blink.

I jerked upright, gasping. Cinth had Ailbhe in a head lock and had wrestled her to the ground. The mystica fae's screams rent the air as the door burst open, and Rowan and Bracken raced inside, their weapons drawn.

"Enough," I yelled.

Cinth let go of Ailbhe, dusted herself off, and stood. Her cheeks were tinged pink with exertion.

Ailbhe was much slower to get to her feet, her pale face already blooming with bruises.

Don't ever mess with a cook.

"I'm sorry," she blurted, flustered for the first time in our acquaintance. "I didn't think you'd willingly drink anything I gave you, so I had to pretend. I knew Rubezahl would be doing terrible things to Lan. He believes that without Faolan, you'll be vulnerable and weak. You had to feel how urgent this was. You're letting everyone else delay your departure."

"Bullshit," Bracken growled.

I swung my legs out of bed. "Ailbhe, if you'd told me there was a way for me to contact Lan, I would have leaped at the chance. Whatever your intentions, tricking me was a mistake." To the others I said, "But she wasn't wrong. Lan doesn't have long."

For all that was holy in this world, we had to go and go *now* if we wanted to save him. "He's going to die unless we take action. Gather the troops. We leave in an hour."

"I need quiet," I murmured to Rowan and General Stryk, who was still simmering in silent fury that we were abandoning careful preparations to save a single person, even if that person was Lugh's grandson and the Unseelie regent.

Whatever. After seeing Lan, I didn't give a fuck what anyone thought.

Closing my eyes, I listened as they hurried away to spread order—and silence—in the three-astride army waiting to sprint through the portal that I may not be able to keep open for long enough.

But if it was incentive I needed, I had it: we had a single day to save Lan's life.

Inhaling, I opened my eyes briefly to consult the Underhill map one last time. Our plan to open multiple portals and drop sections of our army in different locations was officially void. We were going straight to what I believed would be the safest and most strategically sound position.

"As soon as it's large enough, they need to go," I said for the umpteenth time.

Then, submitting to the power, I let it build to the level I'd achieved a few days prior and released it without preamble.

Stampede. A ground-shaking number of fae streamed past, but beyond checking on the size of the portal I'd created to the fae realm, I focused on keeping my breath steady, my heart rate slow, and my thoughts fixed on my goal. On saving the man I loved.

My white lightning covered hands began to tremble.

My legs steadily weakened until I simply gave in and folded to the ground, still maintaining the portal by the skin of a red cap's fangs.

The ground vibrated, and soon my vision seemed to do the same, blurring and wavering.

I held fast to my last encounter with Lan. The sadness in his eyes as he said goodbye in my throne room. He'd expected to never see me again, but I wouldn't—no—I *refused* to lose one more person.

And certainly not him.

There were some things I couldn't do without.

What a fool I'd been.

Arms wrapped under my back and knees, lifting me with ease as my blinks became heavy. Rowan had been delegated to transport me, and he was running, but I didn't dare risk a glance up at him for fear that I wouldn't make it through the shrinking portal. My surroundings were white lightning, and I was lost to it as Rowan plunged into the portal with me in tow.

Upside down. Sideways.

Rowan's arms under my back and knees were ripped away, and I rolled across black grass dotted with golden flowers.

Turning my head with monumental effort, I waited until Bracken and Cinth had cleared the portal, then cut off the—now wisp-thin—flow of white.

The opening between realms imploded, gone.

I lay still, unable to do anything else. Cinth rushed to my side and dropped to her knees. "Alli." She turned shining eyes up to Rowan. "You got her through. I didn't think you'd make it, but you were so fast. Thank you."

His breath caught. "You're welcome, Lady Cinth."

My brows shot up. Lady Cinth, huh?

This time Cinth's breath caught. "Oh, uhm. I. . ." She blinked a few times and then turned from him, clearly flustered as she hugged me tight.

"Mm okay," I mumbled.

She blew out a breath. "I've never seen anything like that. You were scary. Lightning-storm-and-hair-flying scary. If I didn't know you were addicted to tickles, then I may be afraid of you right now."

Slowly, other sounds came to me. The army.

Their murmurs and whispers.

"Did everyone get through?" I slurred. My body was heavy. So heavy I could barely twitch a finger. *Not* the state I wanted to be in to save Lan.

"Everyone," Bracken cut in, wonder in her voice. "That was some serious magic."

Yeah. And I probably had roughly . . . none.

For a long time too—several days if I was lucky. More likely a week.

The physical situation, at least, I could do something about. Intending to draw green energy from Underhill, I didn't question the color when she gave me gold energy instead. I encouraged it into my muscles and joints, whispering strength into my legs and arms. The foliage around me grew and shrank in turn, both of my magics exacting their toll, and by the time I sat down a few minutes later, they were exactly the same as when I arrived.

Rowan dusted his uniform clean. I watched him and General Stryk set about getting the mass of warrior fae into order.

I did it.

I'd gotten the army through, which gave the courts a chance at shutting Rubezahl down for good. As long as Uncle Josef, whom I'd left in charge on Unimak, didn't fuck things up in my absence, most likely as the mouthpiece of Adair, then those fae I'd left behind would be okay. Far more okay than they'd be here anyway. At the end of the day, there weren't many people I trusted anyway.

Bracken extended a hand to help me up. I cast her a weary smile that slipped from my face as a woman marched up through the army.

A woman every Seelie and Unseelie knew.

A woman I'd seen not only through my eyes but Lan's memories.

Ailbhe left General Stryk's side to join me and murmured low. "She comes out of guilt. She comes to salvage her destroyed legacy."

I slid a look at the mystica fae, still uncertain whether bringing her with the army had been the safest option for her. At least here I would know what was happening. I didn't trust other fae not to harm her.

"I would rather be here," she said. "Do not trouble yourself to be my protector, my queen, what must happen, must happen. That you would protect me instead of hurting me is enough. Enough to risk my life sending you to dreamland, and enough to divulge my new suspicions to you when you have a moment spare."

My focus lingered on the mystica fae. She'd told me that Rubezahl believed I'd be weak and vulnerable without Lan.

About Rubezahl's plans? I thought at her.

She nodded, her lips pressed tightly together. "Now I know what the harp can do, I believe I've pieced things together."

Then we must talk as a matter of utmost importance, I thought at her again. *I will summon you as soon as possible.*

She curtsied and backed away.

"Queen Kallik." The woman swept a shallow bow as though her back wasn't used to bending.

I cocked a brow. "Lugh's daughter."

She smiled broadly, and I had to wonder if Ebliu remembered telling her son to leave me half-drowned on the riverbank or whether she knew that I was aware of how she'd beat Lan for having Unseelie magic. "A moment of your time, Your Majesty."

"I have much to do."

"Yes." Her face tightened. "I hear that my son got himself captured." She sighed, setting the end of her spear shaft on the ground and crushing a gold flower in the process. "And mere days after he was made regent of the Unseelie throne. For a moment, I thought . . . but it is of no matter. We all know what he is."

I tilted my head. "And what is that?"

Her gaze darted over my face.

Stepping closer, I looked up into her regal face. Her features were similar to Lan's, but hers formed an expression of conceit and ignorance.

She couldn't have chosen a worse time to open her gob, in all honesty. Despite that, I paused, trying to pick my words with care. Pretending to be one of my advisors had worked well with Rubezahl. . .maybe I'd do that again.

"I am queen of all fae, Ebliu," I said quietly. "So be very careful of what you say next. I do not condemn any fae for the magic they wield. But I will condemn a fae who proves they are not of a certain . . . moral caliber. I have been in Faolan's memories. I have seen who you really are, daughter of Lugh, just as your father saw who you were and, more importantly, who you are not."

Her eyes widened and her throat worked as she swallowed.

Ha! Totally working again.

"I further suggest," I said lightly, "that you set your mind to showing *me* your worth, rather than throwing insults at a man who has proven himself time and again to be a true hero."

That was maybe a little less queenly and a little more Kallik. I had to be giving off some serious heat because she dropped her gaze almost immediately to the spear in her hand.

"That's..." She swallowed once more and started again. "I have my regrets, Your Majesty. Do not believe me free of those. I've made mistakes in the past, and will in the future, I am sure. I came to speak with you of a matter that could help my son. The army whispers that Rubezahl has tortured him. They say my son lingers a hair's breadth from death. Is this true?"

Word spread fast. "It is. Your father is helping to keep him alive, but he can only do so for a day."

"My father," she mouthed without sound. "You really spoke with him?"

More like begged him to help Lan, but . . . "I did. What I told you is the truth. He sees far more of a hero in your son than in you." The words were cutting, but I simply didn't care. This woman ranked higher in my hatred than Adair, something I'd never consciously realized until now.

She sucked in a breath.

Behind her, the armies were in formation. "My time is precious."

Lugh's daughter extended her spear. "This is my father's spear."

Everyone knew that. It was a relic—his fiery weapon that had slayed so many tyrants in fae history. "And I would need that why?"

“Not you,” she said quietly. “Faolan. My father poured some of his life essence into this weapon as a means of protecting his bloodline. If my son holds it, it should help him. I . . . I hope it will help him.”

I searched her face.

Rubezahl might have proven to be a massive dickhead, but his wisdom in some matters was undeniable. He’d once spoken to me about the danger of prestige. How a person, once they were adored, would do anything to maintain that image of themselves.

Although the words and gesture had clearly been difficult for Ebliu, something told me she wasn’t unaware of the eyes on her. The soldiers would just see Lugh’s daughter gifting me her father’s spear, something that might lift her further in their esteem.

Nevertheless, I took it from her. The slight glow it had emanated at her touch died, the essence contained therein recognizing I was not of Lugh’s bloodline.

She bowed, deeper this time. “Thank you, Your Majesty.”

I dipped my head. “May this make up for your past misdeeds, Ebliu. Lugh is watching this moment and weighing your value.”

General Stryk marched up to me, and I turned my back on Lan’s mother.

“They’re rattled but in sound shape,” he reported.

“The sleeping draught?” I asked.

“Intact. The poisoners stored it well.”

Good. We hadn’t been able to transport as much as originally planned, but it would have to do. “We attack at dawn.” Which was maybe three hours away unless Underhill decided to mix things up. Two hours was barely enough time to prepare, but every hour we waited brought Lan one hour closer to death. “Tell General Rowan and give word for the draught to be released as soon as the gas masks have been dispersed to our frontline.”

He snapped his heels together and saluted. “Yes, Your Majesty. And what—”

“Get out of the damn way, you ugly brute,” a voice snapped.

The general’s face twisted in fury, but it promptly faded—clever man—at the sight of a hooded figure approaching, a familiar blooded fae at her side.

“Oracle,” I said respectfully, bowing slightly.

She shoved her hood back, glaring at Stryk with her one good eye, who made the wise decision to make himself scarce. If I could feel anything through the numbness that Lan’s capture had started and the singed insides feeling that portal just inspired, then I’d perhaps laugh at the speed with which he left.

“Queen of All Fae,” the Oracle said. “Still making a mess of things, I see.”

The Oracle looked me up and down, narrowing her one eye. "Rubezahl has Lan."

"I know about that, you little dingdong. What are you doing about the army camped at Dragonsmount?"

A few gasps from those around us reminded me that I should probably chastise her or at least pretend to give a shit about her rudeness. Oh well. "We have a plan. Would you like to be in on it?"

"I can't. I'm the Oracle. But she can." The Oracle pointed her thumb at Devon, who stood just to her left.

Devon's eyes rested lightly on me. "Who helped you keep the portal open?"

My eyebrows slid upward even as my knees threatened to buckle. I drew more energy from the ground. "No one."

Cinth was at my elbow in an instant, shoving food into my hands. "Banana cream pie."

My friend was magical in the kitchen, but not enough to pull a banana cream pie out of thin air. She'd made it before coming. "Banana cream pie" was also our established safe word—something that started from me no longer trusting anyone not to suddenly morph into one of Rubezahl's people. Sure, Ailbhe had done so with honorable intentions, and she'd probably saved Lan's life, but I couldn't be sure it wouldn't happen again . . . and the next time may not work out so well for me.

I took the offered slice of pie and slumped to the ground, crossing my legs in the middle of the field of black grass.

The Oracle sniffed and sat down in front of me with a grace that belied her ancient status. "You finally grasped the lightning."

This pie was probably amazing, but I couldn't taste anything. My mouth was dry, and my taste buds had totally been shot. Like when I drank something too hot, and it burned away all sensation.

Before I could answer her, Devon sat down on my other side. "To pull that much magic means you shall possess no magical signature for the foreseeable future, at least a day or two."

I blinked at her. "What?" Food sprayed from my mouth like I was a heathen. I didn't care. My body was starving.

Devon dusted banana cream pie off the front of her tunic. "That is how Rubezahl hunts for fae. He searches for the magical signatures of those he covets or seeks to destroy. You currently have none."

Her words sunk in hard. "I could slip into his camp." We could save the sleeping draught for a proper battle.

Already on my feet, I did a quick turn. "General Stryk! General Rowan!"

"Yes?" Stryk's voice boomed from somewhere within the crush of the army.

"Attend," I barked the word.

Both generals were at my side in a matter of seconds. "Hold the sleeping draught. New information has come to light."

They shared a look, and I could only imagine what I looked like—my face covered with half the food Cinth had just brought me, my eyes wide, and exhaustion pulling at my features.

In short, I almost certainly looked crazy. Kind of felt that way too, no joke.

"Your Majesty," General Stryk said, slanting a look at Rowan. "Are you sure?"

"Just hold it for the time being while I discuss the matter with the Oracle. She may provide insight into our chances of success." There, that was a little better. Maybe? The two of them saluted, and I saw the look they shared.

They were worried.

I faced the Oracle. "I can't run all the way there. I need something—"

The Oracle nodded. "You need a ride. The land kelpie would be too obvious."

Devon shook her head. "Underhill will assist you. You can use the river system. The water will take you to Dragonsmount in a short time and without detection."

It would? Goddess, of course it would be water. I swallowed the instant fear and pushed back the instant sweat. Why was it always water? "And I just, what, float down the river? Why can't we just do that for the entire army?"

She smiled. "You have yet to understand all that is this place, and how your powers operate within it. Underhill is everything. She is the sand and the sky, the water and the blood within your veins. She is time itself. She is the old and the young and the very essence of the magic we all carry." Devon's voice rose, and the army around us stilled. "Underhill is your goddess, she is your mother and your sister, your enemy and your nemesis. Always she will be with you. Always. Fear her, worship her, *revere* her. And, above all, put your faith in her love of *all* fae. For even when she seems cruel, she does what is needed to see that all survive."

The wind around us had disappeared, but it picked up again as her last words faded from my ears.

"Doesn't answer why I can't stick my whole army in the river," I drawled, wishing I didn't have to do things this way. Devon's eyes narrowed, and I held up both hands. "Peace, friend. I assume it's the sheer number of them that poses the problem?"

"The water is dangerous. Underhill will allow you, Kallik of All Fae, to pass, and only you. She is a sucker for a true love story and will keep her creatures at bay to help you for now. She has reason to be particularly partial to what you and Faolan may achieve together. But you must go without delay." Devon pointed to the river.

My training in the false Underhill was still very much with me, and I yelled over my shoulder as I ran. "If you don't hear from me in six hours, launch the attack as planned!"

Shouts rattled after me, Cinth's front and center, but Devon's words weren't the kind I could or would ignore. Underhill was the boss, and if she didn't want me to delay, then I'd heed her advice. No matter how fucking terrifying it was to dive into water that was dangerous and could kill me in an instant.

I *wanted* to heed her advice. Waiting for the army to ready themselves prior to opening the portal had been torture. The thought of waiting any longer was nearly unbearable, and now that I had a plausible reason . . . well...

Two strides away from the river, I jumped in with my clothing and weapons on, Lugh's spear gripped in one hand. I broke the surface of the still water. Only it wasn't still or silent underneath the gentle waves.

The current ripped at me, jamming me low and thumping me hard into the rocks. And I let it happen. I had to trust Underhill, I had to give in to her will. If she chose to punish me, then I'd take it. She probably had a right to punish me. The Oracle clearly believed I was messing things up. I'd pushed Lan away, thinking we could never be together, yet my heart said otherwise. It said that Lan and I were stronger together, even if the power between us was terrifying.

The water rolled me several times, and I kept my eyes closed. If I opened them, I'd panic, and panic was the last thing I needed to do right then.

Time slid by, and the water smoothed as I relaxed.

I counted the minutes in my head, and when my shoulder bumped into something hard, the water around me receded. I blinked and found myself staring up into the night sky through a thin skin of water. Stars of every color dotted the sky. The same way colors flitted through the dark of Lan's eyes. Everything reminded me of him, and it was like a knife under my ribs.

"You hear anything?"

I froze at the grunted words and the crunch of feet on rocks so very close to me.

"Nothing. Ruby said no one was nearby. Said he'd be able to feel if any assassins approached us. We're just out here in case that prisoner somehow gets up and runs off."

Laughter burst out of the two of them before it shifted to low giggles. "There won't be any running for him in that state. Fool to think he could steal from Ruby."

"Yeah." That second voice didn't sound so sure. "I . . . sometimes I'm not so sure what Ruby is doing is right, you know? Dividing the courts, trying to take over . . . having us torture that fae for so many days. He's the grandson of Lugh, did you know? That seems wrong."

A slap of skin on skin. A grunt. "Don't you be talking like that, Shifty, or I'll smack you harder next time. That's not good talk, bad for morale and all that."

Shifty clearly hadn't sucked down as much tea as his friend. Or maybe he was less of a dick.

"It's just the torture. I know Ruby said he wasn't to live, but the last bit got to me."

"Well, he ain't going anywhere, and fresh air will do you wonders."

Another grunt, and then the sound of gravel and dirt crunching. They weren't even trying to be quiet.

I lifted my head and peered over the shallow riverbank.

The two guards had their backs to me as they trudged downstream. Beyond them were thousands of tents between the two ridges of the valley. And to the left of me, upstream, was a dark gray tent...the flaps tied down.

I drew a deep breath. Was Lan in there? From his torturers' conversation, I'd say he had to be.

Rolling onto my belly, I reached back and worked Lugh's spear between two of the straps securing my swords. Keeping low to the ground, I army crawled with painstaking slowness across the open ground.

There was no place to hide, no place to pause. I'd either make it to the tent or not. But with my magical signature gone, I was a ghost to Rubezahl. From the sound of things, his ability to detect fae had made him—and by default, his guards—cocky.

I kept moving toward the edge of the tent. Sliding under wasn't hard until the spear got caught on the material and tore a hole in the side. I yanked the weapon free and rolled to my feet, spear in hand and ready to fight.

There was only one person in the tent.

Lan was bound to a central pole with thin iron straps. His body was riddled with wounds and slashes from claws and blades alike. What I could see of his skin under the dried blood was ghastly pale. His head lolled, chin to chest, and his dark hair was matted with sweat and blood.

No, no, no, no . . .

A vision of his grandfather flickered behind him. "Hurry, child. I cannot hold him much longer."

Heart thumping in my chest, I lifted the spear and drove the tip into the chains securing Lan's left hand.

The iron shattered like cracking glass, and he slumped to the right.

"Hang on," I whispered as I drove the spear into each point of iron bonds that held him, until he crumpled into a pile at the bottom of the thick pole. I dropped the spear to the ground and pulled Lan's upper body into my arms. "Breathe for me, Faolan!"

"Use the spear." Lugh's voice echoed again.

I lifted my gaze, but he was gone. Juggling Lan's body with one hand, I awkwardly pulled the spear close, laying it across his chest for lack of a better idea. Surely Lugh hadn't meant for me to drive it into him—though at this point, after so much craziness of spirits and drugged tea and whatnot, I wouldn't be damn-well surprised.

There was no sudden jumping up from laying the spear on his chest, no moment of being awake, but his body warmed, a flush appearing between the blood smears and dirt on his face.

The spear lit up, a little too bright for comfort in the dead of night in a tent. I put my hands over it, but it was touching Lan and seemed to be making him better. Or at least *holding* him in this state.

Hopefully it did so until I could get him back to my people.

Wait . . . how the hell was I going to get out of here with him?

The river, that was the only option I had. I needed to at least get him to the other side. Once I was there, I could figure out a different strategy.

"Lan, please wake up. Just for a few minutes," I whispered as I touched his face, brushing away some crusted blood.

Ruby had done this to him. He'd beaten him and cut him and left him to die...to gain what exactly? Lan didn't know anything more than I did. There was no magical word or item that he could have divulged or gained for Rubezahl.

That was why I'd always assumed he'd use Lan as bait for *me*. Yet he'd gone so far that only this spear appeared to be keeping Faolan from death.

Why?

For sport?

That wasn't Rubezahl's style.

I stared at the spear on Lan's chest.

The Fiery Spear. It contained the power and essence of Lugh, just like the harp Rubezahl carried . . .

"You sure you saw something in here, Shifty?"

I jerked. *Fuck.*

"That's not my name."

My eyes widened at the loud thump of a body hitting the ground. What the hell? Had Shifty just attacked the other one?

The tent flapped opened, and in stepped one of the guards.

A guard I knew.

His eyes landed on Lan and me, and he bowed his head. "Your Majesty. You need to get out of here. If Ruby doesn't know you're here already, he'll know soon."

I didn't release Lan, but I couldn't tear my eyes off the fae before me. "Drake? How in the name of the goddess are you alive?" I'd watched Rubezahl *murder* him.

He crouched. "I . . . one of my abilities allowed me to survive."

There weren't many immortal fae at *all*. Only three that I knew of. And—

My mouth dried.

Shifty.

"Damn. You're a changeling?"

He shrugged. "Part. I can only change to one other form. That's why I was being trained in Underhill."

"The missing hand?" Part changelings weren't immortal like full changelings, but from what I knew of them, they had a certain number of lives. They could regenerate, though. It wasn't possible for him to *not* have two arms.

He smiled. "An illusion from Ruby to gain sympathy from you and create a connection between us. The trainers did cut my hand off as punishment knowing it would fucking hurt me as it regrew. Eventually I got it back, of course. Changeling perks." He held up *both* hands. "Look, when I died back on Unimak. Well, using one of my lives clears out any magical holds on me. Resets me almost. I could see Ruby for what he was. For what he *is*. All I can say is that I'm so damn sorry, Alli. I'd beg for your forgiveness for longer, but we've got to get you out of here."

I nodded. "Both of us."

"Of course." He grinned at me. "Much as I'd like another shot at you now that I can show you what I'm capable of with two hands, I doubt I have a chance if you risked coming here to save Faolan."

I ignored the hint of hope in his tone. Because that ship had well and truly sailed. "Help me get him to the river? We'll be good from there."

Drake moved to Lan's other side, and we lifted him between us. I kept the spear pressed against Lan's body, not daring to do anything else, and hoped against hope I wasn't imaging his strengthening inhales or improving color.

We hurried to the river, and Drake helped me to lower Lan into the water. I slid into the water next to him but glanced back. "Drake, they'll know you helped."

He shook his head, glancing back at the thousands of tents. "I'll be okay."

"But you could come with us."

"No," the word ripped from his chest as a growl. "I have unfinished business with Rubezahl." His body shimmered, and a creature that was part wolf and part stag stared back at me. He yipped before bounding away toward a forest to the left of the valley.

I lay flat in the river with Lan and the water flowed up and around us.

Kicking off, I let it carry us down.

Down.

Underhill, please take us to safety.

At this point, pleading with ancient entities was all I had.

CHAPTER 11

Mist hovered like a floating blanket over the river water. Lan and I had drifted downstream a fair bit already, leaving the tents of Rubezahl's army and the valley behind.

"Still with me?" I puffed, kicking hard against the current.

Lan didn't respond. He hadn't so much as groaned or fluttered his eyelids. But the fiery spear still glowed against his torn and cut chest. If I wasn't certain by this point that the spear was the only thing keeping Faolan alive, I would have worried the glowing beacon was attracting every sort of fae predator in our periphery to devour us whole.

But Underhill had kept her word so far—her unpredictable creatures had left us alone.

I wedged Lan against a half-submerged tree trunk and trudged out of the river at last, water pouring from my clothing,

Goddess, I had to get Lan warm and somehow fed and tend to his wounds and—

For a moment, my vision wavered, and panic threatened to overwhelm the fragile grip I'd kept on my control since watching Rubezahl disappear with Lan in tow.

Deep breath, Kallik.

How many times had I nearly lost hope in recent months? If I'd learned anything, it was that I had to just take one footstep after another. That's what I needed to do now.

A branch snapped behind me. With a whisper of steel, I had one of the queen's gifted blades drawn and ready. I gave a cursory glance at Lan to make sure he wasn't going anywhere, then spun into a low crouch, ready to kill whoever and *what*ever I needed to in order to protect Lan.

No one would get between us again.

Devon stepped from the mist; her hands raised. "Easy, Kallik of All Fae."

Sighing heavily, I sheathed my weapon. "How did you get here?"

"One day, you may understand the workings of Underhill."

"Will I be shrouded in mist too?" I replied.

The blooded fae smiled, making me wish I hadn't asked. "You have Lugh's grandson?"

I strode back to him, placing a hand over the spear. "He's in really bad shape. Help me get him out of the water? But be careful of the spear. It's keeping him alive."

"Yes," Devon said, crouching to hook her hands under his left armpit. "I can feel Lugh working to keep him in stasis."

She could? I grunted as we heaved a soaked Lan from the water and onto a ground covering of moss a little way into the cover of the trees. When Ruby discovered his prisoner was missing, he'd send scouts, no doubt. "How long will the spear hold him in stasis?"

"Indefinitely," the blooded fae murmured, already inspecting Lan's multitude of wounds.

I glanced away from the jagged injuries, some days old and others seeping pus as if they'd been infected for weeks. With the time difference between Underhill and Earth, it was entirely possible. Looking at them was almost more than I could bear. I felt each one tenfold. In my very soul and aching heart. I'd fought giants and submitted to entities beyond my understanding, and yet I could hardly stand to look at Lan in this state. I struggled to latch on to the present, and then to find my voice. "So he has time to get better."

"No, I didn't say that."

I closed my eyes. "What do you mean then?"

"We have very little time," she said, looking up at me. "Therefore, Faolan also has very little time. And—" She peered closely at his chest. "—he will not get better."

My heart stuttered in my chest. "There must be something we can do. The wounds are physical. They can be healed."

The blooded fae shook her head. "I suggest you look again."

Already kicking myself, I tuned into my magical sight—and immediately gasped at the ugly and thorned orange tendrils protruding upward through Lan's chest as if poisonous vines had grown inside of him before bursting out. "What is it?"

Nausea churned in my gut, threatening to rise.

"Rubezahl's magic. A curse to ensure Faolan's fate."

I wasn't much for tears in front of others, but some things couldn't be helped. They stung my eyes now. "There has to be something I can do." The words, 'I'll do anything,' hovered on the tip of my tongue, but I swallowed them, knowing it was unnecessary to voice them. Devon would know. "Our combined magic . . . "

Maybe it could sear the curse away?

"Rubezahl is aware of the intricate workings of the magical bond you share with Lugh's grandson. His curse is guarded against such a thing. I would wager a guess that if you attempted it, the curse would strengthen, not weaken."

I crouched and touched trembling fingers to Lan's forehead. If the curse was the spreading kind, then I would have already succumbed to it while carting him downriver. "Where there's a curse, there is a charm to undo it. I don't accept that there isn't a solution."

Devon sat back on her heels. "The strongest curses I have encountered in my time require one of two things. A life sacrifice from someone who is bound to the affected fae—which I imagine is what Rubezahl is after as you would be that person."

Blood rushed in my ears. "The second?"

Her expression hardened. "Faolan, as he is, will not conquer the curse. So he must change."

"Change how?"

She lifted a shoulder. "It is different for all of us. I suggest you cast your memory back to what the Oracle has divulged to you regarding Lugh's grandson."

They'd all been cryptic comments, of course, but one of them floated to the fore of my mind.

"Calm yourself, grandson of Lugh. You must also go, for you, too, are necessary to ensure the correct path for our kind."

She'd gone on to add, *"He will play a part in the demise of Rubezahl. All going well and assuming you two don't revert to being stupid."*

That gave me very little to go on, other than that Lan was important. Regardless, if I'd remembered her words before now, I could have used them to calm General Stryk down about 'abandoning our preparations to save a single person'.

"Fuck." I ran a hand through my slime-covered tresses. I smelled, looked, and felt like a swamp mule. "You can't give me more to go on?

"Believe it or not, Kallik of All Fae, neither I nor Underhill know more. There is a reason the Oracle is allowed space here. She fulfills a role no one else can. She and she alone is privy to the various paths our realms may take."

And the Oracle wouldn't—or couldn't—spill the fire beans. All she could do was pass out cryptic comments. "How can a fae physically change though?"

Devon pursed her lips. "Each of us is a variation on what was once a normal fae—a product of certain stresses or environments. You, for instance, are the only fae of your kind, created by the combination of opposite and equally strong bloodlines. The original mystica fae was created when a toddler was put through horrific trauma and developed the ability to protect himself mentally. Speaking for myself, I faced an inner journey to become a blooded fae. Perhaps what Lan requires cannot be provided to him. Perhaps *he* must find the answer."

Lan was the only one who could break down his walls. Even I'd thought that more than once.

That didn't mean I liked it.

My jaw clenched. "And he's in the perfect state to achieve that."

"There are all kinds of realms," Devon said, not reacting to the bite in my voice. "There is this realm. The realm of humans. And thousands more. You yourself have visited another realm."

I lifted my head. "Dreamland."

The ghost of a smile curved her lips. "It is as good a place to start as any, but do not forget that Lugh's grandson is just one part of what's now unfolding. If you forget *your* path, Queen of All Fae, then you will ensure his death regardless."

My hands curled to fists. Every fucking direction was a dead end. I didn't want to fight this stupid battle when Lan needed me. And yet if I didn't . . . "The harp."

"The harp," she echoed.

I craned my neck, dragging my hands over my face. So tired. But I couldn't stop now, when my magical signature was muted. I still had to put a dent in Rubezahl's magic and steal the external source of some of his power. "I need to get back to the army." My gaze fell to the broken form of the man who meant so much to me. The man I'd die to protect. "I need to put Lan somewhere safe. Rubezahl will track his signature."

"Hard to when the giant has cloaked Faolan in his own magic. The curse does have one downside. His magical signature will be weak and hard to pick up—though it will not be impossible."

There was only one place I could fathom to put Lan. "Can you get me to the Oracle's meadow?"

Devon tilted her head, listening to something—or some*one*—I couldn't hear. She nodded twice.

Was she speaking to Underhill?

"I may transport the two of you," she eventually said.

Good. One more piece of shitty news and I'd detonate. Working quickly, I tore off the bottom hem of my coarse tunic and tied the spear across Lan's chest. "That's better. Let's go."

Devon removed a dagger from her thigh sheath and slashed the blade across the front of her shoulder. Smearing the thick, black substance oozing from her wound over the fingers of both hands, she reached for Lan's forehead with one hand and mine with the other.

"Is that safe for you?" I asked.

"For a blooded fae, there is no safer magic than that which uses the conduit of our essence."

Seemed like an overly long yes to me.

The mist thickened, swirling around us tight. Suffocating. Like a corset drawn inward to a rib-crushing degree, the air pinched at my body until black bordered the edges of my vision.

Then the strings were cut, and the corset fell free.

The mist dissipated, revealing a familiar foliage-covered tower nestled amidst a meadow.

Devon extracted a vial and cloth from an inside pocket, and I only jerked slightly as she wiped my forehead, and then Lan's, clean.

A trail of blood trickled from her nose. Her focus landed on me as though she felt my unasked question, but she didn't offer an explanation.

Was this the price for working her blood magic? Devon was always on the pale side, but a closer look told me she really wasn't looking too flash.

Transporting two people through Underhill likely wasn't as trivial of a feat as she'd suggested.

Cinth exited the tower, the Oracle beside her, as we hurried over with Lan in tow. I thought about asking why Cinth was here, then realized the Oracle would just call me a stupid dingdong for the question.

"Oh, Alli," Cinth whispered, her tear-filled eyes darting to meet mine after a quick assessment of the man in my grip.

I swallowed hard. "He's not in great shape." I quickly filled her in on what had happened, including what the spear was doing now.

The Oracle stood by in mulish silence.

We carried Lan inside, then left him to Cinth and Devon's care. Only then did I turn to face her. I took both the Oracle's hands in mine. "You carry a great burden and a great gift," I said. "And I don't want to make the burden side of what you do worse. So I'll only ask you once. Is there anything else I should or *can* know about my path or what it will take to help Faolan?"

The ancient woman surveyed me, but I got the sense she was looking inward and not really seeing me at all. "Your path and that of Lugh's grandson run parallel, as ever."

"By following my path, I will help Faolan recover." Hadn't Devon implied as much?

The Oracle didn't so much as twitch a facial muscle.

I squeezed her hands. In truth, I'd expected to be met with her usual scathing dismissal. Then I turned from her, going back to Lan. For now, in what little time I could spare before returning to *my* path, I wanted to tend to the man I loved.

The Oracle's weary voice cracked like a whip against my back. "What know you of the harp Rubezahl carries?"

Blinking, I peered over my shoulder. "It lends him great power. Lugh's power. By playing it, he can create the strongest of illusions. He has the power to influence people—to calm or incite them—and transport great numbers between the realms."

The Oracle sniffed. "Is that all?" Limping up to me, she patted my cheek none too gently. Her sole rainbow-hued eye bore into mine. "*Do* stop screwing things up soon."

The Oracle continued into her abode, and I sucked in a harsh breath, my mind scrambling over what she'd said.

Is that all?

I glanced through the open door after her, hardly noticing the bucket of steaming water or clean rags piled next to Lan's frame on the cleared kitchen table. My lips were dry and my mouth drier still. My voice cracked. "I need to learn more about that harp."

Straightening, I felt a foreign wisp of hope curl around my heart.

CHAPTER 12

Of course, finding out more about the harp wasn't so simple. Ailbhe was with my army, and I couldn't be sure she'd have the kind of answers I needed anyway.

Maybe it wouldn't have felt so insurmountable if I'd had months or even weeks to complete the task. As it was, Lan didn't have that kind of time, and my troops didn't have those kinds of provisions, and Rubezahl surely wouldn't wait patiently for me to be ready. I stood in front of the Oracle's messy, stacked-to-the-ceiling library, feeling an exhaustion beyond anything I'd ever experienced before. My eyes were gritty with non-existent sand, my arms so heavy that lifting a finger was akin to moving a two-hundred-pound weight.

A knock sounded at the door.

I didn't turn. The beetroot and cherry smell wafting in confirmed the person was Cinth. She was making tickles again. She put an arm around my waist. "A message has been sent to summon the mystica fae. What else can I do to help?"

I shook my head, but even that felt sluggish and leaden. "I have to find out more about that harp Ruby carries, but there's no time. Ailbhe may have information, but I feel my best bet is to trawl through this mess in here." I blinked, but the blink never ending. I swayed on my feet.

Cinth tried to steer me out of the library. "Alli, you need to rest. Just for an hour if you won't sleep longer."

"Lan doesn't have extra time, Cinth." I whispered. "You sent a message to Rowan too?"

Her arm tightened around my waist. "I did. Told him to hold his position. The Unseelie are masking the army as requested."

The unspoken 'but' was that masking the entire army would weaken the Unseelie. Like me, they couldn't keep going indefinitely, and I still needed them to face Rubezahl, most likely sooner than we'd ever feel ready to do so.

I stepped farther into the room and forced my eyes to focus on the spines of the books *not* covered by mountains of parchment. "I'll look through the books, and if they're no good, I'll hand them to you to stack outside the door."

She let me go, and my legs folded under me. Logically, I knew she was right, I was beyond any level of fatigue I'd ever faced. No amount of drawing from the earth would re-energize me. My kind may be magic, but fae still had a point of no return, and I was there.

On my butt and there to stay, I reached for the first book.

"Magical Creatures and Their Habitats." I handed the text to Cinth, and she tossed it out of the room. I was too tired to ask her not to be a monster with books—she'd never liked reading anything but recipes.

Digging deep, I forced my hands and eyes to keep going. For Lan.

"Freeing Magical Elements." Toss.

"How to Deal with Trackers and Ascendants." Toss.

"The Pack Habits of Luthers."

"Vissimo Hierarchy—Common Misconceptions About Modern-Day 'Vampires'."

The books numbered many, but the subjects weren't at all what I needed. I kept going, handling one at a time until my vision blurred and all I could see were the titles.

Anything that wasn't in a language I knew was ruthlessly thrown out the door by Cinth.

"Alli, you've been at this for an hour, and we've got nothing." Cinth's voice was gentle as she pushed a plate of food in front of me. I hadn't seen her leave to grab it.

"Eat," she hushed. "You can still look at the titles. I'll show them to you, you say in or out, okay?"

Tears sprang into my eyes at her understanding.

I nodded, accepting the plate and starting to eat. She'd made tickles again, but she must've added pixy dust into the batter. A warm sensation flooded my mouth as the dust soothed an ache in my throat that I hadn't even noticed was there.

Cinth held a book up. I shook my head.

Another.

Another.

I finished the food and took a mug from her, holding it tightly in my hands. The warmth of the stone seeped into my palms.

So sleepy.

Eating may help me in the long run, but right now, it was only exacerbating my stupor.

"Is this even a book?" Cinth scoffed. "More like someone's art project."

She'd picked up a thin book the height and width of a doormat. Actually, thin was an understatement. The tome couldn't contain more than twenty pages, if that, and it had no title. She barely showed it to me before chucking it overhead. My eyes tracked its journey to the door and caught the faintest flutter of gold inside.

A drawing?

"That . . . could be something." I slurred.

Putting down the mug, I crawled after the sorry excuse for a book. It was perhaps a dozen pages long, hand-stitched together without even a proper cover. But we were looking for something different, weren't we? Different could be good.

I bent and scooped the bound pages up. Someone had stitched the thick parchment together with a deep blue and green thread.

This was more like someone's journal than a book, really. I swallowed hard as a strange sensation pressed in on me. The feeling was one of expectation and familiarity. Of warmth.

I briefly considered the possibility that it had belonged to one of my parents before discarding the thought. This was a poor man's journal, not forged of silver and gold. Whoever had put it together had done so with hands that were larger than a typical fae's.

I flipped over the journal again. A smudged fingerprint marked the back, as if he'd put it there accidently. I laid my thumb over the print and, as expected, the edges of the print spread far past my own fingertips.

"This belonged to Rubezahl," I whispered.

Cinth scrambled up next to me. "Are you sure?"

I showed her the print. "He made this. It's a giant-sized journal. It has to mean something." At least, I *hoped* it did, more than I'd ever hoped for anything. We hadn't found anything else of significance, and we'd made only a tiny dent in the library's contents.

Maybe, just maybe, the journal would contain insight into the harp or the giant who wielded it.

Still, I found myself hesitating to open it, although not because I was tired.

I was afraid.

At each turn, I seemed to encounter something worse. What if that happened again? What if somehow this knowledge showed me there was no path to defeating him?

Or...

"What if I see something that makes me empathize with him?" I asked, though my entire being shied from that after what he'd done to Lan.

"It won't." Cinth's voice was firm. "You know that."

Despite everything, I wasn't so sure. There were a lot of parallels between us. He'd been cast out from his family and the person he loved, abandoned to the Triangle with no one at his back to help him. "We shared a common path for a time, Cinth. I can't deny that I understand him."

Her hand settled on my back, lending support. "If you wish to show him mercy when he is on his knees, then it is in your power to grant it. But we must drive him to his knees first, Alli. For all fae. For Faolan."

She was right. I shouldn't worry about that before reading whatever these pages contained. Especially when the thought of Rubezahl on his knees just filled me with grim satisfaction. Still. This felt like a huge moment. One I needed to experience in private. "I . . . give me my drink."

Cinth handed it to me. "Need to see Lan?"

I nodded and left the room, working my way around the piles of books we'd reviewed and rejected, down the hall, and into the room where Lan lay on a bed under a pile of blankets. The tip of the fiery spear poked out over his left shoulder, the spear still very much attached to him and almost as hot as a fireplace throwing off waves of heat.

I sat next to him and set my drink on the side table. "I can't . . . No, that's not the right word. I don't *want* to do this without you, Lan. I will fight for you here, but you must fight to remain with me from wherever you are."

Setting the booklet on the bed, I flipped it open to the first page. The printed words were neat, tidy, and so unlike the penmanship I'd expected to see.

I read aloud to Lan.

I saw my beauty today.

She gifted me a rare smile, and if ever I thought my soul would be free of her, her smile erased that hopeful belief.

Anna is so young to have this mantle pressed on her. Too young. It breaks my heart daily to see her killing herself to play the part. I could make this easier for her to bear. If only she would allow me to stand beside her instead of behind her, then I could relieve her of such burdens.

I cannot remain idly by when a union with me is the perfect solution.

I believe I have an answer. A way to sway her heart.

I know that I am a giant, and no matter how small I try to make myself, that truth shall remain. Anna though, she is not like the others, she sees only the heart of a person, and I cannot believe that she would turn me away.

Not once I prove my worth to her.

I swallowed hard and found my hand moving to wrap around Lan's far too cool one.

The Seelie king came today.

He kept his admiration of my Anna well hidden, but I was watching. I saw it shine from his eyes as plainly as others likely see it shine from mine. She is a dark star in the endless night sky. She is mystery and beauty, intelligence and fire. I worry that the king, whom many refer to as the everlasting light, will manage to dazzle her . . . but no, I will not think like that.

She has my heart, and I cannot believe she would cast me away. I will speak with Ebliu tomorrow. She has a lead for me.

"He knew your mom, Lan." I breathed out the four words and once more wondered at Ebliu's reasons for giving me the spear for Lan. Had she truly wished to help Lan, or was it a ruse to get the weapon closer to Rubezahl so he might steal it away?

Was Lugh's daughter a traitor?

My mind tried to fit the pieces together, but my mind was far too sluggish.

I reached out and took the drink Cinth had made for me off the table. The first sip set my mouth curling into a grimace. “Espresso?” Cinth knew I hated this human stuff, but maybe the caffeine would help where no magic could. I went back to reading.

> *Ebliu has given me information to help me find it. I believe I will be successful.*

“Definitely a traitor.” I whispered, eyes glued to the page.

> *I have it!*

> *The music is beyond beautiful, I played for my Anna, and she begged me to stay all night, strumming the harp. This is just as I’d hoped. The harp gives me a worth that all can now see.*

> *That I can play it at all speaks of* my *worth. Anna knows it. Even the Seelie king can see.*

> *I, an Unseelie fae, carry the harp of Lugh, and can produce its glorious music as well as the famed hero ever could.*

There was only one more page, and fear filled me that the journal entries would end before providing me with what I sought.

> *She cast me out.*

And in doing so, she has shattered my heart. I played for her, I gave her my special tea to open her to my worth. That is all I wanted, for her to see that I am deserving of her love. I am *worthy of her love, and yet still she cast me out.*

My Anna called me a monster.

There were great stains on the paper.

The remnants of teardrops shed by a giant.

My heart clenched. I didn't want to feel anything other than hate for Rubezahl, not after all he'd done to harm me and others. But I'd been unwanted. I'd been cast out and framed and chased. Yet with all that, I'd still chosen to do what was right. Maybe I could just feel sad and frustrated for the path Rubezahl had decided to walk instead of taking other, better paths.

I leave now for the Seelie king. Perhaps I can use him.

For if I cannot have Anna, then no one can. I must make sure that the darkest star does not join with the everlasting light.

She will never have a child that is not mine.

"Not creepy at all," I muttered.

The harp will help me.

I will play for her one last time, while she sleeps.

"Fuck." I turned the page, but there was no more from the young giant. No more peeks into his twisted psyche.

I closed the pages and stared down at Lan. There was only one thing I could connect from the entries in my current state—that Rubezahl, an Unseelie, had wielded a Seelie weapon. That meant *my* Unseelie could do the same.

The Oracle had warned that Lan must walk his own path if we were to succeed against Rubezahl.

"The harp belongs in your hands." Certainty burned molten within me. "Just like the fiery spear. Did you know that when you went to take it from him? Did you know that you were meant to play it too?"

The instrument had always bothered my Unseelie. I'd thought it was because the power Ruby wielded with the harp was unsettling to him. Maybe Faolan had even believed that was true. But on a deeper level, had Lan's body or mind recognized the harp? Had the harp called to the grandson of Lugh? And had it dredged up old fears of unworthiness?

I closed my eyes. "Cinth, I know you're there."

"Quite the story," she said from the doorway. "What are you going to do?"

I turned my head. The edges of her body were blurry to my exhausted eyes. "I'm going to crawl into bed with my love and try to reach him in dreamland. The harp is important, and I have no idea why. I have every intention to pray to the goddess for help figuring out what the hell to do."

Cinth forced a smile. "Then I wish you sweet dreams, sister of my heart. But don't go fucking him while you're there. You had your chance in Underhill last time, and you didn't grab the opportunity by the balls. We don't have time for you two to go knocking boots now."

I managed a weak twitch of my lips. "Roger that."

Cinth loaded me into bed, and I curled up next to my cool-skinned Unseelie, wrapping my arms and legs around his body. “Please don’t let me be too late. Please don’t let him die.”

Because the world still needed the grandson of Lugh. *I* needed him. And, most especially, the fae would need him once I faced Rubezahl and gave my life to stop him.

I only hoped the love of my life would one day forgive me for the lies I would utter to get us there.

CHAPTER 13

Summoning the visual of eerie mist and sparkling bubbles, I tried to draw forth the high-pitched tinkle of bells. The last time I'd visited dreamland I'd been drugged by Ailbhe. Any worry I'd had about finding my way back melted away as exhaustion dragged me under. *Helpful.*

Smiling, I opened my eyes and glanced down. Yep, naked.

Dreamland didn't believe in clothing. And it apparently didn't believe in exhaustion either. The vitality coursing through me made me realize how much like warmed-up death I'd felt a mere minute ago.

The sparkling bubbles were just the same as last time.

Lan. I had to find him.

Setting my mind on my Unseelie, I started wading through the orbs, but they became thicker and thicker, sticking together and crowding my progress.

Grunting, I put my shoulder into the job, spreading my feet into a wider stance to help.

"Sparkly fuckers," I cursed.

I threw my weight against the next set of twinkling bubbles and bounced off this time, hitting the bubbles behind me and rolling to a stop in the eerie mist.

"Lan?" I called.

This had to be harder because of his state. I'd heard him sigh last time, then he'd just appeared past a bunch of these bubbles.

Remaining where I stood, I inhaled and closed my eyes. Tuning into my magic, I sent out indigo tendrils. Feelers. They hit the shining orbs and, like the slowest game of ping pong ever, ricocheted between the bubbles at a languid pace. At least my magic worked in this place, though it wasn't achieving what I wanted.

"Lan?" I shouted. "Lan's granddad?"

Grandpa Lugh didn't shout back.

Like everything life and fate and the goddess herself had thrown at me in recent times, there had to be an answer to the puzzle. The difference now? Time had run out. This puzzle needed solving yesterday.

Worrying at my bottom lip, I mentally stuffed the blue Seelie part of my essence deep within me, leaving only purple Unseelie magic flowing from my hands. I shooed more tendrils toward the bubbles, hoping Lan's Unseelie magic would call to mine.

I got to my feet, listening for the tiniest sigh or scuff. Nothing.

Maybe opposites would attract. It was worth a shot before unleashing lightning in dreamland. I wasn't eager to confirm whether it would ricochet in every direction off the twinkling orbs, straight into my face.

Calling the purple Unseelie magic home, I released the Seelie half of my power. Blue poured from my hands, and I whispered to the tendrils, *Find Lan.*

The blue bounced away.

And I kept listening.

Time worked differently here and standing idly without action unnerved me. The last time, Cinth had burst into the room to tackle Ailbhe seconds after I'd entered dreamland, yet I'd spent at least ten minutes speaking to Lan and...well, he'd been focused on other things too. I also couldn't discount that it might work differently this time since my physical body was in Underhill, not the human world.

Nothing.

Lightening it was. I really hoped fried Alli wasn't on the menu this evening. Calling forth the two halves of my magic, I did the visual exercise of layering them on top of each other and dissolving them to one.

A faint scream tore the air.

It was Lan. I felt that down to my very being.

I jerked, eyes widening.

None of the lightning I'd built within me had released into dreamland. My Seelie power had done the trick. I shot Seelie tendrils in the direction of the scream.

Waiting was torture, but nothing like Lan had endured at Rubezahl's hands.

A pained groan followed the scream.

"Lan," I shouted.

I shoved into the balls, pushing them aside with as much difficulty as if they were thick mud. In seconds sweat dripped from my chin and ran in rivulets down my neck and back. With each step the path became more difficult, and physical strength wasn't enough to break through the barrier. Disregarding fears of becoming fried Alli, I blasted the orbs with my lightning, sending them flying away.

Wow. So much more efficient.

Striding between the balls, I sent more of my Seelie magic out at intervals, adjusting my direction as needed.

Before me stood a shimmering wall. One I recognized without having seen it before. This was the barrier of Lan's mind.

"Lan," I whispered against the shimmering surface.

An agonized howl answered me.

Tears sprang to my eyes. I eased my hands through the wall and reached blindly. There was something in there. A foot? I grunted, trying to balance so I didn't fall inside. That would put me inside his mind and a heavy weight in my gut warned me doing so was unnatural and forbidden.

An ankle.

I heaved backward with all my might.

Lan's legs appeared in dreamland, entirely limp. Choking on fear, I hauled the rest of him through, falling hard onto my butt in the process. *Please don't let him be dead.*

Before I could get to my feet, a hand reached down, and I gaped at Faolan, now standing over me.

"How?" I gasped. "You were screaming, then so still."

He lifted a shoulder. "It is this place, I assume. The pain I felt didn't follow me here."

I took his hand and launched into his arms. "Faolan!"

His strong arms wrapped around me, and I sobbed against his chest. "You idiot. Why did you go after the harp like that?"

He eased one of his arms free, only to take a loose strand of my dark hair and hold it to his nose, inhaling. "I had to go. Something in me needed the harp. I didn't understand it at the time, but as soon as I set my hands on it, I knew. The harp has been calling to me, Alli. I can't fathom why, but it whispers to me day and night."

"You're meant to play it," I said.

Faolan inhaled sharply. "What?"

"I'm almost certain of it. Being able to wield it has nothing to do with whether a fae is Unseelie or Seelie. Did your grandfather say nothing?"

"I see him, but he cannot break his healing chant. I believe it's the only reason I've lived this long."

His words only filled me with fear . . . and *fury*. Despite his obvious suffering, I was so *mad* at him. He'd put all fae at risk by going in blind. We'd needed to deploy the army early, and with less sleeping draught. But truth be told, I only cared that he'd put *himself* at risk. "Since you were taken, life has been a black void." It wasn't like me to be so forthcoming, but truthfully, the words still did sum up the yawning hole within me when Rubezahl took him.

"Alli," he whispered against my neck. "Forgive me. Before the curse takes me, tell me you won't remember me with anger in your heart."

I pushed away from him. "I can't promise that."

Shock lit his features. "Grandfather has been keeping me alive through his spear, but it can't last. The curse Rubezahl cast has rooted deep in my heart. Nothing you do can remove it. You would let things end this way?"

"The way you were going to let things end between us on Unimak?" I challenged, frustration leaking into my words.

I hadn't come here to fight with Lan. I'd come to hold him close, but my wounded feelings insisted that everything come out.

His gaze narrowed. "*You* ended it. You ended our balcony meetings."

"Which I did because you were doing what you damned-well always do—you were pushing me away!"

Faolan clenched his jaw.

I blew out a breath, some of my anger deflating. "It's true. You let yourself believe all that crap your parents put in your head about your magic making you evil. Worse, you let it come between us. So, yes, I ended the balcony meetings. I'll even admit that part of the reason I did it was the pressure of being queen and my worry that the courts wouldn't accept us being together. But the real reason was because I couldn't bear for you to leave me again."

He stepped forward.

I held up both hands. "How am I meant to trust you when you don't even trust yourself? You've already decided to give up."

"You can't help this time—"

I exploded; hands clenched into fists. "Do you think I would've entered dreamland without looking for an answer first?"

He blinked, saying hoarsely, "Something can be done?"

Closing the distance between us, I rested my hand against his jaw. "Something can be done. Devon gave me a hint—well, half a hint. You know what she's like."

"I do." Lan cracked a smile, and the remaining anger gushed out of me.

I took his hand, and he intertwined our fingers. "You're right about one thing."

"Just one thing?" he teased.

I considered that. "Yes."

Faolan gripped my chin and whispered a soft kiss on my lips. "What did Devon say, Orphan?"

"Only two charms exist to counter Rubezahl's curse. One requires my death, but the other..." My gaze flew to his dark gaze and the glints of rainbow within. "The curse is linked to your essence. If you alter your essence enough, then the curse cannot maintain its hold. Its roots will slip away, and we can expel the curse without ending your life."

Lan's jaw worked. "Did she tell you how to alter my essence? Does she mean my magic?"

"No, grandson of mine," a deep voice rent the air.

Heart galloping, I shifted my gaze toward the voice as Lugh himself appeared through the bubbles.

The Seelie fae hero inclined his head in my direction.

I bowed my head in return. "Thank you for keeping him alive."

"The fiery spear is anchored to your world; unlike this form I wear in dreamland. Through it, I am able to maintain my magic indefinitely, though it requires my full concentration."

Ebliu had said as much, and Devon too. Of course, Devon had also pointed out that it wouldn't do us much good since there was an army days from attacking us. "Is your harp the same?" I asked.

He glanced at his grandson. "It is. My harp must be returned to our bloodline. That is imperative."

"The harp represents half of Rubezahl's power."

"Yes," he said seriously. "And half of yours."

I frowned. "Mine?"

"Through my grandson, yes."

Lan and I exchanged a glance.

Faolan spoke first. "I definitely have to wield the harp?"

Lugh nodded. "You must."

I rubbed my temples. "You won't be able to wield a cucumber unless you figure out how to alter your essence."

Unfortunately, Lan looked about as clueless as I was on that front.

"I tried for years to alter my essence," he said. "I'm Unseelie. And if that's something I can change, then I haven't figured out how."

Lugh walked to his grandson, placing a big hand on his shoulder. "Your magic is merely the color of your essence, not your essence itself. You *are* Unseelie. That will never change, nor should you seek to alter it. But I believe you have the answer to what you must do to defeat the curse."

His grandson stared at him, saying hoarsely, "I don't understand."

"You do."

Understanding dawned in Lan's eyes, and he instantly closed them.

"What is it?" I demanded.

"Part of his essence is masked by the belief that what he is, is wrong."

Lan had told me of his childhood struggles. That he, a fae of Lugh's line, had been sorted Unseelie was something he perceived as a failing, and it had absolutely shaped the man he'd become.

It was the reason he had so many barriers up.

It was the reason he kept pushing me away.

Faolan's belief that he was evil inside was the reason he believed himself unworthy.

My voice was low. "He has to overcome his aversion to being Unseelie."

Lan had opened his eyes, and he and Lugh were locked in a silent battle.

"So, I'm supposed to sit here and give myself a pep talk?" Faolan said between gritted teeth. "How is that going to help? We won't even know if or when I've managed it."

Lugh gripped his grandson's jaw. "I live in death, watching over you and the world. When the woman I must call daughter began to fill you with fear and self-disgust for your magic, I would occasionally step into your mind in an attempt to undo the damage." He glanced at the shimmering wall behind us. "Alas, I have told you my influence in this form is no match for magic anchored in the world of the living. While you would often rally after I whispered to you in dreams, her words soon overpowered mine. And so, I was forced to watch as you tried to fight your heart and mind. It was a ripe punishment from the goddess for the mistakes I made in life. One day, you closed the door to your mind, and I could no longer gain access. It was the day the Oracle sorted you to the Unseelie court."

Lan's throat worked. His hands trembled. "I think I remember you. I used to think I'd gone crazy."

Lugh smiled. "Do you recall what I would say?"

Lan watched him wordlessly.

His grandfather drew him into his embrace. "That I had never loved anyone more. That if your fears were a dagger, I would let it stab me one million times rather than let it so much as prick your skin. You are my grandchild in heart and deed, not only blood. Every breath you have taken has filled me with pride. And just as the goddess may have punished me for my failings, so she has rewarded me for my heroism. With you."

Faolan looked at me over his grandfather's shoulder, shock and fear coating his angled features.

Lugh released him, and I'd never seen Lan looking more like a boy than in that moment.

"I don't know how to accept what I am," he admitted, defeat clear in the sagging of his shoulders. "How am I meant to undo everything I was told for so long?"

The fae hero tilted his chin. "The hardest battles are the ones no one sees, pride of my heart. No one can do this but you. But there is a way to know when you have succeeded."

I shot him a look. "How?"

It was Lan who replied. "The spear?"

Lugh smiled again. "My weapon glows at your touch. But you will find there is a difference between recognition and acceptance. When you find acceptance within yourself, the spear will accept *you*. That is how you will know your essence is altered. As for the journey to get there . . ." His grandfather turned and began to walk back to the shimmering wall. ". . . neither the Queen of All Fae nor I can help you with that."

I looked helplessly at the man I loved. "There's nothing I can do?"

Halfway through the barrier to Lan's mind, which I hadn't dared to enter, the fae hero met my gaze, then looked to his grandson. "Join your queen in life, pride of my heart. Or me in death. The choice is in your hands."

I walked away from dreamland with only Lan's lingering kiss on my lips. My raging headache nearly matched the pain in my heart.

Truth was a terrible master.

Faolan's journey was his, and his alone.

There was nothing more I could do but wait and hope that he had the strength to change—that he would choose life over death.

That he wound finally believe in his worth.

I cupped my head in my hands and drew in a shuddering breath before turning to the man I loved, who lay silent beside me. Leaning over, I pressed my cheek to his and whispered, "Come back to me, Lan. Please."

His body didn't so much as twitch. There was no new warmth radiating from it after our dreamland meeting. I fought tears, losing the battle when one escaped and ran from my face onto his. I didn't wipe it away.

"You have done all you can." Devon's voice rolled over me, and I lifted my eyes to hers.

"Have I?"

Her smile was sad, as though she already knew the outcome and it was one I would not like.

"Some paths are meant to be walked alone," said the blooded fae. "Faolan must see his path through to the end. Just as you must do with yours."

I wondered at how much she understood because I didn't care for her wording. End of the path . . . did that mean she thought he was going to die? She hadn't been there with Lugh and Lan and me in the dreamworld.

Had she?

I frowned as a dribble of blood trickled from her ear. "Devon . . . Are you okay?"

"A messenger has arrived." She cut me off with a wave of her hand. "From your army. I do believe you are needed, Queen of all Fae."

I swung to sit on the edge of the bed, and only remembered Rubezahl's journal when it fell to the ground. The journal had told us something, but I felt there was something else there too. Another connection that my mind hadn't quite latched onto. I'd go through the entries again when I had time.

Filled with new determination, I hurried down the halls of the Oracle's home and through the kitchen, where Cinth handed me a star-shaped filled pastry without a word.

Goddess.

I nodded my thanks as I wolfed down the meat pie. The tender, smoky flavors slid down my throat, battening down the empty ache in my stomach. Cinth followed after me, shoving a cup of something into my other hand.

Pausing with the cup pressed to my lips, I strained to remember today's password from our list. Remembering which day it *was* proved a feat in itself. *Ah, yes.* "Passcode?"

"Ogre's ass crack."

Correct.

I downed the drink as if I were on a professional drinking team.

"Maybe not so fast . . ." she muttered.

Too late.

It was True Heat, a healing drink laced with spices that burned my mouth and throat *all* the way down. I thumped my chest, gasping, but as the heat receded, so did the fog in my mind and the headache pounding my brain

Who knew?

"Running off somewhere like your boobs are on fire again, I see," the Oracle called.

Wincing at the visual, I breathed out, and my lips tingled with heat. "Once my mouth stops burning."

"Bah!" she roared. "We used to drink True Heat through our noses in my day, Dandelion."

My brows rose. No kidding.

Out the door I went, fully expecting bright sunshine to greet me, but an overcast evening sky and pouring rain met my eyes instead. How long had I spent in dreamland? An entire day?

The messenger stood waiting.

"Bracken," I said.

She bowed. "Queen Kallik. A report from the generals. There is movement in the giant's army. We are losing our window of opportunity. We have two hours to make a move. Perhaps less."

And Devon had somehow known this before Bracken's arrival.

She'd known I would need to leave Lan to face his path so I could stand with my army against Ruby. I'd chosen my fae subjects over Lan before, and it had led to him sneaking into Ruby's camp to steal the harp . . .

Everything in me protested a repeat of that. Yet everything was different this time around. Now, I had no choice but to watch him battle from afar.

"There's something else," she said. "The mystica fae you summoned, Ailbhe, has disappeared. No one saw her leave. Rowan had escorted her to a tent. Trusted guards were there to keep her safe. When a meal was taken to her, the tent was found empty."

My eyes closed. "Rubezahl got to her." I knew how—he'd used the damn harp to jump around. But how had he known she was even with the army instead of on Unimak?

The answer hit me like a wall. Her magical signature. "Fuck," I roared. He'd make more brainwashing tea with her blood.

He'd *hurt* her. Maybe even kill her.

She'd had something important to impart to me, too, about the harp and Rubezahl's plan. *Why* didn't I just take five damn minutes to talk to her at the time rather than waste time speaking with Lan's mother?

I gripped my hair, taking steadying breaths. It felt like every step I took forward was leading to five backward, yet I had to keep lifting my damn feet in the hopes I'd somehow make it to the finish line.

Okay. *Breathe, Alli. You can only work with what you have.*

Everything Bracken just reported pointed to one course of action. I knew what had to be done. "We go now."

Bracken bowed from the waist.

I glanced back at Cinth, who stood behind me. "Stay with Lan. Please."

She and Lan were my only true family. They had to keep safe. Her face tightened, and tears pricked at the corners of her eyes. “Don’t you fucking die on me, Orphan. Or you’ll not see any sweet treats from my ovens in the afterlife.”

She’d used Lan’s nickname for me . . . and a sob built in my chest.

I caught her up in my arms and held on tight to the person who was more sister than friend. She squeezed me back, enveloping me in the aromas that were so uniquely her. Cinnamon and spice, sweet and salty.

She was one of the few places I had to call home.

And sometimes the truth was too harsh to utter. Sometimes it was kinder to voice hope, no matter that I couldn’t guarantee anything. “I won’t. I promise.”

Cinth let me go slowly, as if she could feel the lie between us. Her brows furrowed, and I had to look away.

Devon stepped up beside her. “I will go with you into battle, Queen of All Fae. Underhill has deemed that I must be present to witness and assess the fight.”

Like . . . she’d score it out of ten?

Whatever. I’d be glad for the support of a blooded fae. “We have to hurry. What lies between us and Ruby’s camp in Dragonsmount?”

Rain splattered down around us, and a boom of thunder rippled through my body, reverberating in my chest and calling to my lightning like a long-lost lover.

I clamped down on the urge to join with the storm around us.

This was not the place.

Nor did I have any magic left to me. Which would be an issue in itself for the battle ahead.

Devon stared off into the distance. “Plains that can present as whatever Underhill desires in the moment. And the dragon wings that you crossed to find the Oracle.”

Bingo. I'd remembered the terrain from Rowan's map correctly. My experience over the dragon's wings would give us something of an edge if Rubezahl decided to meet us halfway.

"Is there any way to get a message to the generals? We need to release the sleeping draught now." Aside from Devon's teleportation, which I really wasn't sure she should do again given her constant nosebleed going on, I only knew of one other speedy means of transportation in Underhill—though I was certain the Oracle had her own means of jumping around too.

I peered out across the meadow of alicorns and found the single land kelpie. As if feeling my gaze, he reared his head back and looked at me.

"What the fuck are you staring at, dumdum?" he bellowed across the meadow.

I strode toward him, but a glittering gold on the ground to my left stopped me in my tracks. The gold wound into the distance, a path. Clearly a path for me.

I focused on the land kelpie again. "I know you think I'm a fool. I also know you hate Rubezahl. I need to get a message to my army to release a sleeping draught. Then I will meet the giant on the wings of the dragon. I would have you with me when I do. Let's see if he can keep his footing there, shall we?"

The land kelpie drew close and bared his overly sharp teeth. "A chance to see the giant tumble on his great ass? You jest. You tease. You tempt."

I shook my head. "I do no such thing. You can kick him in the kneecaps after I take him down."

"Aside from spreading my seed, that is my heart's greatest desire."

Too much info. "I need to take this path for now," I said, nodding to the glittering that he likely did not see, "but will you tell the generals that—"

The land kelpie took off with a leap, kicking his heels high and letting out a tremendous fart that put the thunder to shame.

"We ride!" he roared and was gone in a tinkling of icicles, racing toward my army.

Okay, then.

"Can you trust him?" Bracken asked.

"I trust his hate of Rubezahl, and he does carry me on occasion." I stared at the path that had extended beneath my feet, sparkling and beckoning. "Meet me at the edge of the wings, Devon. We fight for all fae, for Underhill."

Bracken, Devon, and Cinth all reached as though to stop me as I took a step down the path. But the Oracle smiled and tipped her head my way. "Walk your path, Kallik of All Fae. And find your strength."

My strength?

My magic?

She had to mean my magic. My stores were completely empty, and if I went into battle like that, I wouldn't just die—I'd die without casting a single blow.

I took another step, and it felt as though a shot of lightning had burst up my limbs and into my torso.

I'd thought I was meant to walk alone, but a split second later, Devon was strolling beside me. Her nose and ears trickled blood as a voice that was definitely not her own rolled from her mouth.

"Young," it said. "You are so young and yet you are my only hope."

Power poured out of Devon—a terrible, ancient power that drove itself into my bones and brutally resonated there like a tuning fork.

I didn't know if I should bow or fall flat onto my face. "Underhill?"

"Yes, infant. We shall together walk. But understand balance is that which must be sought. For to exist without it is to exist no more. You . . . the fae . . . soul creations of mine . . . none without balance may exist."

"I'm trying to restore balance," I said.

Her eyes never looked my way. She walked steadily down the path, the words falling from her mouth.

Her chest rattled like a Nut Snake. "Balance is me. Good is me. Hurt, yes. Kiss, yes. Heal, yes. Lose. Win. Balance is all, and good. Good must be in us. And here. Only balance and good."

"You're saying Ruby has to win to maintain balance?" Making sense of her words wasn't easy with half my mind tucked away with my army and the sleeping draught. Besides, Underhill needed English lessons.

She turned Devon's head toward me, but Devon's eyes did not look out at me. Eyes were the window to the soul, and I was seeing Underhill's.

Brilliant white, flecked with all the colors of the rainbow. Like Lan's. Like the Oracle's. Only in reverse. And where their eyes sucked me in and made me think of the universe and the night sky, hers . . . they were creation itself—all the world was and ever would be. They were the beginning and the end of our world encapsulated. Time immortal.

Balance is me. Good is me. Hurt, yes. Kiss, yes. Heal, yes. Lose. Win.

I'd been shaken before, but it was nothing to the way my body quivered in her presence. Or this part of her she'd managed to stuff into Devon's body.

The edges of her eyes bled, her version of tears, perhaps? "*You* are balance, Kallik of all Fae. You are good. Remain such."

Her eyes closed, squeezing blood in a torrent out over Devon's cheeks.

She slumped, and I barely caught her before she hit the ground. The glittering gold path faded, and I blinked to see that we'd already reached the edge of the dragon's wings.

The five-minute walk had transported us miles upon miles.

"Devon?" I shook her gently. The blood coming from her was thicker, more than a trickle sliding from her mouth, nose, eyes, and ears. Her skin was waxy and cool to the touch and had split where it was thinnest, over her cheekbones, brow, and jaw. Hosting Underhill was no small thing, I gathered, but she still breathed.

Thank the gods I didn't have *that* burden at least.

I ducked low at a sweeping *whoosh* of wings overhead and covered Devon's body with my own. I craned up and spotted the blur of the pixie troop.

"Oh, shit." I whispered.

The pixies were going to spread the sleeping draught, and I had no magic to cloak us.

"Devon. I need you to wake up." I shook her again.

Nothing.

I stared in the direction of the blowing wind, and a string of curses flowed from my mouth.

I didn't have time to get us both out of here.

The ground under us was rock, and the dragon's wide membrane wings lay ahead. My mind worked rapidly as a crazy, absolutely fucking nuts idea came to me. "Hell, it just might work."

Devon wouldn't be hurt by the sleeping draught. She was already down for the count, so I patted her on the head. "Sleep well, my friend. Dream of large, muscled men."

I raced toward the edge of the rocky ground as the wind pushed at my back. Hopefully in encouragement and approval of my wild plan?

At the juncture between stone and dragon wing, I dove and slid forward on my belly. Jamming my knee against the cartilage edge of the membrane, I grabbed the edge of the dragon's wing, swinging underneath.

My crazy idea? I was now living it. Clinging onto the underside of a dragon's wing for shelter.

Any hope of quietly waiting out the sleeping draught on was squashed as I peered into the darkness.

"Fuck me!" I nearly lost my grip.

A ginormous dragon eye stared up at me, unblinking. Its gray magic stretched toward me. Hanging and helpless, I couldn't do anything when the tendrils touched me, tapping on every nerve ending and leaving a painful sharpness in its wake. The magic scented every ounce of my fear, making my heart pound.

As if with the twist of a dial, the creature magnified those fears and the stabbing pain along with them.

A grunt escaped me as my arms shook.

The dragon blinked, and a forked tongue flicked out between its teeth.

Nausea rolled through me, sweat beading from every pore in my damn body, including my palms, which was bad news since sliding off the edge of the dragon's wing was about the worst thing that could happen.

I smiled at the dragon. "Hi. Just . . . hanging out a minute. You don't want to go up there. Sleeping draught in the wind. It'd knock you right out. Trust me. Balance, you know. We need to keep balance. Hurt, yes. Uh, what was the other one? Kiss, yes. Good. Bad."

I was babbling. But when you were staring into the eyes of a creature capable of torturing and eating you, and that creature had a mouth big enough to snap up ten giants in one go, and its magic literally induced fear and pain . . . well, all that would make a person babble.

The dragon's eyes were a deep, dark red, and I could feel the Unseelie magic coursing through it. Its mouth opened slowly, displaying teeth that sparkled even in the dim light under its wings.

They weren't the yellowish-whitish shade I'd expected.

More like a yellow. Wait, orange.

Red?

"Oh shit," I whispered. A molten flicker in the back of the dragon's throat told me I was out of time under here.

Flames licked upward, past its teeth, and roared toward me like galloping kelpies.

Sleeping draught it was!

I adjusted my grip and pulled myself up, swinging my legs over the edge of the wing. Heat blazed behind me.

Go, go, go!

I leaped across the divide and rolled across the stone ground I'd come from, not daring to stop. When I met with a softer surface, I simply grabbed Devon and kept rolling.

Because those flames? They were targeted at me, and assuming they didn't have a mind of their own was a sure way to become Flamé Alli, as Cinth might say.

Dragon fire coursed along the grass toward me, and my momentum slowed. Shielding Devon, I watched the flames bear down on me, at Underhill's mercy once more.

Because if Underhill didn't need me anymore, I'd be dead before the battle with Ruby even started.

CHAPTER 15

I choked on a shriek as flames licked my boots.

But I didn't meet a blistering fate because the tendrils of fire curled in on themselves. Devon was motionless beneath me as I watched, eyes huge, as the dragon flame was sucked away from me, like a fish being reeled through water.

The dragon's snout was just visible under its slightly raised left wing, and as the last wisps of orange and red retreated into its mouth, it hiccupped smoke and grunted in something akin to shock.

Hiccupping smoke again, it gave a mighty rumble, then peeked at me with one gigantic dragon eye. It blinked, multiple eyelids squelching.

I waved. "Thanks?"

Though I suspected the dragon wasn't the one to thank. He seemed as confused as I felt.

"Hey . . . big fella. Just a friendly warning that judging by the sound of things, my army isn't too far away." I tilted my head, realizing the mighty rumble from before couldn't just be blamed on the dragon moving. "Make that real soon. Is there a certain way you'd like us to, uh, get on you?"

The creature couldn't fail to notice us.

And he didn't appear to care. Belching more smoke, the force of which knocked me over, the dragon retracted once more, lowering its wing.

One eye on Underhill's beastie, I crouched over Devon.

Shit. She was *really* not looking flash. Blood poured from her eye sockets, nose, and ears.

Her inhales were steady though.

"Queen Kallik!"

I glanced into the distance and spotted Rowan, magic swirling around his throat. My army was a rippling sheet of black and gold. The fae had entered in a strip of dark Unseelie and another strip of glinting Seelie, so for the two colors to be mixed like this would give me the fuzzies if we weren't on the cusp of a battle that would likely leave many of them, and probably me, dead.

I picked up the blooded fae, cradling her in my arms. She felt light, far lighter than she looked. Rowan ran forward to join us.

"Report as we walk. Devon needs help," I said to him.

We strode back toward the army.

"We thought the sleeping draught might've gotten you. The pixies spotted you here."

"I hid under the dragon's wing."

He frowned, glancing back. "What dragon?"

I jerked my head. "That whole membrane-looking thing over there is a set of wings. The dragon's body is beneath them."

Rowan stumbled. "That's *nothing* like the dragons in training."

Nope. That had come as a surprise to me too on my first visit. Although fake Underhill could be felt and heard and seen, it failed miserably at mimicking the wonder and utter strangeness of the real thing.

"What do the pixies see?" I asked.

"The sleeping draught took down Rubezahl's frontline. They didn't dare fly beyond that to check."

I nodded. "What of the sleeping draught?"

"It has dispersed. They watched for long enough to ensure Rubezahl didn't gather it and send it back our way."

Good. "We must strike without delay." The draught was strong, but I'd been stung by the prowess of Ruby's magic and intellect enough times to know we didn't have much time. He was too quick for us to dawdle.

Small stones leaped underfoot at the approach of my army.

General Stryk led the procession. Well, a few steps behind the land kelpie, who'd clearly nominated himself as regent in my absence.

"Thank you," I said to the land kelpie.

"Now, where's the oversized fucker?" he replied, scanning the horizon.

Shaking my head, I passed Devon to the general. "She needs immediate attention—from a fae who can be trusted."

I liked Devon, cryptic though she was. Besides, not treating Underhill's mouthpiece with the proper respect seemed like a good way to get myself dead.

Pixies darted to and from Rowan before blurring back across the dragon's wings. They came in a steady stream, giving my Seelie general a live feed of the other army.

I joined him. "What's Rubezahl's position?"

"He's advancing. Twenty minutes from the wings."

He'd left Dragonsmount. Which, if I had to lay a wager, he'd only done because his frontline was down for the count.

Rowan hummed. "I don't think he'll step foot onto the membranes."

No, he probably wouldn't risk it, but . . . "His army will. There's no way he can allow us to reach the other side. We'd be able to jump straight over his frontline and annihilate his army."

Which is exactly what I intended to do.

Rowan hesitated. "Queen Kallik, how was Cinth when you left her?"

He and my friend had fallen hard for each other. It was hard to understand when my experience with Lan had been a desperate battle from the get-go, but I didn't doubt the feeling I saw in her eyes, nor the feeling I now saw in his. I held his gaze. "She's safe. And we're going to do our absolute best to get back to her. Copy that?"

His swallow was audible. "Copy that. Having someone to return to changes things."

Was that what Rowan had needed to unlock every bit of his potential? Someone to fight for? I thought of Lan. Perhaps the same was true for me too. "Do her proud, General."

Rowan stood to attention. "Of course, Queen Kallik."

"Ready?" I asked the land kelpie.

"As ready as an asshole after consuming too many cloud plants," he answered.

That . . .

Nope, not asking.

I leaped astride him, gripping chunks of his frozen mane.

General Stryk returned. "I have your . . . friend . . . with our healers. They will do all they can for her."

I regarded the two leaders before me. "General Stryk, take the right wing. General Rowan, you take the center, either side of the dragon's spine so you can still bounce. I'll take the left wing. I think Underhill has warned the dragon to stay out of this, but relay to the force that the dragon could take large sweeps with its tail. And obviously there's the head to think of, and it *does* include a fiery booby trap."

The Unseelie general nodded curtly. "Fear not, Queen Kallik, the army is prepared. We are well-versed in the drills you ordered."

Good.

I peered across the membranes as my two generals barked orders to the army to split into three. Across the other side were thousands of outcasts under Rubezahl's control. And I had to make the decision about how we would treat them.

My gut churned at the idea of slaughtering them. Hadn't I been a victim of the giant's tea until recently? If anything had happened differently, I would be with him still. What if I was standing there and needed someone to show me mercy?

And yet . . .

Hesitation could kill us all.

Bres had spent years in Underhill hammering it out of us during sparring for that very reason. If I told my army to disarm and contain, to hurt but not kill, then that order could claim *their* lives.

If I managed to hit Rubezahl hard now, then I could be in a position later to spare lives later. With that mentality, I could *almost* convince myself that I'd be able to sleep at night if I somehow survived this. I'd never wanted to be a leader simply because I'd never wanted to make these calls.

I nudged the land kelpie until I was facing the army. I didn't have magic to amplify my voice, so they'd have to use magic to sharpen their hearing.

"Today, we fight to live another day," I said. "We fight for our freedom, and for the freedom of those still on Earth, human and fae alike." I steeled myself. "Today, I fight without mercy, and I ask that you do the same."

Underhill always had an odd stillness to it. The air was denser than on Earth and sound didn't carry the same, but it seemed significant the army didn't make a single sound either.

This was a new position for me, but I'd helped lead the Untried for years during our tests. Bravery was catching.

In each of these soldiers was the deep drive to leave a legacy. To be a hero.

To become a Lugh.

I smiled coldly and drew my sword, holding it high. "Tonight, we cut off the giant's head."

My proclamation was followed by the ringing hiss of thousands of fae drawing their swords. "*We cut off the giant's head.*"

"Left flank," I told the land kelpie.

"I have ears, imbecile," he replied.

Trotting to stand before the far battalion, I met the eyes of the nearest soldiers but was careful not to wave or make any other foolish gestures. I needed to appear untouchable, just like Queen Elisavanna had always appeared to me.

They had to believe me invincible as the sounds of the approaching army swelled louder. It was almost worse to be able to hear Rubezahl's approach without yet being able to see his force, and if my army knew I was going into this without magic and with very little plan other than to 'steal the harp for Lan,' then I had a feeling they'd disperse in every direction. They wouldn't care about my one advantage—that Rubezahl still couldn't track me.

Be untouchable.

I held my sword high, voice still magically amplified. "Forward march!"

My stomach flipped, and I released a long, steady breath, my heart hammering with the knowledge that I could have just hours to live.

So could the ten thousand soldiers at my back. If we failed here, the first their families heard of their deaths might be when Rubezahl waged war on Adair and Uncle Josef back on Unimak.

"Hey, you got a name?" I asked the kelpie.

It felt wrong to go into war on his back without knowing his name.

The land kelpie snorted. "Why the hell would I tell you that?"

"You don't have to give your real name. Just a fake one will do."

"Kallik."

I rolled my eyes as he launched onto the dragon's left wing, and we started bouncing across. The land kelpie kept our trajectory low and the angle acute, so we shot forward without becoming targets for the enemy army in the not-so-far distance. "How about 'asshole'?"

"How about I kick you in the teeth?"

I smirked. "I Kick You in the Teeth. I like it."

He was silent. "Kikuindateeth . . . It does have as certain ring to it."

My brows rose as I scanned for the dragon's head, then his tail. But so far, my hunch had been borne out. My new beastie friend wasn't going to be a second adversary. "Seriously? That's what you want to be called?"

"Do I have to spell it out for you, imbecile?"

Guess not. "Kikuindateeth it is," I muttered.

I checked the position of the fae at my back in relation to those ahead. The danger was that they could close around us if we kept too central. I held my sword high, then extended it to the left. *Spread wide.*

To my far right, General Stryk echoed the order.

The clanging of weapons filled the air behind me, but a deep bellow of thunder rose before us.

I still couldn't see Rubezahl's army, but they were running.

At this pace, the new front lines would reach the wings within minutes.

Sword high, I tipped forward. "Faster."

Kikuindateeth didn't argue, grunting as he kicked harder off the thin, vein-streaked membrane under hoof.

I gritted my teeth. It'd be close.

Fire exploded to my right. *No, wait.* It had come from a catapult.

My focus shifted to the fiery ball aimed for Rowan's battalion.

Water burst from our frontline, extinguishing the catapult. But I winced as it collected fae mid-air and more upon landing.

More cannon balls launched from Rubezahl's side.

I tracked them back to small groups of giants standing on outcrops of stone as their outcast brethren sprinted toward us.

Rubezahl was trying to slow us down.

"Too late this time," I whispered.

The edge was in sight.

Very few outcasts launched onto the wing to attack us, their line a poor attempt compared to ours. *They*, untrained and driven by fury, weren't the problem.

They were just in the way.

Metal singing, I swiped clean through the middle of an outcast descending from an uncontrolled bounce.

Blood sprayed my face, and mentally locked away in battle mode, I pushed aside his top half, vaguely noting the gray tinge to his skin.

"The last bounce is a big one," I told the land kelpie. "Make it count. See the outcrops with the giants? That's our goal."

This was where everything could go horribly wrong.

My army had to dismount from the wing and land in roughly the same place.

We launched high, and I swung my sword through an arrow targeted at Kikuindateeth's neck. He plucked another one from the other side, chomping down to snap it before spitting it out.

We descended, and I readied myself, brandishing my dagger in addition to a gifted sword. Always good to have a weapon to wield in close quarters too. But my movements slowed as my scanning eyes picked up something I hadn't yet seen.

Some*one.*

Horror choked in my throat even as disgust surged up from my stomach.

It was Ailbhe. Or it had been before her body had been lashed to a wooden pole and carried by the frontline of the outcast army like a war banner. I could see she was dead. Drained—always fair, her skin now held a gray tinge.

Air whooshed past my ears as our descent continued.

She'd chosen the right side. She'd helped us. All I'd needed to do was protect her. No matter her words absolving me of that role, guilt swarmed me at the terrible sight of her.

"For Queen Kallik."

The battle cry rose in a roar, jolting me from my sickened shock. A beat later, my earlier resolve started to mount again, reinforced by the sight of Ailbhe and how Rubezahl was using her dead body against me. I might not want to fight these people, these victims, but it was the only way to save my people from fates like Ailbhe's.

She'd met a tragic end. An unfair, gut wrenching end.

And I didn't save her from Rubezahl.

But I could save others from his endlessly brutal ambition.

I circled my sword three times, and the fae behind me unleashed columns of fire toward the outcasts on the ground, waiting with pikes raised.

They scattered, although some were not quite fast enough.

The flames cut off, and the land kelpie thudded onto the hard ground. I gripped on tightly as he ran to clear the area for those behind us, coming in on their own leaps off the wings.

This . . . this was not going to be pretty.

My fae landed all around me. Some behind, but many in front.

Screams filled the air as some impaled on the outcasts' iron-tipped spears.

Yelling wordlessly, a battle cry that crawled up from deep in my belly, I swiveled my sword and cut through an arm. Bending forward, I shoved my dagger into the base of a man's neck and yanked back, turning my face from the jet of blood.

I leaned forward. "Kik, keep moving!"

I circled again, slashing to keep crazed outcasts clear of my four-legged ride. Our archers had remained on the dragon's wings, using the height advantage to their favor. Most of the other soldiers had landed and were convening in the center. The bulk of my army split Rubezahl's in half. He couldn't surround us.

"Split," I roared.

The command was repeated down the line. My fae divided in half and faced outward to the fae that had once been like them.

But not any longer.

Their skin was mottled gray. Some were missing teeth. Some only had a few clumps of hair remaining.

It was something I'd seen before and misunderstood as madness.

Not anymore.

This was what happened when a fae was drained of their magic. Rubezahl was draining his army of life to save his own worthless hide, even as Underhill tried to replenish them. This was why he'd wanted to fight here. Because those he was feeding on would never truly die.

Bile surged up my throat, but I forced it back.

"Charge," I bellowed.

CHAPTER 16

The army around me surged forward. Healthy, vibrant fae full of life and energy facing down a ragtag bunch of outcast fae whose lives were being drained to protect their master.

Not their leader, their master.

"Kik, get your worthless feet moving. Let's find Rubezahl!" I snapped the words as I drove my heels into his sides. The only way to save any of these outcasts, and I *did* want to save them, would be to kill the giant. And I only had my brain and weapons to achieve that, and Underhill's help if she deigned to give it. *Somehow*, I had to kill him and sever the ties connecting him to his unwilling slaves.

That was their only hope, and it depended on our speed.

Kik let out a fierce bray and leapt forward, a tremor running through him as I let my heels drum his sides, urging him forward, pushing him hard. I held tightly to an icicle with one hand and swung my sword without mercy with the other.

"Now this is more like it!" Kik bellowed. "I like it rough!"

I didn't have time to ponder that comment too much as he angled his head down and charged across the hard ground, hooves sending up a drumbeat matched by my heart.

Blood and screams. Dying fae surrounded me, and it didn't matter that some of them were mine and some were not.

They were all mine to protect.

They'd *been* mine to protect.

I steeled myself against the horror rising in my heart and mind.

"Hurry, Kik!" I brought down the flat of my sword behind me and smacked his ass. He squealed, kicked out, then picked up more speed.

I grimaced. He really did like it rough.

To my right, a gray-skinned fae lunged with a spear, and I cut the weapon away, swinging back and severing his head in the next breath.

These were my people, and I was sworn to protect them. Yet here I was, slaughtering them.

"I'm sorry," I whispered, feeling the guilt vibrate within my very soul,

There was a moment of pause, like the world around us froze, and then the footing below us shifted suddenly

Sand dunes shot up, towering over us in height, encompassing both armies. Bodies were flung left and right as fae tumbled into the valleys between the dunes, unable to keep up with Underhill's ruthless change. I'd been assured by Ailbhe that this was the one place in this realm that never changed, but it appeared Underhill had decided to take an active role in this shitstorm.

"Sand! I hate it when she does this! Underhill, you're a miserable bitch!" Kik hollered, and I didn't disagree. Our battle would be harder in the sand, but I wasn't about to call Underhill a bitch out loud.

Kik sunk deep into the sand—his body had been made for the ice and cold, not the slick desert dunes we now found ourselves in.

I leapt off and scrambled away from him. "Meet me if you can! Otherwise, I'll kill him without you." That should put a bee up his ass.

"Goddess be damned!" Kik roared as he sunk up to his chest and stared hard at me, chagrin written clearly across his face. "Perhaps I should not have called her a miserable bitch."

"Yep, you fucked that one up." I shouted over my shoulder as Kik began to profusely apologize to Underhill in his loudest, whiniest bray.

I sprinted up the next dune, feet light on the sand as I pulled gold energy from the ground without conscious thought. I still had no access to *expending* my indigo magic, and usually that would mean I couldn't draw magic into me either, but it seemed like Underhill was willing to replenish me with her power—just like she'd helped me immediately after I stepped through the portal with my army. Her gold snapped and danced its way through my body.

The gold sharpened my vision and leased new energy to my muscles.

She was helping me.

The fae I could see were struggling with the sand dunes, much as Kik was, but to me the ground felt hard-packed, perfect for running. My feet didn't sink in or leave imprints at all. "Thank you, Underhill," I said, never feeling more grateful for her aid.

I reached the top of the first dune.

Finally, I saw him.

The giant who'd lured me in. The giant who'd betrayed me. Who'd betrayed us all.

Rubezahl.

Four sand dunes away, he sat on what could only be called a throne of stone and branches. He wore a crown made of similar material, and I honestly could not imagine why anyone would choose to wear something so uncomfortable.

"Come then, Queen of All fae." He drew out the words, his voice heavy with sarcasm, but the slight widening of his eyes made me wonder if he was surprised to find me so close. Losing my magic had its upsides.

He sneered. "Let us see you face *me*, the King of Underhill."

"Ballsy," I whispered under my breath. "Way too ballsy. Underhill won't stand for that."

But then why wasn't Underhill sinking him up to his chest like she'd done with Kik? Burying him up to his rotten, black heart so I could lop off his head and free the fae captured in his seductive net?

I couldn't wait for him to come to me. I had to go to him, and he knew it.

A quick count showed me fifty wild fae stood between the giant and me, each with very little damage. No gray skin, no missing hair or teeth. These were his best warriors, and he'd leave them hale for as long as he could.

So they could fight his battles for him.

Coward.

"Damn it all," I muttered to myself, thinking of the promise I'd made to Cinth not to die.

I'd felt like a liar then, and I still did. Because I was an awesome warrior. But was I fifty-wild-fae awesome?

And even if I *was* fifty-wild-fae awesome, could I get through them and still be in giant-killing awesome form?

Experience told me nope.

But it didn't matter. I had to try.

I started down the dune at full speed, sprinting straight for the giant and his fighters. Shoving my dagger in my thigh holster, I drew my second gifted sword.

At the bottom I engaged the first ranks, twin blades swinging. I didn't look at their faces, didn't acknowledge they were fae, or even alive.

I couldn't.

Training.

This was just training, and I would do what I must to end this battle.

Wild fae fell at my feet as though I were cutting off daisy heads in the fields around Unimak. They may be his best warriors, but they preferred their bow and arrows.

And I?

I preferred close combat and the high ringing of my blades.

Even as the wild fae fell, I felt the truth in my very bones. There was no way I'd make it through.

When all else fails?

I sucked in a breath. "The tea he feeds you holds the blood of the mystica fae. The tea allows him to control you!"

Swing, parry, thrust, a spray of blood across my cheek. "He fed the tea to me too! He's killing his own arm to feed his power!" Duck, kick out a knee, slash across the throat, take a blow to my side. "Look at your friends, at their skin! They're gray! It's all him." I gasped and dropped to a knee, rolling to avoid losing my head to a savage blow.

Staggering slightly, I stood.

The wild fae turned as a unit to face me. Their eyes blank.

"They cannot hear you, young one." Rubezahl chuckled. "I have plugged their ears with wax and made them see you as the monster you are. There should never have been a child of the Seelie and Unseelie. You are a monstrosity. I thought that perhaps you would be the answer, but I can see that you are a poison to my people. A mutt."

He didn't stand but sat and spoke as his fae launched themselves at me.

"Look at you, starting a fight that is killing hundreds, perhaps thousands of the people you were sworn to protect. That is. . . if you are even properly coronated? Or did you manage to avoid speaking those oaths too?"

My arms grew tired, and I struggled to keep my blade up, to stop the cold hard iron that slashed toward my face and limbs. I stumbled back a few steps just in time and sucked in a ragged breath as I drew more gold energy from Underhill again, thanking her quietly for her help.

The boost gave me what I needed to down three more of the giant's men. Three more.

Forty plus left. Only a few of that number were injured by defensive blows.

"You will never reach me." Rubezahl said, his once kind, twinkling eyes hard. "You will die first. You know this."

Maybe I would have said something in response, but as I opened my mouth to speak, a spine-tingling howl cut through the air.

I sucked in a sharp inhale.

The men in front of me didn't even see the pack coming. Their ears were plugged solid after all.

A flash of gray and black. The rippling of winter coats that stood out against the desert sands, the bright gleam of wicked teeth.

"Drake?" I shouted his name.

"For the Queen of All Fae!" he howled in his changeling form to the others with him, who were a mish-mash of various animals. They slammed into Rubezahl's men like a tidal wave, washing them out of my path.

My heart constricted. "Thank you."

"Kill him, Alli," Drake yelled, yelping as he took a kick to his shoulder. "Kill him quickly!"

I was already running toward the giant who stood before his throne. Rage rolled over his features, and amid all this, I wondered how I'd ever thought him kind and gentle.

Rubezahl pulled the harp from its fastening at his hip and put his large fingers to it. The harp that could calm a wild fae. That could calm a giant and steal its urge to fight. The harp that could transport huge numbers between realms. If he calmed my troops enough, they'd stand still as his slaves slaughtered them. He could simply whisk them back to Earth for all I knew.

"You fear me so much that you'd use your harp rather than face me?" I slid to a stop at the base of the sand dune he stood upon, craning my neck to see him.

The sand shifted beneath my feet, and the ground groaned as the dunes decompressed, sinking away until we were on flat ground once more. It turned marshy and wet as trees shot up around us, some of them spearing wild fae and changeling bodies on their lethal tips.

A blast of humid heat rolled through the air, turning cloying in my throat, and water seeped through my boots, rising to my knees.

Didn't matter. I sloshed toward the giant.

A chance. I only needed a damn chance. But without my magic, I already knew what the outcome would be. "I will drop my weapons if you drop your harp."

From behind me, Rowan bellowed a "No" as I stared the giant down. I hadn't realized they were so close, and it renewed my resolve. I had to buy my troops and generals time to surround Rubezahl, even if it meant sacrificing my life.

Sheer numbers could overwhelm him so long as he didn't have the harp.

"A deal struck in Underhill must be seen through to the end." Rubezahl declared. "And so, it will be always between us henceforth in this realm—no weapons but the magic we each carry."

Fuckity shit, I *was* a big dumdum. But I needed him to put down that harp, and time was wasting and all . . .

I nodded. "So be it."

He dropped the harp, and I drove my swords into the soft muck of the swamp around us.

I stared at his magic swirling around his body, black with hints of green. Unseelie magic through and through. Not once in all the time that I'd known him had he revealed his magic in this way. "Why have you never shown your magic? Ashamed much?"

He smiled as we circled one another, ten of my strides for one of his tiny pivots. "Never. But there are many who judge me for being a giant, let alone the most powerful Unseelie ever born."

I couldn't help it—I snorted. "I doubt that very much. Elisavanna—"

"Did not ever fully grasp her magic. Even at the end, I *let* her beat me," Rubezahl said. "I let her sacrifice herself because it served my purpose to bring you here. Because here . . . *here* I am king. Underhill stands with me in all things."

Unless she was two-timing me, I was pretty sure she was on my side.

Most of the time anyway. "Did you feel anything when Elisavanna died? Can you feel *anything* anymore?"

The giant's lips spread wide, and there wasn't so much as a flicker in his eyes. Gone was the twinkling blue I'd sought comfort in. A darkness lingered there now. "In my mind, she died long ago."

I lowered my voice. "And yet you still pleaded with her before the end, did you not?"

His smile faded and churning fury replaced it that was almost foreign in its intensity. Rubezahl was more inclined toward mild reactions that hid a horrific agenda, in my experience.

I widened my stance. "Tell me then. . .if you don't wish to speak truth on that matter. . . Who killed my father on your orders?" So many mysteries solved, and many more half solved, but this mystery would always plague me if the answer remained buried.

Rubezahl recovered his wide smile. "Truth is what you desire? This gift I will grant you. Because part of me still wishes that I had been able to save you from these choices you are making."

My choices. He wanted to criticize *my* choices?

I didn't take the bait.

The giant crouched, locking his gaze with mine. "How I wished to be the one to shoot the arrow into his body that was as weak as his magic and mind. I've dreamed of his death for decades; of all the ways I might do it. And yet, in the end, I had to relinquish those wishes and dreams. There was some satisfaction in ordering a wild fae—the very first fae your father outcast to the Triangle, actually—to make the kill."

And there it was.

Adair was innocent. Of this. Rubezahl had murdered my father. "You knew they'd blame me?"

The giant chuckled. "No, but I should have guessed they would do such an idiotic thing. Does it not rankle that you fight to protect the very people who accepted you as the archer when you stood *beside* the target at the time? How can you care for them?"

Well, I wasn't sure I did, really. But that didn't change that I'd do the right thing by them. "Because someone has to. Someone must protect them from fae like you. And now that I've given you a truth for a truth, we're even."

"It is so. And there is nothing left but to begin." Rubezahl flicked a finger at me, and his magic sought me out, the blackish-green ribbon of power turning into a literal hand with more fingers than any humanoid would have.

I did the only thing I could. Diving beneath the knee-high water, I kicked *hard*, gripping onto the slimy plants lining the bottom to pull myself along.

I listened as the ground shook slightly in front of me. Rubezahl stepped one way, then the other.

He couldn't see me? He still couldn't track my magic, but was Underhill cloaking me now or was the water just that murky?

Either way, I had to keep still.

I turned to lie face up, gripping the plants on either side of me. The surface above rippled and danced as Rubezahl's magic sought me out.

I'd wait here until he expended more of his reserves.

But this was Underhill, and I should have known lying quietly while my enemy tired himself out would never be allowed.

Between one blink and the next, the water whooshed away as if a plug had been pulled in the gigantic tub that was this realm.

I rolled onto my belly and shoved to my feet, water and slime dripping from my body. Rubezahl had his back to me, and I seized my moment like a feral animal, my mind clinging to survival.

Running hard, I leapt forward and landed on his back. He grunted and reached back for me, but I hung far enough down that I was untouchable.

Murder swam in my vision, and I pulled on every ounce of gold I could summon, shoving it into my hands in a desperate bid for my magic to give me added strength. Fae were strong as it was, but this was giant skin.

I drove my hand through his left side, aiming upward for his heart. Through the tough flesh I pushed, twisting hard and drilling into the giant. His heart was deep. My stomach flipped as my magic twitched and seeped from my fingertips, making me the very weapon I needed.

Yes.

I pushed harder, submitting completely. Pouring my very life into this job, this sole task that I'd been bred for.

"No!" His voice boomed through the air, and the sweet sound of the harp pulsed around us. *Sweet . . .sour . . . pain.* Flavors and smells blended with the sound of the harp, as if Rubezahl were pulling on all my senses at once.

Cheating, he was cheating.

And if he was cheating, then why did Underhill do nothing?

My spine arched in response to his music. My fingers spasmed, and I fell backward. Eyes open, I stared at the sky as the colors slid from white to green, yellow, orange, blue, red, and then to a deep purple like my magic. *Indigo.* More and more, Rubezahl pushed the magic of the harp through my limp body. And it dug at my mind. My *heart.* The essence of who I was.

I wasn't breathing. Because the harp didn't wish me to do so anymore.

The sky called to me, singing of sorrow and despair. Indigo deepened until blackness reigned, and night no longer revealed more than streaks of purple hue. Hints of color stained the stars, and my mother's face smiled down at me. Not Elisavanna—my real mother. The one who'd carried me inside of her, the one who'd loved me as hard as she'd lied to me.

Child of mine, your time is nearly here, she whispered in Tlingit.

The world slowed, and the sky drew closer. I was done. My death was coming.

But I wasn't afraid.

No, this was almost a relief. An end to the loss, the pain, the . . .

I was so tired of fighting.

His hands caught me—had I still been falling? I wasn't sure—and the giant leaned over me so that he blocked me from the night sky and my mother's smiling face.

Blood trickled from his mouth, nose, and eyes. He gave a long, slow blink. "I am taking your power from you. And with it your life, young one."

I blinked. *I know.*

"You do not fear death?"

His question was odd, the strangeness of the remark reaching me even in the deep-rooted peace that had started to fill me, and I wondered at his words. I was not afraid.

Should I be?

Why was I not afraid?

I frowned, looking past him to see the sky was back where it should be. My mother's face was gone. Death had receded, but I could see my energy and magic spooling out of me and into him. My hand fell to the side and brushed through a scattering of flowers that had bloomed around us in what used to be a swamp.

All the worries, all the fear, all the what ifs fell away, dropping from me like a heavy winter coat.

My submission to both sides of my magic was total, and I understood that the submission I'd achieved until now was a laughable thing.

The power inside of me curled upward, and I smiled as it arced out of me, my body arching from the force of it, and collided with the magic of Lugh's harp and Rubezahl.

He screamed.

The drain he'd put on me reversed. My energy, my magic, and my life came flowing back.

And my smile grew wider.

"Impossible!" Rubezahl's fingers clenched around me as the blood flowed faster from his nose. "If I cannot take your power, then I will kill you the old-fashioned way."

The indigo sky around us cracked with a sudden rip of thunder. The skies opened, throwing down curtains of rain that sparkled like diamonds.

And glinted with my indigo magic.

The power that only I carried.

"Not today, you oversized bastard," I whispered.

I reached down deep for my power, connecting to Underhill, feeling her energy billowing around me. He'd cheated by using the harp. There were no longer any rules. Even so, a burst of flames, orange, red and gold, shot toward us, slicing through three of the giant's fingers.

The flames dropped as Rubezahl bellowed, and I rolled onto the ground, groaning.

A hand caught me under the arm, and I staggered upright to find eyes as dark as the night sky staring back at me.

A fiery spear was clutched in the handsome man's hand, and the flames licked over his skin, not burning him in the slightest.

"I'm sorry it took me so long," Faolan said. "But I'm here now, my love. I'm here."

CHAPTER 17

Two armies clashed around us. A giant stood not thirty feet away, quickly getting over the burns dealt to his hands.

But my gaze was locked on Lan, on this new version of the man I loved. Handsome beyond reason before, he was now so radiant I couldn't find words to describe him.

Lan's walls were gone. He exuded a confidence that stole my breath more assuredly than Rubezahl had just tried to drain the very essence from me.

"You're here," I said hoarsely.

Expression solemn, he nodded. "I am here."

With effort, I dragged my focus from him to Rubezahl, and the reassurance I'd felt moments prior—bolstered by the giant's failure to take my power—was amplified tenfold by Lan's presence and that of his spear.

I smiled at the giant, who appeared almost pale, his uncertainty shaving years off his age and making him look like a child caught in a trap of his own making.

His fear was a soothing balm. I relished in it—for all the fae he'd used and killed to arrive at this spot in Underhill today.

"This is over, Rubezahl," I announced.

Lan stepped forward. "You have something that belongs to me, giant."

And it glinted at the ancient fae's hip.

"Faolan," Rubezahl answered. "I would ask how you evaded my curse, but I see that you have had help. Tell me, how is Lugh? Still dead?"

Lan stepped forward, a hunter with his prey in sight. "My grandfather is well."

Rubezahl gave a slow nod, and I could see him gathering himself. Pulling his shit together. "He will be proud of you. There are none who have evaded that curse in my lifetime. To achieve fundamental change is a feat comparable to the successes of your ancestor. I admit even I do not have such an ability."

My stomach clenched as Lan circled closer, but this was his battle. Once he had the harp? Then it would be mine.

I gathered Underhill's golden power, preparing to step in as needed.

Lan circled his flaming spear with a dexterity and speed that spoke of months of practice, even for a trained warrior such as himself. How long had he stayed in dreamland?

"That doesn't surprise anyone," Lan told the giant. "Being that my power is superior, it would be wise of you to hand over the harp you stole."

Rubezahl's lips curved. "Me, steal? My, my, Faolan. I have stolen many things, but the harp is not one of them."

"I'm sure you love to tell yourself that at night."

"Love. Therein lies the story. Is it not funny how one person pines for another even as another pines for them? And so it was that the harp first came to me. For as I watched Elisavanna—" the giant smiled cruelly, "—your *mother* watched me. There was no need to steal the harp, for she offered it to me. Well, she offered me the exact information I needed to find it, I should say."

Faolan's eyes narrowed. "Her? Part with her father's objects of power? Never."

And yet a tightness in my chest told me Rubezahl was wielding a brutal truth. The journal. He'd mentioned in it that Ebliu had given him a clue or a lead. The next passages had mentioned the harp, but those prior to it had not. "He's telling the truth, Lan. Ebliu has worked with Rubezahl for a long time."

"I admit, she epitomizes everything I hate in the court fae," Ruby said, facing Lan as he unhooked the harp at his side. "But she was very, very useful. Love made her that much more pliable to my tea. Enough to turn a mother against her young, monstrous Unseelie son."

Faolan sucked in a breath.

I circled the other way to give him time to refocus. "Just one more despicable act to add to the rest. You sure are getting repetitive. There is one thing stronger than your tea though."

The giant cast me a lazy, dismissive look underplayed by the tension evident in his shoulders. He did not want to be caught between me and Lan. "And what's that, young one?"

"Regret. How do you think we got the spear? Ebliu herself delivered it into my hands for her son."

His mother's paltry effort to right her wrongs.

Yet Lan would be dead if she hadn't.

The giant dipped his head. "Why, yes. That is why I killed her."

There was a pregnant beat. A pause. A sigh in the very fabric of Underhill.

Then Lan roared with fury, charging the huge fae. Rubezahl thrummed on the harp, and I dropped to my knees as a cacophonic boom rippled outward in a wave.

I gasped, gathering gold to me in a demanding draw.

But Lan wasn't on his knees like me and everyone else within view. He charged on, and Rubezahl's eyes widened. He hadn't bothered to draw another weapon. He hadn't thought he needed one.

Such was his arrogant belief in the power of the harp.

Yet it appeared the harp didn't have the inclination to work against its true bearer.

Lan spun the spear, and yellow, orange, and red flames arced around him and Rubezahl, tightening, drawing them together. An arc of the deepest red morphed to a wave of black magic that glittered with every color imaginable. It lashed out at the giant, cracking like a whip as it connected with the massive hand holding the harp. The faces of the surrounding fighting fae not forty feet away were washed with a hundred different hues from the explosion.

The giant bellowed but didn't release his hold, drawing his Unseelie magic into the palm of his other hand.

I fisted my hands, getting to my feet.

Drawing more gold still, I whispered it into my white lightning and let it fly.

My indigo had been depleted. Believing the same was true of my white lightning had nearly killed me. How could the power from Underhill ever deplete unless she herself faded from being? No, I'd merely exhausted my ability to be her power's vessel for a time. Sipping at her golden tendrils had restored me.

Rubezahl reeled back from my strike. My attention, however, was on the braid of flame forming under Lan's instruction. I shied back from the pulsing heat as he raised a hand, wrapped the flaming rope around the giant's wrist, and pulled.

This was no mere physical battle, and I blinked into my magical vision to watch the real combat.

Rubezahl's ugly black-green power was wrapped around the harp like a parasitic vine, but the magic of the spear combined with Lan's essence was yanking at it like the weed it was. I gasped as I saw Lan's magic for the first time since he'd exited dreamland. His essence was no longer the darkest of crimsons but a black just like that flaming arc littered with every color of the rainbow.

"Yes, Lan," I whispered.

He was freeing the harp from Rubezahl's claim.

The giant's bellows as the flames charred through his flesh and bone were lost to me as the final claws of his hold on Lugh's instrument were ripped out.

"No! It's mine," Rubezahl said through pained howls.

Lan walked calmly around to stand before the giant. "It was *never* yours. Some things are more than us, King of No Fae."

My gaze fell to the giant's arm. What remained of it.

And curiosity was my downfall.

Rubezahl roared, swiping to send Lan flying with the harp and spear. I charged, flinging out white lightning at his knobbly knees. Green magic deflected my blow, swallowing it whole before slamming toward me in a solid wall.

I obliterated the wall, staggering at the physical energy it cost me.

"Alli!" Lan shouted.

He ran toward me, and as green magic filled the very air, I raced toward him. The better strategy would surely be to divide and conquer an opponent of this size, yet a strange certainty had filled my body.

I reached for Lan.

"This ends, Kallik of No House," Rubezahl said, his terrible voice crawling between the space that divided us.

Lan and I touched, and a furious bray sounded. I turned to see Kik galloping directly for the giant, but I released Lan at the sight of the woman who sat upon his back.

The giant hadn't seen Devon—or he didn't care. The green magic he'd been accumulating compressed into a dagger over his head, a tiny, lethal vessel.

The tip gleamed, pointing directly at me.

I drew white lightning to my hands as Rubezahl screamed, shooting the dagger like an arrow from a bow. I'd been able to stop his wall of power, but this?

Lan's fear-filled shout overrode my senses. I threw up a shield of blazing white, but the dagger sliced through it akin to a hot knife in butter.

Faolan choked and raised the harp in front of the dagger's target, my heart.

I was thrown.

Ears ringing, my sense of up and down void, I hit the ground in a roll, and landed in a heap facing Rubezahl.

I watched as Devon slid off Kik, who immediately galloped to the giant and kicked him in the head with savage force. My brows still worked, and they rose as Rubezahl's blue eyes rolled back in his head.

We had him.

He'd put everything into that dagger, leaving nothing in his reserves because he'd believed he could not be beaten.

I struggled up to my hands and knees, but another glance at the giant froze me to the spot.

Devon walked over to him and spread both of her arms wide. The very air before her ripped and stretched, widening until another Underhill scene was evident through the portal.

What was she doing? I staggered in her direction. "Devon!"

She brought the portal down over the giant like a blanket. I broke into a painful, limping run. “What the fuck are you doing, Devon?”

The blooded fae glanced back at me but didn’t hesitate as she finished her task. She began to shrink the portal, and my heart sank as the portal disappeared, leaving thin air where Rubezahl had lain.

I slowed, unable to believe what I’d just seen. “You are with--”

This entire time? She’d been on *his* side? But Devon was the mouthpiece of Underhill, the fae realm’s physical vessel.

And if Underhill was on Rubezahl’s side, then we were beyond fucked.

Devon turned, blood pouring from her eyes, nose, and mouth as she faced me.

“Why did you do it?” I whispered.

Her eyes rolled back in her head, and I let her fall to the ground. We’d nearly had him. We’d been so fucking close. And she’d betrayed us.

Underhill had betrayed us.

Kik trotted toward me, but I ignored the land kelpie, scanning the landscape.

Lan was kneeling, his back to me, and something about the hang of his shoulders had me breaking into another run.

I could feel every muscle and bone in my body—or so it seemed—as I slowed by his side. “What’s wrong? Did you get hurt?”

“Hurt?” he asked, lifting his head. “I’m not hurt.”

My gaze dropped to his lap and what sat there. *Oh shit.*

“The dagger,” he choked out, holding up the mangled bit of gold clutched in his hands as if it were a dying bird.

Maybe Rubezahl wasn’t in control of the Seelie harp anymore . . . but he’d ensured no one else would be either.

It was bent and twisted beyond recognition.

I blinked as a thick white smoke poured from the instrument, only it had more substance. Lan wasn't reacting, and it became clear why when, eventually, a woman stood before me.

A woman in battle attire from an era long before my birth.

I stared at her, and she tilted her chin, meeting my gaze with unfaltering confidence before walking away and fading from sight.

We hadn't thought beyond taking the instrument from the giant, but as I gazed upon what was left of the harp, I saw a golden pathway begin to close in my mind's eye.

A cold tendril wrapped around my heart as I realized that wielding the harp had been just as important as reclaiming it, if not more.

While the battle with Rubezahl was over for the moment, Underhill was not done with us. Not by a long shot.

As I stood staring at the place where the giant had been, the land heaved and cracked open with a groan that sounded as if the very core of Underhill's existence was tearing. The groans turned to bellows, then howls and screams that had those around us clamping their hands to their ears.

I felt Underhill urging us to move, to get the hell away from this place of death and blood. Why, I didn't know.

But did I still trust her?

I spun in a crouch as my army was driven to their knees by the pressure. Rubezahl's army . . . they were on their asses and facedown for the most part. Unconscious or dead, I wasn't sure.

Their deaths weren't on Underhill's head though. How many of them had Rubezahl killed in those last moments he'd been connected to them? How many had he drained?

I stumbled as a chunk of red rock shot up beneath me. We had to move and move *fast*. Regardless of whether Underhill meant us harm, it was obvious she intended for us to move.

I wove magic around my throat to amplify my voice, thanking it extra hard for being accessible to me since I'd felt so vulnerable without it. "Gather those that live! We take them with us! *Everyone* who lives."

"Where?" Rowan used his own magic to be heard over what felt like the world breaking to pieces.

Fuck, it really was though.

I bent and scooped up Devon the traitor, throwing her over my shoulder like a sack of potatoes.

I wanted to get the army and injured back to the Oracle's valley. They wouldn't all fit inside her home, but the meadow was the safest place I knew.

The problem was getting there.

To my left, Kik shook his head, icicles clinking together though I couldn't hear them over the din as the land opened around us.

Unfortunately for me, the land kelpie decided to trot over. "How did you let him get away? I didn't think you could be more stupid, imbecile, and yet somehow you defied the odds! Sweet goddess, you are a fuck up!" he barked.

Glowering, I walked to his side and slung Devon on his back, then reached around and grabbed his nose before he could pull away. I dug my fingers in and twisted a handful of the soft flesh. The move worked with naughty horses, why not a naughty land kelpie?

He grunted, and I pulled him by the nose until he was close enough that I could lower my voice and still be heard. "We need to get them back to the Oracle. All of them. Lead them. Now."

He blinked, eyes watering with the pain. He tried to grimace, but my hold on him wouldn't allow it. We locked eyes and he started to curse. Phew, he knew some words, but I maintained my hold until the last, defiant f-word and then c-word came out of his mouth.

"Fine," he spat, showering me with spittle in the doing—no doubt on purpose.

I let him go, once more wrapping my voice in magic to amplify it. "Follow the land kelpie to safety!"

The army slid into formation, most of my people carrying one or more of Rubezahl's fallen fae.

Head erect, as though *he* were the crowned leader of the army, Kik led them from the heaving landscape that was ever unpredictable, and away from the dragon's wings, that seemed to stay in the same place. I watched as they entered the swamp where I'd fought the giant in, then continued retreating until I could no longer see them.

As the army disappeared, the land settled with a sigh. Only then did I let myself turn to Lan, who was still on his knees.

"If you do not like bloodshed and battles," I said with more than a trace of bitterness, directed at Underhill, "perhaps you should not have stayed my hand from ending this fight once and for all." I waited, but there was no reply from the fae realm.

Not so much as a hiccup or fart.

And I now had other concerns.

I crouched next to Lan. That light I'd seen in his eyes, the change that had been wrought in him in dreamland was still there, but there was deep sorrow too.

The harp had been completely destroyed by Rubezahl's magic.

"Lan, I'm so sorry." I touched the edges of the broken harp, and he placed a hand over mine and wove our fingers together.

Lifting our joined hands, he kissed mine. "I would give up all I have to protect you, Orphan. They're precious heirlooms, but they are only things. They're nothing compared to what you are to me." His eyes met mine. "And I would give them all up to keep you whole, do not ever doubt that."

There was no magic in the world stronger to me in that moment than the unfaltering belief that he meant every word—that to him I was more precious than anything.

I leaned into his side, and we clung to each other, the harp—what was left of it—and spear pinned between us. He tipped my head back and kissed me, lips searing against mine, marking me as clearly as I was marking him. So long as we had each other, what else did we need in this world?

We were both alive, and that was worth pausing for a kiss or two.

Or more if I could wrangle it.

A moan slid from his warm lips, and I found myself straddling his lap. His hands circled around my hips and worked across my ass, pulling me tight against his hardness. Each dig of his fingers had me arching into him, pressing and moving against him. I couldn't get close enough. If we hadn't been out in the middle of Underhill . . .

A crackle of energy pinged between us, soft at first, then strong enough that I yelped. The sharp jab of a different kind of magic all but threw us apart.

Wide-eyed, I touched my lips, which were swollen and hot from his kisses. But it was the two items still touching him that drew my focus. "What *was* that?"

He waggled his brows.

"No. Not that." Though I had every intention of exploring his hardness at a later date.

The harp—what was left of it—emitted a faint glow around the edges. The spear was lit up too. Not with red flames this time, but blue and white.

"I don't know. They've never glowed like that." Lan stood and grabbed both heirlooms.

Had it happened because we were touching?

"We should go," he grunted. "Before Underhill remembers she doesn't like us and decides to send something else our way."

I flinched, because he wasn't wrong. The dragon wings we'd bounced over shifted, a baleful red eye peeking out at us.

"Yeah, time to go." I agreed.

Lan strapped his spear to his back so he could offer me a free hand, the other cradled the ruined harp. Once more we wove our fingers together, and I looked down at our interlocked fingers, blinking into my magical vision.

My indigo essence split apart and wove around us like a hug, and his magic—still black with flecks of all colors—did the same.

"They look happy." I said without thinking, then shifted my gaze to Lan. "Is it weird to see magic as happy?"

He laughed softly. "Maybe? But weird is what we do, Alli. Nothing about us or this journey to find each other has been normal or predictable. So why shouldn't our magic be happy when we're touching?"

True. We were weird with a capital strange.

We walked after the army, following the beaten path they'd forged with ease. I half expected a new monster to jump out, but there was nothing. Almost as if Underhill slumbered. Or maybe she was hiding, embarrassed that her mouthpiece had stopped me from killing Rubezahl.

"What happened back there?" I asked. "We had him, and Devon fucked us over."

Balor's balls, we'd *had him.* Now the giant was off somewhere healing, plotting some new tactic to destroy us. And he had full knowledge of my reserves and Lan's new toy.

Shit, Ruby could hole up and lick his wounds for decades, *centuries.*

I groaned, already running through the nightmare of Ruby potentially aligning with my stepmother against me. That was a pile of shit I did *not* need to dig through. He could so easily feed her tea and recruit her—and my half sibling in her womb—to his side.

Lan shook his head. "I don't know. Devon didn't seem all that sure of what she was doing. It was as if she didn't want to let him go either. But that doesn't make sense—I thought Underhill was on our side. For a moment there, I thought . . . I thought we were done."

Yep.

I took in the scene in front of us as the realm shifted once more. We'd been transported to the top of the ridge overlooking the Oracle's valley. Flowers surrounded us, miniature clouds hovering over them. Tiny miniature birds darted to and fro, zipping here and there with soft chirps. The scene soothed my aching weariness, but it didn't take my mind from the tasks that lay ahead.

Before I reached my army, I wanted to have answers. I wanted to be able to tell them something about what would come next. A leader without a plan was not much of a leader at all.

Pausing at the top of the hill, I peered down into the valley. The army was spread out beneath us. Tents had been erected, and I had no doubt healers were working overtime on the injured fae.

My attention shifted back to Faolan. I looked down at our joined hands, then at the magic buzzing around us, alive in its own way. "I spoke with Underhill before the battle."

Lan startled. "You did? What did she say?"

"That the battle with Rubezahl was all about balance. What she seeks is not for good or bad to win, but for balance to prevail." I frowned. "Could that be why Devon took Rubezahl out of range? Except that doesn't make sense, not really. Are we meant to battle endlessly? Because that doesn't fit with what the Oracle has hinted at either."

Lan did not have an answer for me, but someone else did.

"The amount of death and life has to be balanced," a voice said, and I turned, expecting a fae.

What I saw was someone else entirely.

The winged snow cat and her cubs that Cinth had introduced me to back on Unimak padded toward us.

"How do you know this?" I watched her closely as she drew near. I didn't bother asking how she'd come to be here. She must have slipped through the portal with my army.

Her blue eyes showed a wisdom I wouldn't have expected from a cat. Her cubs tumbled and played in her wake, leaping through the tiny clouds and yowling as they got shocked with miniature lightning and drenched with rain. The birds darted around them, drawing them farther down the slope.

The mother cat sighed. "Balance is the natural world, young fae. There must be the correct amount of prey for the predators to survive. If you kill off the predators, the prey bloom and become too much for the world, and all will suffer. That is what I know. The giant . . . he is a predator. He is part of the balance. I say this as someone who is a predator in my own right."

She butted her head against my hip, rubbing her face, neck, and body against my thigh. "The mother of all mothers knows this and more."

I blinked, and she moved on down the hill, her cubs following her, still playing and tumbling along.

"He *is* a predator," Lan mused. "But do we really want to keep him alive? How is that good for our world? That can't be what Underhill wants."

I touched my fingers to my forehead, seeing a vision of Rubezahl and me laid out on a field of battle. Both of us unmoving. The image was there, then gone in a flash. "I . . . I don't know." If the winged snow cat was right, Underhill might keep us from killing Rubezahl.

Forever.

I couldn't do this forever. Even the thought of continuing this fight until the winter solstice threatened to crush me.

Someone from the army spotted us and a shout went up through the men and women who'd fought for me. Who'd fought for all the fae, Seelie and Unseelie alike. *That* was a beautiful thing.

I lifted my hand and smiled, forcing my feet to carry me forward.

Lan kept up. "This could cause a serious issue, Orphan. How the fuck do we catch the giant if Underhill keeps helping him? Will caging him satisfy this world's need for balance?"

Caging him would take his power away, so I thought not—but we didn't have a cage for him anyway, so it was a moot point.

I swallowed hard. There had to be a way around this conundrum. If Rubezahl was a predator, then what did that make me? Prey who fought back? Would my life count as the balance needed to keep the realm stable? Because, if so, I could see a way to end this war. It just wasn't the outcome I wanted.

A life for a life, just like the vision had shown me.

Lan tightened his hold on my hand. "I can feel you shaking. Talk to me, Alli."

His words were lost to a roar, the hero's welcome that went up around us. The army was ecstatic.

Oh, no. They thought we'd won. The cheering went on and on, and through it I found the eyes of my two generals.

They weren't cheering.

They knew.

Drake stood with a group of men. They seemed to be a unit, and I wondered if they were also changelings. Drake's eyes said the same as my generals' eyes. He knew the truth too.

And the Oracle was nowhere to be seen.

I lifted my free hand and the cheering slowly faded. "My friends, my . . . my family . . ." My throat tightened as I realized that they truly were my family. People who depended on me to live. My children.

And my heart told me I was going to have to say goodbye to them all in order to save them. The good, the bad, and the in between. Because they were all my responsibility. "Enjoy the respite, you have earned it."

The cheering blew up again, with the clattering of weapons on bucklers. I kept on walking, Lan at my side. My generals joined us, as did Drake. And when we passed the Oracle's home, Cinth stepped out and fell into step with us, too, her hand slipping into my free one. I squeezed hers tightly, silently praying that she'd understand my choice one day.

And that Lan would too. He may need to be at the final battle, too—that much seemed inevitable—but that didn't mean he had to share my fate.

Because sacrificing my life for the sake of balance *had* to be what Underhill wanted. All the effort I'd expended to understand her and the power within me had been unnecessary—all I'd needed to do was roll over and die.

I clenched my jaw. My feet took me deeper into the pasture around the valley where the alicorns grazed, oblivious to the army around them.

I stopped in the center of the lush pasture and stared back at the fae army, who believed themselves safe and victorious.

"They need to leave," I said. "All of them, we have to get the army out before nightfall. This valley will not protect them."

Rowan startled. "But we're not done. The giant lives."

"I know, but it won't take an army to kill him. His people are gone, drained, or with us and injured. We'll need to contain them until the tea wears off, and we don't have the space to do so here." I made myself look at each of them in turn. "Underhill demands balance above all else. Rubezahl no longer has an army, so the fight would be unbalanced should ours stay. She will find a way to even the odds. The final battle must be one on one."

Predator and prey.

"No, Alli." Faolan tightened his hold on me. "The battle isn't going to happen without me. There are too many signs to ignore. We face Rubezahl together."

My attempt to get him to leave had been half-hearted at best, and I agreed that there really *were* too many signs to ignore. Lan wouldn't die along with me though. I didn't know exactly how I'd save him, but I would. With my last breath, I'd make sure of it.

Cinth snorted. "What he said. You can't actually believe we'd leave you here to face that monster alone?"

I thought about all the challenges I'd faced alone in my life. My stepmother and her absolute hatred of me. The loss of my birth mother. The burden of being an outcast. The destruction of Underhill. My father's rejection of me, until the end. I'd faced those things without flinching, growing stronger with each step.

Until this, the last one.

Until the end.

"I am still the queen. Am I not?"

Rowan and Stryk both bowed from the waist.

"As my queen commands." Rowan said first, and Stryk mimicked the words through a mouth twisted in distaste. He didn't agree with me.

Cinth folded her arms over her ample bosom. "That won't work with me, girlie. I'm staying."

Rowan looked from Stryk to Cinth, his eyes warm with admiration. "If Cinth stays, then so do I."

"And you'll need help finding him," Drake said. "Which means I'm staying too."

Lan tightened his hold on me but otherwise said nothing. There was no love lost between him and Drake, but Lan knew that my heart only had room for one.

I put a hand to my forehead. “General Stryk, you will take command of both armies. *You* are in command of the courts, not Adair or my uncle. Ready the armies to return to Unimak via the portal.”

“As you command.” He bowed again. “And if I may say one more thing?”

Don’t see why he’d stop now. “Of course.”

“Kill him. No matter what else you do, Queen of All Fae, kill him.”

I smiled, my lips straining with the effort. Because keeping my end of this promise would mean giving my life. “There is no other way.”

Chapter 19

Wrapped in a towel, I crouched before my pack, dragging out the only set of leggings and tunic that weren't drying or covered in blood and gore. As it was, if Cinth hadn't brought my pack to the Oracle's, I'd be a bare-assed queen right now.

The army was gone. And the only people who remained either belonged in Underhill or had simply refused to budge.

The others were scouring the Oracle's mess of a library for anything to do with Underhill's balance complex.

I pulled out my leggings and squinted as something rolled under the bed before stopping with a light thud.

Bending forward, I reached under the bed.

The door opened.

"Just goes to show," the Oracle muttered behind me. "I can't foresee everything. Never knew an eyeful of your vagina would be in my future."

"Your problem for looking." I grunted, closing my fingers around the small object. It gave me a slight prick, just like before. *Huh.* Even with Lugh's prompt and my own rampant curiosity, I'd completely forgotten about the puzzle game taken from Elisavanna's desk. Perhaps warring against a giant was a good enough excuse. . .

I sat on my haunches and turned the toy over in my hands. Seelie and Unseelie magic still twisted through the game. *Just like me.*

"What's that, Dandelion?" The Oracle walked to stand at my shoulder.

I hummed. "A puzzle game I found in the Unseelie queen's quarters. It's like those toys fae used to give to toddlers. I always wanted one. They used their magic to figure out the puzzle. That's all I remember. This game has Unseelie and Seelie magic within it, and I can't help but feel the queen meant it for me."

And a tangle it was, of thin and thick curves, with columns and a sole straight rod.

"Idiot, your mother," the Oracle said.

The Unseelie queen had been a lot of things, but an idiot wasn't one of them. "Why do you believe that?"

The Oracle huffed, bringing her cane down on the wooden floor a few times. "Sometimes the path before us is obvious and wide enough for a fucking herd of alicorns to go down. She chose the tiny, thorned path. She could have ended Rubezahl early on, but she let him live long enough to find the two weapons that would ensure his rise to power, putting herself in a position where she had to unify with the Seelie king to create a series of children who stood as their only chance at taking Rubezahl down for good."

A series of children. “How many? I know the last spirit was my sister.”

“Five.” The Oracle sighed, never looking wearier. “And I watched each of them fail despite my best attempts to guide them in the limited capacity I am granted.” The ancient woman tilted her head up. “Am I to be blamed then when the limitations of my role becomes too much? No, but still, as one power fades, another grows elsewhere. I know this. And perhaps my frustration was always meant to reach this level.”

The words didn’t seem like they were for me.

I watched her, searching her wrinkled face for any clues that would help decipher her words.

She shook herself, then glowered at me. “Go on, Dandelion. Untangle it then.”

“I don’t know how. I never had one of these toys.”

She muttered something about me being stupider than a toddler and left the room. Between her and Kik, I’d be in danger of developing a serious complex if I let people’s insults get to me.

I blinked into my magical vision and studied the looping Seelie and Unseelie power around the statue. Submitting to the seamless merging of my power, I let the magic fill my palm, directing it into the statue, which began to contort and writhe in my hand.

I peered closer. That curve there was just filled with Seelie power.

Peeling back the Unseelie part of my magic, I directed the blue portion of my essence into the curve. With a low hiss, the curve pulled free of the rest, sticking out at a weird angle.

Childhood Alli was intrigued by the toy, not gonna lie.

As the statue writhed, I tried to make sense of the mess. There. A column that seemed freer than the rest. Unseelie this time.

I directed red magic into that one.

Instead of remaining attached to the rest of the contraption, like the first curve I'd loosened, the column fell away, landing in my palm.

Transfixed by the challenge, I kept working, separating the columns from the curves. As I worked, the curves started forming a shape.

The sole straight rod was last, and unlike the rest, it pulsed white.

I pushed lightning into it, and the rod fell away from the other pieces.

A song filled the air, warming my very soul in a way no one or nothing but Lan had ever managed before. The pieces of the toy floated free of my touch and lifted to hover overhead. They began to spin. Faster. Faster.

Then the song suddenly cut off, leaving an ache in my chest, and three pieces lowered into my palm where before there'd only been one.

I stared down at them in awe. One was obviously a spear. Lan's spear. I picked up the largest of the remaining two. A braided archway.

A portal.

But the last . . .

I set the spear and portal down, then picked up the third and smallest item. It was the harp. Yet this version of the instrument was different than the original. Five strands of lightning strung this harp, looking far more like hair than a string, however.

I set the harp against my lips. "What the hell do you mean?"

Nothing happened.

Dang.

Elisavanna had clearly left the toy out as a message to me. Only I could have untangled it. And just like when I first found the statue, I knew in my heart that it meant something.

My guess? I needed all three of these things to stop Rubezahl.

Was her clue still relevant? It could have been meant for the last battle, and if so, it was null and void. But something made me think not, and after a tense beat, I realized what I was picking up on.

The harp.

Why would the instrument appear different now if she hadn't known it would be damaged?

My inhale caught in my throat. Were we meant to fix the harp?

Lan. I had to find Lan.

We had to fix the Seelie weapon.

Those two words—*Seelie weapon*—stopped me in my tracks because they were an exact echo of what the Oracle had said not an hour prior.

She'd spoken of a Seelie weapon carried by an Unseelie.

One of Rubezahl's journal entries swam to the forefront of my mind.

That I can play it at all speaks of my worth. Anna knows it. Even the Seelie king can see.

I, an Unseelie fae, carry the harp of Lugh, and can produce its glorious music as well as the famed hero could.

Unseelie and Seelie.

"It wasn't his power that allowed him to travel between the realms," I whispered. "It was the mixture of his Unseelie magic with the Seelie magic of the harp." I'd assumed the harp was the reason he was able to leap between realms, but it was good to understand *why* the harp enabled him to do that.

Wasn't that exactly why I could do it? The only difference was that both halves were contained within me.

And that meant—

The door opened.

"Now that's a sight for sore eyes," Lan's deep voice curled around me.

A glance down told me that the towel had fallen from its position over my breasts, probably long ago. My hair was mostly dried too.

I stood and faced Lan, gripping the three metal objects. "I figured something out."

"That you should never wear clothes?" he murmured, stepping closer with the grace of a predator. He stopped, a wrinkle forming between his brows. "Around me, that is."

My lips curved. "That seems more like something you've figured out."

"I figured it out long ago."

The spear pricked my thumb again, and I jolted out of the haze Lan always seemed to cast over me. "Rubezahl can't leave the fae realm."

Faolan met my gaze. "What? How do you know?"

I quickly explained my suspicions to him. He was clenching his jaw by the end.

"What is it?" I asked.

"I just spent five hours in that dust pit of a library searching for answers."

My lips twitched. "What a shame. You should know that I'm the smartest fae around this joint. There's something else."

I passed over the tiny harp. "Thoughts?"

"Only a small bug could play this."

A snort escaped me. "Seriously though. Tell me what you'd think if you found it with these two other things." I passed over the portal and spear.

He looked at the three objects, and his eyes rounded. "Portal, spear, and harp. But . . . this isn't like the harp was."

"I found them in Elisavanna's desk. They were wrapped up together in one of those toys fae children play with, only the magic was Seelie and Unseelie. I'm assuming my parents made it together and left it for me. The harp *is* different. It's like they knew Lugh's instrument would be damaged in the last battle."

His gaze lifted to mine. “You think it needs to be remade?

I nodded a few times, recalling the blue and white glow. “The harp still has some power, Lugh’s power, but it’s not the same.” I had a strong inkling that the spirit woman who’d poured out of the ruined instrument had been the rest of the harp’s power. “The Oracle told me that as one power fades, it grows elsewhere. Lan . . . we need to replace its power. And we need to do it before facing Rubezahl again.”

“Oh,” he said wryly. “Is that all?”

I quickly dressed, and we strode down the hall to the kitchen.

“Figured it out, Dandelion?” the Oracle said, puffing on her pipe in her rocking chair.

I cut to the chase. “Do I need to recapture the spirit who possessed the harp, or does it require something else?”

Lan grunted, sliding me a surprised glance, but the Oracle smiled. “Good luck trapping that feral bitch again. She won’t go back in there for anything.”

Okay. “What needs to go into the harp?”

She rolled her eyes. “Still asking me questions. Have you learned nothing?”

Yep, I’d learned that her ramblings often gave things away. “Can you point me in the right direction?”

The Oracle lifted the hand with her pipe and pointed it through a curtain blocking off a room adjacent to the kitchen.

Lan ducked through ahead of me, and his growl alerted me to something amiss. It didn’t take me long to figure out what. When I stepped through, my gaze landed on the blooded fae.

“You look like shit,” I told her.

Dried blood covered her face in dark brown smears. It was as if her body was splitting from the inside. Bruises marred the skin under her eyes and beneath her cheekbones. “I feel that way, too, Queen of All Fae.”

She called me queen of all fae, yet she’d cut the legs from under me. “Why the fuck did you help Rubezahl?”

Reclined on the bed, the fae met my gaze. "I have told you why. You know the answer to your question. You just don't want to fathom what it means."

She was wrong. I'd already fathomed what it meant.

I wished there were another way. With Lan beside me, alive, I didn't want to believe that my path ended in an early grave.

Or, more likely, being feasted upon by Underhill's beasties

I warned her with my gaze not to say more. Lan couldn't know. If he learned the truth, he'd never let me do what I needed to do. "If there must be balance, then the prey must have her weapons, so her strength matches the power of the predator."

The ghost of a smile danced on Devon's lips. "Is that what you are?"

"Is that not what Underhill has decided?"

"Do not attempt to interpret the complexities of Underhill's decisions, young fae. Instead, change as she changes, and understand that nothing, not your desires and hopes or your anger and sadness will affect what must come." She coughed and fumbled for a cloth to wipe fresh spurts of blood from her chin. "Ask what you have come to ask."

"The harp. We need to replace its power. What can do that?"

The blooded fae rested back. "Your answer lies in the meadow."

I perked up. "Really?"

"Leave me now."

Lan did as she asked, but I stopped just before ducking out of the curtain. "Will you be all right, Devon?"

Traitor she may be, but when all was said and done, she was Underhill's vessel and probably as tightly trussed by her role as the Oracle was by hers.

The blood fae sighed. "It is not yet my time."

But it would be soon? My stomach churned with the conviction that all our fates—even that of this realm—were tied to the next battle that would occur.

Shoving away the feeling of doom before it settled over me, I marched past the Oracle snoring on her rocking chair and out the front door, nearly colliding with Lan.

He'd planted himself there, his arms crossing as he peered out at the meadow with a baffled expression.

I tracked his gaze to the only occupant of the meadow, likely because he'd kicked everyone else out or they'd grown sick of his colorful vocabulary.

Underhill hated me.

"Kikuindateeth," I muttered, eyeing the grazing land kelpie.

That four-legged asshole was the key to fixing the harp.

Chapter 20

"How are you going to convince him to help?" Lan asked as we studied the land kelpie.

I stared at Kik's large ass, which he kept firmly turned in our direction, almost as if he knew we were discussing him. The question was a good one. The land kelpie was helpful when he wanted to be, and only then.

No, let's be honest. He did what he wanted, when he wanted. Rubezahl had made sure the four-legged creature would never truly trust another fae again.

"I don't know." I put my hands on my hips. Despite his aversion to Ruby, he was unlikely to give up his hair willingly.

Rowan and Drake stood to the left of the Oracle's tower home, their heads together. They'd been friends when we were training in fake Underhill.

I shook off the sensation that we were there again. Training and Untried, facing challenges no one, fae or human or otherwise, could truly prepare for.

Cinth ducked out through the door. “So, what’s the plan?”

Her voice spun Rowan around. *Selective hearing much?*

Cinth pretended not to see him, though I noted she drew in a deep breath that made her breasts strain at the top of her corset.

I raised an eyebrow, and her pale cheeks pinked up. *Yeah, that’s what I thought.*

Rowan and Drake joined us.

“We have to convince the land kelpie to help us.” I said, “We need some of his mane or tail hairs.”

Drake grunted as if I’d kicked him in the balls. “You do know that they won’t give up their hair for anyone? They’re more protective of their hair than unicorns or alicorns .”

I hadn’t known that, but I gave him a quick nod. “Right, so you see the problem. We need it. He’s going to fight us. We have to win.”

Kik swung his head and bared his overly sharp teeth in our direction. “I can feel your imbecile eyes on me. What the fuck do you want this time?”

Lan leaned in close, putting his mouth against my ear. “Do we just ask? Might he be willing if he knew that the cause was great?”

After a brief contemplation, I shook my head. “That might make him more likely to turn us down.” With Kik, you just never knew. “I think we are going to have to surprise him.” To Kik, I called, “Shut your damn horse mouth,” to alleviate his suspicions. Hopefully.

I motioned for Rowan, Drake and Cinth to follow me inside the Oracle’s house again.

I sat at the lone table, and the others joined me. The Oracle still snored away in her chair outside of Devon’s room.

"Do you need his mane or tail hairs?" Cinth asked. "Does it matter which?"

Another good question. "No idea. We take what we can get and work with it. But getting anything is going to be tough." I found myself turning toward Drake. "How did Rubezahl catch him the first time? Were you there?"

Drake nodded slowly. "Yes. He used the harp, knocked him out, then trussed him up and brought him to camp. Really wasn't much work."

I grimaced. "That does not help us one whit. Why would Kik help us restore the instrument that helped capture him in the first place? Anything else you can remember? I mean, Kik is savvy and doesn't seem like the type to let someone close if they mean him any harm. He had to know Rubezahl was up to something."

Drumming his fingers on the table, Drake tipped his head back. "There was . . . I don't know if it was a female land kelpie, but it was another kelpie and a pile of food. That kept him distracted long enough for Ruby to get close."

Cinth smiled. "I could make him a big pot of bruadar. I've taken him other food before, so he'd never think anything of it."

"Think we could slip some sleeping draught into it?" Rowan asked, and I wrinkled my nose at the thought.

Though we still had some of the sleeping draught left from the battle, using it on Kik felt like something Rubezahl would do.

Cinth immediately shook her head. "No, it would throw off the recipe."

"And he'd notice," Drake said. "Land kelpies have a great sense of smell and taste. The bruadar *could* keep him busy. Then I could sneak up behind him in my wolf form and try to take him out."

"I don't want to hurt him," I said. Although we needed his hair, I didn't want to be like the giant. Forcing people to give up their autonomy.

I paced the room. "If I ask him, I tip our hand. *If* we make a move, and he gets away, then we'll have lost our chance."

"So we do both," Lan said, a slow smile sliding over his face. "Ask. If he says no, we attack."

Kik would probably say something far more colorful than 'no', but it was all we had.

Lips pressed together, I dipped my head. "Let's do it."

Cinth got to work on the bruadar, shooing the boys out of the kitchen.

"You. Stay." She pointed a wooden spoon at me. "We haven't had a good girl's chat in some time, and I've missed you."

She was right, with everything that had happened these last weeks, there hadn't been a lot of time for a talk. I'd missed her too.

"What's up with you and Rowan?" I dove right into the deep end as she began to mix stuff into the heavy cauldron over the open fire. The smell of cinnamon was the first thing I picked up on, but after that, it was just a mixture of spices I didn't recognize.

"I think he's the one." Cinth didn't miss a beat as she worked her magic—literally—on the dish our lives depended on. That thought made me smile.

Cinth, a cook, was saving us all.

Without her and her cooking, we'd never fix the harp, and if we couldn't fix the harp there was no way we'd stop Rubezahl.

Then her words sunk in. *Whoa.* "You think he's . . . Seriously? It's just so fast. And I don't mean that in a bad way. You've always taken your time with guys. . .had you spent time with Rowan prior and I had no idea?"

Because coming from her, that was *huge.*

She tucked a strand of hair behind her ear, and again I could see the pink stain on her cheeks. "No, we hadn't seen each other since the orphanage, and I'm pretty sure that I couldn't stand him back then." She laughed. "My feelings caught me by surprise in a huge way. What I felt when I saw him kind of. . .obliterated what I thought I knew about love—that love only comes with time and work. As it was, this situation has sped things up, I know. Without impending death, the speed of it might've made me hesitate. But war. . .loss. . .it put my feelings —and his—into perspective. There might not be time for us, so why waste what we do have?"

"Wow, Cinth. That's huge. I mean, you two make sense in a way. I couldn't have seen you with someone who didn't understand where you were from." They'd both had the same start in life. That was why Lan and I made sense too. He may have been surrounded by riches, but ultimately, he'd had a family that turned their backs on him.

She smiled shyly. "It's so different with him. The feelings aren't just lust. He's kind and thoughtful. And he doesn't pressure me to flash him or let him into my bed. He's not like the others."

"No one has ever asked me to flash them," I muttered.

She shot a look at my chest. "Well . . . "

I snorted. "Thanks."

A handful of something stringy that looked like pasta was pushed into the pot, and steam rose around her in a cloud.

I thought about what was coming. What I had to do once the harp was restored. A weight slid off my shoulders at the thought that she'd have a companion by her side.

"I'm happy for you." I stood and hugged her from behind, squeezing her tight. "He's a good one. You just keep your wooden spoon on hand to keep him in line."

She patted me, then all but shoved me back. "No peeking at my recipe."

I obeyed, chuckling. "Even if you gave me detailed instructions, I wouldn't be able to duplicate it. I don't have a single skill in the kitchen, as you know."

Waving her spoon, she motioned again for me to sit. "What's happening with you and Lan now? He really has changed. He seems lighter and more open since breaking the curse. Did you bang him?"

My brows shot up. "I wish. Give me an excuse, and I'll be there."

"Do you need one?"

I pulled a face. "No. More like time."

"You're a queen," she murmured, face gleaming from the steam pouring out of the bruadar. "Demand time."

I thought about my dark fae. *Mine.* He would always be mine, even after I was gone. We'd always been intertwined in ways beyond my understanding—our fates, our magic, as though born to be together. This had seemed to be true for my parents too. Maybe soulmates did exist for fae, I wasn't sure. I just knew, inexplicably, that our connection would last through the grave and beyond.

He would be alone after I was gone, and my heart thumped hard with that thought. Because when I'd thought he'd left me alone here, it had been too much to bear.

My throat tightened. "He's the one. But you've known that longer than I have."

"Sure as shit on a pixie's ass. I've known that you two would be in each other's lives since he saved you from the water. Since he read to you in the orphanage. I knew it would be a romantic thing since you kissed his eyeball and he chased you all the way to the Triangle. I've watched him wait for you, Alli. That man loves you beyond reason, and you love him the same way. The world just had to be ready for that kind of love to shine." She tapped the side of her pot and turned to me, her eyes widening. "Are you crying?"

Yup. Because she was right, Lan and I had always shared a connection, but the world had never wanted us to have each other. It was irony at its finest that we'd finally found a path to one another, and I would have to leave him soon.

And I wished in that moment that I was the sort of person who could say 'fuck the world' and 'fuck all the fae and all the humans' and 'they can solve this unholy mess themselves,' but I just wasn't.

I never had been. Underhill didn't need to ask me to remain good. I just was. To my loss at times, more times than I could count lately. I couldn't deny that the temptation to turn from that path had occurred to me several times.

Cinth's arms came around me, and I leaned into her. This was the last moment I could give myself to feel the weight of what was coming, to let the sadness and grief flow. Sobs heaved out of me, and Cinth rocked me like she'd done when we were little. Not once did she ask me why I was crying. Not once did she try to stop me. Sometime in the middle of it, however, I felt her tears on my cheeks.

She *knew*. Without a single word between us, she understood that there was a final goodbye in our future.

When you were this close to a friend, they could read your mind a little.

"I could not have asked for a better sister." I whispered. "You know that, right?"

Her eyes flooded with tears as she sat back. "There's got to be another way. Tell me there's another way."

"There isn't." I wiped her tears away. "If there were, I'd take it in a flash."

She closed her eyes, and tears streamed down her face. "Does he know?"

"Not that Underhill demands balance in the final battle. A life for a life. He doesn't know that he'll remain with the living either." Technically, if balance was the aim of the game, then Lan's death would upset that balance. So maybe if I couldn't find a way to save him, then Underhill would intervene. I could only hope that she would.

Cinth tugged me close. "*I* want to stop you."

But like me, like every woman who'd faced an impossible decision or task, she knew what needed to be done. One life was worth saving hundreds of thousands of fae and humans alike.

"I will always be with you." I choked on the words.

Sobs wracked her body.

"What are you two doing?" The Oracle's voice cut through the moment, and I turned to see her stirring from her slumber. "That's not how you go into a battle! Crying? Are you weak *and* stupid?"

Cinth dashed away her tears and went back to the bruadar, stirring.

"Shouldn't we cry when death and pain is imminent?"

I turned to see Devon standing—wobbling, really—in the curtained doorway to her room. "If love and tears and heart were a part of all battles, then there would be less blood and death and sorrow. Perhaps that is the better way. Not to hide what we feel."

I wasn't sure if she was talking as Devon, or if Underhill was peeking through again. Blood trickled from both her ears, but it wasn't any more or less than before.

"You should lie down," I said, wiping my face. "You've done enough."

"We all do what we must, Kallik. Remember that."

How could I forget? Though I hadn't meant the words as a jab.

"The bruadar is ready," Cinth said. Her voice was hard. She might understand that I would do as I must, but she didn't like anyone else pushing me in that direction.

My friend grabbed the entire cauldron and heaved it out of the fire. She grabbed a single bowl, then lugged everything past the Oracle and out the door.

"Good luck." Devon said.

I nodded, then followed Cinth. A few strides and I caught up to her, taking one side of the cauldron. "You want him to have the whole thing?"

"He's a land kelpie. I assume he's like most four-legged creatures and doesn't know when to stop."

We walked out into the field. The three men were already in position, waiting for their moment. If it was needed.

I hoped it wouldn't be, but I could feel the energy around us shifting. My gut said that Kik wouldn't give up his hair without a fight. But I had to at least give him the chance.

The land kelpie ignored us until we were setting the cauldron down a few feet from his nose. "What do you two nincompoops want?"

I motioned to Cinth. "We have an offer for you. I need four strands of your hair—"

"No."

"In exchange for a cauldron of bruadar." Cinth said.

His ears flicked forward. "Bruadar? That hasn't existed since —"

Cinth smiled and put her hands on her hips. "Since I brought it back, dumdum."

My lips twitched. If anyone could spar with Kik, it was Cinth. Perhaps he shouldn't challenge her when she was dealing with the knowledge that I was going to die.

His nostrils flared, and he drew in a deep breath. "It can't be. I've not tasted that since . . . not since I was still on my mother's biggest tit."

As always, he gave new meaning to the word crass. He took a step and Cinth held up her wooden spoon. "Bruadar for the hair."

His lips curled back, and he lunged at her. "I'll have it either way. You're just a cook!"

She whacked him with the spoon, right on his nose. Three times in rapid succession. "You will give me the hair, or you get nothing. Alli, get out of the way. I will deal with him. I'm in a mood."

I'd experienced Cinth in a *mood* three times in my life.

"Cinth?" My eyebrows shot up, and I motioned for the men to draw closer.

"I've got this, Alli." She growled. "Nobody takes my food unless I choose to give it to them."

A wooden spoon. She was taking on a land kelpie with a wooden spoon.

And she was going to win.

I backed the fuck up.

"Kick his ass!" Rowan shouted as Kik lunged for the cauldron again. Cinth moved lightly, jamming the pointed end of the wooden spoon up his nose.

All four of us winced.

Kik bellowed and lifted a front hoof to strike her.

"Watch it," I yelped, but she simply stepped to the side, as graceful as any dancer.

"Damn, my woman has moves!" Rowan crowed, and we watched as Cinth and Kik circled around each other, her spoon still jammed inside his nose.

"Give me the hairs," she said, calm as a summer's day.

"No!" he bellowed, trying to rear up. She changed the angle of her spoon until I could see the outline of it high up in his face, almost poking through the skin.

I rubbed my nose. *Fucking ouch.*

Cinth kept dodging his hooves. "I could do this all day. Rowan, would you like to take a bowl and have some bruadar?"

"With pleasure," he said, and bent to pick up the bowl she'd brought out.

Part of her plan, clearly.

Rowan sipped some of the steaming liquid out and then proceeded to moan as he ate whatever it was the bruadar had become for him. "Incredible," he said, eyes twinkling.

Kik moaned. "That's mine!"

Cinth dodged another blow from a front hoof. Yet Kik didn't try to snake his head around to bite her—stubborn though he was, he probably realized that would be a good way to get the spoon jammed all the way up to his brain.

Still, the asshole was headstrong enough to keep this going for a week. We needed something to tip the scales in his mind. And there was only one entity—other than the goddess he'd once transported—that I'd seen sway him. I looked at the ground and thought about how Underhill had sunk him to his chest.

"Underhill wishes you to help us," I declared.

"That bitch doesn't care about anyone!" he roared, and then I saw his eyes widen.

I laughed. I hadn't even twitched my magic. "You should have learned your lesson the first time around, Kik."

There was no need for me to soften the ground this time.

Underhill did it for me.

The land kelpie sank to the base of his neck, and Cinth motioned to me with her free hand. "Take the hairs you want."

I approached him from the side. "You could have made this easy, Kik."

"Fuck off, you mouthy, filthy mutt. Ouch!" he brayed as Cinth dug in harder with the spoon.

"Don't you talk to her that way," my friend spat. "She's going to save us all, you ungrateful equine! You show her the damn respect she deserves!" And then Cinth burst into tears, and I quickly cut off a hunk of Kik's frozen hair. As soon as I did, the icicles at the tips began to melt.

Cinth yanked her wooden spoon free of Kik's nose, and everyone winced yet again at the wet squelch it made. She turned and marched toward the Oracle's house, crying hard.

Gripping the kelpie's hair tightly, I picked up the cauldron and presented it to Kik. "Here. So that you can't say you got nothing, asshole."

He narrowed his eyes. “Why did your friend start crying? I didn’t hurt her.”

No, he hadn’t. And as stubborn as Kik was, I had a feeling he wouldn’t have. There was just something untouchable about a great cook.

“I did,” I told him softly.

I composed myself and turned to the other half of my soul. “Ready to make a harp with me, hot stuff?”

CHAPTER 21

Lan and I sat cross-legged at the outer border of the Oracle's meadow. The twin suns still peeked over the gold mountain range in the distance, and the tarbeasts we'd encountered before wouldn't be out for at least another hour. Though I hadn't seen or heard any in the last few days. Bile rose in my throat at the thought of them feasting on the corpses left behind on the battlefield.

"Any previous undisclosed experience in instrument making?" Lan asked.

I dropped Kik's long white hairs beside the mangled remains of the harp. "Nope, you?"

"Funnily enough, no."

"Well, the harp contained Seelie power, like your spear, so I'm assuming Seelie power must go back *into* it."

Lan glanced at me. "You want to give it a whirl?"

"Might as well. We've gotta start somewhere." I lifted my palm face up and let white lightning fill it. Peeling back the Unseelie red, I smiled briefly at the friendly blue dancing between my fingers. "Let's give you a new home, huh?"

I pushed the Seelie tendrils toward the harp, trying to whisper them through the gold frame.

The blue laved over the surface, but it didn't absorb into the harp whatsoever.

"Next idea," I declared, dropping my magic.

Lan grabbed a hair. "How do we incorporate these?"

"I thought those would become the strings, but how do we get the shape back?"

Frowning, Lan grabbed the harp and extended it to me. "Here, take one end."

I did so, and we both yanked our side. "Put your feet against mine, so we can get more traction."

We grunted, each gripping a side of the harp, and pulled with all our fae might. The harp slipped from my fingers. Lan whomped flat on his back as I cried, "Oops."

The instrument went flying through the air.

Lan groaned. "Some warning would've been nice."

"Warning?" I scoffed, leaning back on my hands. "Who do you think you're shacking up with?" I'd said it glibly, but the words hit me hard—we wouldn't get to shack up together, would we?—but my pallor went unnoticed as Faolan grabbed his spear.

"Watch this," he said smugly, crossing his legs at the ankle.

The spear glowed a fiery red, and with a low, sad song the harp zipped back to us as though hooked on a line.

Huh. That was pretty cool. "Nice party trick."

"Isn't it? I guess grandfather's weapons have spent a long time together."

I suppose they had. "Do you think the spear could help fix it? The harp didn't let my magic in, but it might accept help from a friend."

"What if the spear melts it?"

I pursed my lips. "A giant wall of Rubezahl's magic didn't melt it. The harp is stronger than it looks. We could use it as our last attempt if you're worried."

"Do we *have* any other ideas?"

"I usually just blast things with lightning and hope for the best," I deadpanned.

We grinned at each other.

He put the harp and spear down. Leaning over, Lan then brushed my dark hair back over my shoulder. I'd kept it loose while it dried from my earlier bath, and it fell in soft waves. "You're beautiful, Alli."

I nuzzled into his touch. "You're getting off topic."

"Am I? Should I stop?"

You're a queen. Demand time. "As queen, I order you to attend my bed this evening."

Laughter choked in his throat. "Am I your mistress now or something?"

I smiled and pressed my lips to his, pulling back and sighing out, "Or something."

"I accept." Lan's mouth moved over mine, and he ran his hands up my arms, kneading as he went.

When we separated, I cocked a brow. "How did I end up on your lap?"

"Magic."

Rolling my eyes, I wiggled until he widened his legs, and I could sit on the ground between them. "Let's give the spear a go."

Lan hooked his grandfather's weapon and held it in both hands, caging me between the weapon and his body. I blinked into my magical sight as he directed his Unseelie power into the spear.

It awakened in response, and I blinked, just managing to prevent myself from shying away as flames licked up the shaft and gathered on the gleaming tip.

"Scared?" Faolan whispered in my ear.

I sniffed. "Get on with the lightshow, mistress."

Behind me, his body shook with his low chuckle. Lan extended the spear and touched the tip to the harp. The flare of gold and fire made me turn away. Eyes streaming, I squinted through the shining aura.

"It's accepting the flames," I hushed. "What do you feel?"

The fire was permeating the metal whereas my magic hadn't.

Lan said, "It's not holding. The fire is flowing in and out."

He severed the flow.

It was something though. "We need to figure out how to make the magic stay in."

"I'd rather do this." He pressed kisses up my neck. "You smell so sweet."

Shivers wracked my body. "Mmm?"

"Mmm," he echoed in a deep rumble. "You know how I know you're turned on?"

I grinned at his use of the words he'd said in the cabin, not far from here, during our previous stay in Underhill. "How?"

"Those little gasping breaths you're making."

I rested back. "You know how I know you're turned on?"

"Last time it was my erection on your thigh."

Correct. "And this time it's on my back."

We laughed together.

I slapped his leg. "Stop distracting me from saving the world. We've got to figure this out."

"Yes, Queen of All Fae."

Twisting, I blasted him with a look so dry it'd evaporate oil from a pan.

He bowed his head. "I am but a humble mistress."

I snorted. "You're never going to let that go, are you?"

"Not while it makes you laugh, Orphan."

Crawling a short distance away, I wiggled my butt for his benefit, then sat cross-legged again. "Try blasting it again."

Lan called the spear's flames and directed them at the harp. "They're not even going inside now."

I looked between us. "We're not touching. Maybe we need to be touching."

I shuffled back and rested a hand on his thigh. Immediately, golden fire beamed from the spear.

"Your Seelie magic, Alli," he said quickly. "Try it again."

I was already there, peeling away my Unseelie power. Tentatively, I pushed magic down my arm, then shifted my grip to his hand. My magic was a #1 Lan Fan and curled about his fingers before I urged it onward to the shaft of the spear.

The result was immediate.

A whining hum filled the air, vibrating in pulsing waves that shook my very mind with their intensity.

"The spear," Lan grunted. "It's heating up."

More than usual?

"I can't hold it," he said in surprise, voice tight with pain.

We were close. I could feel it. "What's happening?" I couldn't see through the glare cast by both artifacts.

"The spear is melting," he said in horror. "Or destroying the harp. I can't see the tip anymore. Alli, I can't hold it much longer."

What could I do? Maybe we just had to go for it. "Push, Lan. As hard as you can. I'll do it too."

He tensed under my hand, his entire arm shaking with the force of holding the spear. I gritted my teeth, unable to keep my eyes open as the light increased ten-fold, along with the pulsing waves of power echoing from the two weapons.

Kik's hair!

Opening my eyes, a mere sliver, I felt around and eventually found the coarse strands. This was a theory only, and a wild one at that, so I made sure to only take a few. Drawing as close to the flames as I dared, I scattered the hairs over top of them.

"I'm going to drop it," Lan shouted over the din.

"So let's give it everything we have," I yelled back.

I shoved my Seelie magic into the shaft.

Boom!

The surge of power sent me tumbling across the surface of the meadow, legs over my head. I came to a sprawling rest, lying with my face smooshed into a flower. As I groaned, one of the tiny clouds drifted closer and started to rain on me.

Because that was just my life.

I pressed up and hobbled back, stretching down a hand to help Lan stand because he'd been propelled by the explosion too.

"No, thanks," he winced, spreading his palms for me to see.

I gasped at the charred and blistered skin. "Shit. Let's get you to the Oracle." Or maybe Devon could help him.

He clenched his jaw. "Harp first."

We walked to the huge, singed circle at the edge of the meadow.

"The spear is gone," Lan said dully.

I fell to my knees. "It's still here. It's just got a new home inside the harp."

And the harp was shaped just like the one in Elisavanna's puzzle.

I yelped at a scalding pain in my pocket. Reaching inside, I tossed the molten objects to the ground, rubbing my thigh.

The pieces of her puzzles glowed, and as we looked on, the tiny spear dragged along the singed meadow floor to the equally tiny harp. It curled around the toy version of Lugh's instrument and then melted away into nothing.

"It was meant to happen," I whispered. "The harp absorbed the spear. The only Seelie power strong enough to replace the spirit that was released was another of your grandfather's relics."

Lan rubbed his jaw. "Strength wasn't the issue. I think it accepted the spear because it was familiar."

The harp was back, but the spear that Lan had worked so hard to claim was now gone. "Are you all right?"

My Unseelie bent to pick up the stringless instrument. "I won't look as cool with a harp. But if it was meant to happen, then standing in the way wouldn't have changed a thing." He raised his rainbow gaze to mine. "How about we string this up?"

I leaned down to grab the remaining kelpie hairs.

"Hold on," he muttered. "There are tiny cracks all over it."

I shot a glance at it. He was right. Orange light flickered through the lines. "I can see the flames inside." I sucked in a breath. "That crack just got bigger."

Lan swore. "This one over here too."

"Shit, do you think it will explode?" If so, there was a serious time limit for finding Rubezahl.

Pounding hooves had us both whirling.

I'd expected to see a furious Kik bearing down on us, but instead an alicorn cantered toward me and Lan, slowing to a trot and then a walk before stopping before us. Her coat shimmered with hidden colors, like the gleaming surface of a pearl.

She was beautiful.

I bowed slightly, lifting my hand in a sign of peace—thumb and first two fingers touching, ring and pinky finger flared, palm toward the one approaching. "Greetings, my friend."

She whinnied softly, and the sound contained a hint of inquiry.

"Hold up the harp," I said. "Maybe she needs to complete the process."

Lan did so, stepping closer to Underhill's graceful creature. She tossed her mane and then reared up, striking the air with her front hooves.

Something was wrong.

And I was coming to realize that many wrongs could be righted by touching Lan—when we worked together, everything was easier, and it felt better too. Joining him, I gripped the harp, too, wrapping my other arm around his torso for good measure.

She nuzzled my hand holding Kik's hairs. I quickly draped them over the harp, then resumed my hold on Lan.

The alicorn nickered, dropped to the ground, then touched her nose to the harp.

A string of sorrowful harp music filled the air, circling us in a gentle cyclone of the warmest breeze. The hairs slipped into place across the harp, bound by forces invisible to my eyes. I inhaled, letting the beauty of the melody fill my heart and soul, unable to prevent a wide smile.

The alicorn raised her head again, then extended a foreleg and bowed back.

"The cracks are gone," Lan said, then winced as the harp shifted against his burns.

The alicorn set her nose to one of his arms, and there was a lesser melodic ring. A beat later, Lan held up an unblemished hand, and awe filled his voice. "You healed me."

I bowed deeply. "Thank you for helping us. Truly."

Or should I thank Underhill? Nah, I was still pissed at her for throwing the last battle.

I took the harp from him as the alicorn left. "Are your hands all fixed? I have ideas that involve them, and if they're still injured, then you'd just have to sit back and let me do the work."

He cocked a brow. "They're fixed, but even if they weren't, what's a little pain in the scheme of things?"

We started back to the Oracle's house, where I could already see the old woman outside, tapping her cane on the ground in agitation.

"The harp is fixed," he said. "Where does that leave us now?"

In a stronger position.

Though there was no point in us possessing either instrument if we had no one for it. "Think Drake and Rowan are having any luck out there?"

No idea. But you would've thought a giant of his size couldn't have many hiding places.

"You know what they say?"

My lips curved. "If you want a job done properly, do it yourself?"

I meant that, but I also wanted to heed Cinth's words. *Take the time.*

My days in both realms were numbered, and that meant my time with Lan was ticking away before my eyes.

"Want me to speak to Kik about carrying us?"

Yeah, right. The only place he'd carry us now would be to the fiery mouth of the dragon. "No."

"Maybe Devon could make a golden path to save us time."

"No."

"I'll grab supplies then. We'll take the opposite—"

I looped my hands around the back of his neck. "No."

His rainbow gaze found mine. "No?"

I kissed him. "No. Tonight is ours, Lan. Tonight, I don't give a single fuck about giants, harps, or asshole kelpies. Got it?"

He stroked my cheek with his knuckles. "Yes, my queen."

CHAPTER 22

Lan slung the harp over his shoulder and lifted me as he stood, as if I were light as a feather. Which, for clarity, I was not. My arms were still looped around his neck, and I jiggled the hilt of one of the twin blades strapped to my back, so it wasn't jutting into his jaw. Romantic gestures like this really weren't made for people armed to the teeth.

"Where?" he asked.

That single word stumped me. Crap, he was right. *Where* was the question of the day.

I opened my mouth, but nothing came out. The Oracle's house held far too many people. Underhill was not a place to go wandering about looking for a place to get naked and sexy. Where could we be together without being disturbed? Even an hour would be a boon, though I'd take more if I could get it. Scrap that, I was going to take them.

I peered around. "I don't know." Then I tapped him on the shoulder, and he slowly set me down. My bare feet buried into the soft grass of the meadow. For just a moment, I thought I saw a line of gold rushing to the tips of my toes. Underhill's magic? She'd only shown me a golden path a few times so far. It had to mean something.

But why would she care whether Lan and I had a few hours to ourselves? It wasn't as if Underhill was rooting for me to get laid. She just wanted me to die in a balanced way.

I wiggled my toes, and the gold lines wrapped around them and then zipped away.

Lan stepped behind me and swept my hair to the side to kiss my neck. "I will follow you anywhere, Alli. You know that."

I leaned into him, wishing I was naked and writhing with his hard body instead. The thought rippled through me, hitting me hard. What if Drake and Rowan returned in the next few hours with Rubezahl's location? What if this was the last chance we had to have this experience?

Please don't take this from me too. Let me have my goodbye with Lan.

"For fuck's sake, you two could not be more stupid if you were thrown out of a dumbass tree and hit every idiot branch on the way down."

Lan and I turned. There was no rushing. Only one person would speak to us like that. Kik had joined us, hide still covered in dirt, his face covered in bruadar. There was something in his eyes that I couldn't quite understand. Was he . . . sad?

"Get on," he demanded. "I'll take you somewhere quiet. Dingdongs."

The discrepancy between his words and his sentiment had my head spinning, but Lan didn't hesitate. He all but threw me onto

Kik's back, then leapt on behind me, his arms circling my waist. The land kelpie took off, galloping from the Oracle's valley.

"Where are we going?" I tugged on Kik's mane. We couldn't go too far. I had to be ready for Rubezahl when the time came

My body tensed at the thought, my mind teetering on the edge of panic, and both males felt it.

Kik glanced back. "You aren't going to cry, are you? I have a place that's nice enough. I hate it when women cry for no reason."

With everything going on, he thought I didn't have plenty of reasons? Still, he hadn't uttered a single curse, and I had to wonder if he was high on whatever dream grass he'd imagined the bruadar to be.

A flash of Underhill's magic zipped down Kik's mane and into my fingers. Warm. Comforting. *Ah.* Right. Kik wasn't helping out of the goodness of his icicles. He had been prompted by Underhill. Those zips of gold said it all.

Was this Underhill's last gift to me? A night with Lan?

I bit my lower lip to keep it from trembling. I didn't want to be grateful when Underhill was demanding I give up my very life. In all honesty, though, part of me had known from the moment I first ran to the Triangle that the odds for my long-term survival weren't great.

Underhill's bullshit aside, I was grateful for her blessing now.

Lan's arms were warm around me as he held me steady. "What's wrong?"

"Just . . . stressed." I said, not lying. I *was* stressed. About what was coming, yes, but not because I knew it would end in my death.

I was stressed by the thought of those I would leave behind. By the good times I would miss with them. That was where the pain came in. I was so lost in thought I didn't notice where the land kelpie had brought us until he slid to a stop.

Kik paused long enough for me to take in the perfectly arched bower made of willow branches woven with lilac and wisteria—purple blooms interspersed with tiny white snowdrop flowers, petite and impossible in this balmy climate. Yet was *anything* impossible in the fae realm? Because here they were.

At the center of the bower was a bed strewn with petals and sheets that looked silken to touch.

Beautiful.

"Get the fuck off." Kik bucked, sending us flying.

Lan grunted as I landed on top of him.

"Sorry." I rolled to my feet. "Knew his manners would wear off sooner rather than later.

Kik snapped at the ground that was softening beneath his feet. "I did what you asked!"

The ground solidified again, and Kik wandered off, flashing his asshole at me and Lan and letting out a deep fart that had me backing up despite the distance that was already between us.

I put my hand to the ground and whispered my thanks to Underhill, quietly so Lan couldn't hear. "For whatever time we have, I'm grateful."

My body tingled, the magic of Underhill whispering over me in veins of gold. Everywhere her essence touched, my skin glowed. The dirt and grime of battle fell away, and my clothing was transformed into a gossamer dress. The light purple material had flecks of gold running through it, just like Underhill's magic. This was clothing meant to be taken off. I ran my fingers through the translucent skirts, wondering at the way they flowed like water. It felt as if I touched nothing. As if I *wore* nothing.

Was Underhill *actually* rooting me on? Because she felt like my wing woman right now.

I looked up and sucked in a sharp breath. Lan stood across from me, his hips wrapped in a swath of material that fell to mid-thigh. *Old school fae style.* I approved. The fabric was the deepest ruby red, drawing attention to the ridges and lines of his chest. His hair was pulled back, and every angle of his face seemed highlighted by a fire that didn't exist. Perhaps the fire was within him.

I could take being burned.

I'd lean into his flames for as long as I could.

His chest rose and fell a little too fast to be normal as we exchanged stares, drinking each other in.

"You are a goddess," he whispered. "A part of me thinks this can't be real."

"I feel the same. Only you're not so much a goddess as a god." I let a slow smile steal across my mouth and deliberately set aside my fears and worries. This was our time. Blessed by Underhill to have it, I would take all I could without question.

I took another step, and he matched me. Another. Another, until our fingertips touched, a sizzle of energy heating each digit. Our magics rose, dancing the way they'd done so long ago in Rubezahl's outcast home. They tightened like bands across our wrists. A little bit kinky and not at all unpleasant.

Heat burned low in my belly.

I wove our fingers together until we were hanging onto each other as tightly as we'd ever done.

"This is how it should always have been, my love." He lowered his head and moved to kiss me.

And Goddess knows I wanted him to, but I couldn't resist.

I turned my head at the last second, and he kissed my closed eyelid, his lips pressing into my eyeball. For a leaden moment he just stood there in confusion, his mouth pressed to my eye. And I stood there, smiling, *knowing* that his mind was wondering at the odd feeling under his lips and trying to make sense of it.

Unable to contain myself, I burst out laughing.

He pulled back and wiped my eyelid, shaking his head as he laughed with me. "I'll never forget that day. I couldn't believe you tried to kiss me, and I . . . I was glad, even though I knew I would have to tell you off. But to kiss my eye!" He laughed harder, rainbow eyes swirling. “I cherished that memory in my darkest moments. I always will. Maybe it’s only appropriate that our first kiss was as odd as the match we present to the world.”

I ran my fingers over his stubble while my heart did some serious flipping out in my chest. “It was perfect. I didn’t think so at the time, but I do now.”

Growling, he tugged me hard against his chest, stealing away my laughter with the intensity of his gaze. Tucking both my wrists behind my back, he pinned them there, fanning the flame within me.

“Such cheek from a queen,” he said his voice low. “I would say it’s unseemly.”

I batted my eyelashes at him. “What are you going to do, spank me?”

“Not unless you beg,” he whispered, and damn it if my legs didn’t give a suspicious wobble. Fire rolled from my lower belly and pooled deeper yet, filling my body with want and need that only Faolan could cure.

Lan held my wrists with one hand, and the other he kneaded up my back. He swept his fingertips across my collar bone, then traced his way up my neck to my jaw. Each touch was heartbreakingly gentle for a warrior and a man who’d been trained to fight, kill, and be all around unyielding.

He was treating me as if I would break when I had at least as many scars as he did. “I could touch you for the rest of my life and not get enough of the feel of your skin—” he dipped his head and kissed along the path his fingers had traced, “—the taste of your body—” he nuzzled up my neck to my ear and into the edge of my hairline, “—the smell that is you and you alone.”

I closed my eyes and fought to be present in the moment. To be patient. Our long-contained emotions and desire and magic rolled freely around us, sweeping me up in the thick wave, drowning me in the heady sensations of Lan’s touch. Of him loving me.

"I love you, Lan," I gasped. "No matter what comes, know that I love you."

His mouth made its way to mine, and he kissed the corner, the bottom lip and finally, when I groaned, covered my lips with his own, speaking between kisses. "You have my heart, for now and forever, Alli. My orphan. My fae queen."

He let my wrist go and crushed me against his hard body. The flimsy material swathing me was thin enough to leave me with no doubt Faolan wanted me through and through.

Yet even with the time it had taken to get us to this moment—our whole damn lives—he wasn't hurrying. He wasn't rushing to finally do the deed, and his restraint was driving me wild. *Mad* in a way no other trial of my life had managed to.

My hands had frantic minds of their own as they dug into his shoulders, then slid down his back to his very nice ass in something close to desperation. The roughness of my touch drew a low growling moan out of him. I took two handfuls of the wrap around his waist and yanked him, step by step, into the bower.

I wanted him in me.

I wanted to feel his body on mine.

There was so much I wanted from him that panic to get it was clawing up my throat.

The back of my knees hit something soft, and I let myself fall backward onto a bed made of ferns and rose petals. The sheets felt as silky as they'd looked.

He followed me down into the softness, bracing on his elbows above me.

A lump rose in my throat.

"This is a dream," I whispered as I stroked a hand over his face. "One I don't want to wake up from."

How could I ever get enough of him?

Lan pressed his lips to the sides of my face. "Why are you crying? Alli, talk to me."

I closed my eyes and shook my head slightly.

"Just kiss me, Lan. Just love me. I want everything you have to give." I reached for him, dragging him into another kiss that left us both panting.

Sensation rocketed through me as the heat between us flared and danced, Lan circling his mouth around my nipple through the wispy excuse of a dress I wore. My back arched, and he held me there, drawing me higher as his free hand slid between my legs.

Only it wasn't just his fingers he drew across my lips and clit.

Lan's magic coursed over my body—electrical vibrations, heat, and then shivering cold chased one another in rolling pulses with each stroke of his fingers.

Fuck!

"Lan." I bucked my hips as I cried out his name. He stayed where he was, preventing me from wiggling away. Not that I wanted to go anywhere, but it was too much.

The sensations tore down any modicum of control I'd hoped to maintain.

"Good, Alli?" he murmured against my mouth, his smug-ass smile saying it all. He *knew* it was good.

"Fucking amazing," I whimpered. "Don't stop."

"Not done yet." He kissed me, drawing his tongue across mine before he traced kisses down south. Across my chest, down over my belly, pausing at a few scars on the way, then settling across my aching heat.

A sigh left my mouth that had him chuckling.

Magic hands, magic mouth as they say.

His tongue laved across my aching center, and with it came another rush of his Unseelie magic that had me moaning like a wild thing, thrashing on the bed and unable to help any of it.

Part of me knew this wasn't entirely fair.

I wanted him to be reduced to wildness too.

I couldn't reach anything except his upper body, so that would have to do. Seeing as I had no idea what I was doing with 'magical sexy,' this would be interesting. I wove my fingers through his dark hair and unleashed a trickle of magic, sending it down his spine and directing it across his ass.

He yelped as the tendril swatted his butt, but his yelp turned into a rumbling growl.

I grinned before realizing the growl wasn't from him.

No, no, this could not be happening again.

Underhill, you fucking led us here.

A howl cut through the air, and I scrambled upright as Lan pulled away. "Underhill, the least you can do is give me some different damn clothes." I tagged on, "Please."

Golden veins slid through the bower and wrapped around my body, creating an outfit fit for a queen. Slick fitted pants and a loose top, both in a pale gold matching Underhill's magic. A cloak as light as my skirts had been hung from my shoulders, and I could feel the weight of a crown on my head even though I couldn't see it. No boots. My feet sunk into the soft ground, and I wiggled my toes.

It was a crappy consolation prize. I swiped up my twin blades and dagger from where I'd dropped them while in lust's haze.

"What's happening?" Lan said, a beat behind me, as naked as the day he was born.

"Lan, too, please." I touched my fingers to my lips, tasting the tears that coursed down my cheeks.

We'd been so close.

I'd nearly had something to strengthen me in my final moments.

Why had she taken that from me?

Or perhaps she'd done it for Lan. Was he meant for another?

That was as unbearable a thought to me as death itself.

Another howl cut the air, and I recognized it now that my body wasn't in the throes of passion.

Drake.

I gave Lan a slow nod, his body now covered in a warrior's garb, trying to keep my bitter disappointment under wraps. He would expect more time. More moments between us. He didn't know our only chance had been ripped from us.

Because I was about to meet my destiny.

CHAPTER 23

"Where is he?" I shouted at Drake as Lan and I sprinted toward the changeling

A glance back told me that our Underhill bedroom had already sunken into the ground, and grief swept through me in a sickening rush before I hardened my mind to what lay ahead.

The path I was on was set—there was no going back.

Drake swung his stag head our way, then took off on his front hooves and his back legs, which were huge wolf paws.

This was his second shape—a combination of creatures.

The ground morphed almost immediately, and a forest shot up underfoot, one made entirely of gold.

Drawing golden energy from the fae forest, I whispered it into my indigo and spurred my legs and arms to pump harder. I was flying along beside Drake. The slight widening of his gaze showed his surprise that I could keep with him even in his changeling form.

His eyes slanted back, and I peered around for Lan.

Oops.

Spotting him through the gold branches and leaves, I sent a bolt of my power back to aid him. We slowed until he caught up.

"Thanks," he said drily.

His voice rumbled through me, eliciting shivers. My body was still having whiplash from what we'd been doing in the tent.

Drake didn't stop until the Oracle's tower abode came into view. Everyone had gathered outside.

"Report," I said to Rowan.

He straightened. "We found Rubezahl. West of here."

"In the Caves of Honor," the Oracle interrupted. "Which is why we never thought to look there."

An unfamiliar image flashed into my mind—a system of golden caves with yawning entrances that wormed their way deep underground. My mouth dried at the image. Where the fuck had that come from? I blinked a few times, and said in a dry voice, "Tell me about them. Why would Rubezahl have gone there? And why wouldn't you think he'd dare go? I suspect it's not just because he's dishonorable."

"Finally asking the right questions," the Oracle said. "The caves are dangerous. They shift with Underhill, but they follow patterns that can be predicted. Many say they are the strings Underhill plucks to change the rest of the realm."

"Rubezahl knows the patterns," I guessed.

"Yes," she said. "Honorable or not, the caves are no place for one who has not learned them. Tunnels collapse, sinkholes appear, and walls slam together with more force than a giant's fists without warning."

No wonder he was there—if he knew the caves, he could set up trap after trap for us. My eyes narrowed. "How did you find him?"

Drake had shifted back to two feet. He straightened his tunic. “We were scouting the area, and I saw him plain as day at the entrance of a cave.”

I blinked as the caves flashed into my mind again. “The middle one.”

He frowned, exchanging a surprised look with Rowan. “Yes. How did you know?”

Good question. I’d never been to the caves before, and I couldn’t imagine why Underhill would help me if balance was the objective.

But in the next blink I saw myself in front of the same cave. Even as my heart hammered at the pictures in my head, I said, “I must go there. He won’t come out. I’m betting he showed himself on purpose.” He could, after all, sense others and their magic.

Cinth cracked her neck. “When do we leave?”

There’s no we.

I fixed the chest harness on, then tightened the holster for the dagger around my upper thigh. That felt better.

Here was the hard part. “I need the rest of you to go back to Unimak.” And I needed Lan to leave me the harp. I refused to believe that he had to be present to wield it. He had to be safe. His part was done and over. Now it was my turn to protect him.

Silence.

I tilted my chin. “This part is for me alone.”

“Is it?” the Oracle murmured. “That’s not what I see.”

I took a closer look at *her.* The ancient fae’s hands shook. Sweat beaded on her brow, and her knuckles were white from where she clutched her cane.

If I asked whether she was okay, she’d hit me.

I met her rainbow gaze. Was it me or were there fewer rainbows swirling in that eye of hers lately? “What do you see?”

“That there are many caves and only one of you.”

Her comment was far less cryptic than those she'd made in the past. This time, instead of seeing myself standing in front of the cave, I saw me and my friends standing in front of several.

"Never narrow the lens," the Oracle murmured, looking into the distance.

I frowned. "Sorry?"

She snapped her head back and glared. "Can't an old woman mutter nonsense in fucking peace?"

There she was.

My weak heart wanted my friends to come, if only so I could have them close for another hour or two. Was it that weakness that had me clinging to the Oracle's words? "Okay. You can all come with me."

"I'm glad you've realized the inevitable," Faolan grunted, adjusting the harp slung over his shoulder. "We weren't going anywhere you weren't."

When the time came, I'd leave them behind. And when the final moment was upon me, I'd leave Lan behind too. Somehow.

"Here," the Oracle muttered. "Let me help. What a lot of dumdums that you are." The old woman turned from us, and magic surged in a whoosh before a portal expanded before us.

My jaw dropped. "What the hell? Since when can you make portals?"

"Since always," she said. "How do you think I got to and from the Earth realm back in the day?"

"By the entrance."

A shadow flitted across her rainbow iris. "Indeed. That did become the smart choice while it was functional. But we both know the entrance was a scam for a long time. But you, my child, must be smarter than I ever was." She lowered her voice, her focus shifting to Lan. "Protect him. He is your life as you are his, as he was mine."

We were back to cryptic. But I'd never heard her use that sorrowful tone before. "Are you going to be all right?" I asked.

She took a breath and smiled. “Yes, I will be. At last.” Her brows slammed together. “You think I’m going to stand here all day with this portal open? Get out of here.”

I heard Drake yelp. He and Rowan were first through, then Cinth. Lan stepped one foot through, then held his hand back for me. His rainbow eyes—far brighter than the Oracle’s—swept over my face. I took in the slight wariness in his gaze. Damn, he was on to me.

I’d definitely need to sneak away.

“Thanks,” I said to the Oracle.

“Fuck off, Kallik of All Fae.”

I placed one foot in the portal. “No queen?”

Her answer was lost as I stepped through. Peering back, I sucked in a breath as the Oracle collapsed to her knees. She looked up at me through the portal and winked.

Then the opening was gone.

“Up there,” Rowan said, pointing.

He needn’t have bothered. The golden glow from the cave system was a beacon—magical and physical. I shoved aside my worry for the Oracle.

“What’s the plan?” Lan asked. “Divide and conquer?”

I didn’t want anyone other than me to enter those caves. The giant’s plans weren’t always clear, but this one was. His magical reserves would still be coming back. He wouldn’t waste them on a face-to-face battle with me. Nope, he was trying to use his knowledge of Underhill against us. And I didn’t have time to learn the network of caves. None of us did. “No one will enter. We’ll all gather at a cave entrance. I want everyone to whisper at first, then use magic to project your voices. We want him to think we’re all inside searching.”

A slow smile spread across Lan’s lips. “Trickster. I approve.”

We started up the slight rise from the thorny purple and ruby red bushes surrounding us.

An eerie feeling crawled up my spine at the sight of those yawning gold entrances. This was exactly like what I'd seen in my vision. *Underhill, you creepy bitch.*

A wrinkle between my brows, I said, "I'll take the middle. Lan to my right. Cinth, left. Rowan beside you and Drake on Lan's other side."

"Why?" Cinth asked.

I shrugged one shoulder. "Because." *The pictures in my head said so.* That was not an answer I wanted to give out loud.

"Good enough for me." Drawing out her wooden spoon, she took the cave entrance to my left, and the others spread out.

Sliding my dagger free, I planted my feet in the gritty sand-like dirt of the middle cave. I whispered, "I'll take the middle cave."

Sure enough, the cave took up the sound, carrying it inside.

I nodded to Rowan, who spoke.

Lan was next. "Keep quiet."

Drake signaled me, his head tilted, and eyes narrowed as he listened intently. He then sniffed the air and pointed, circling a finger. Rubezahl was somewhere between me, Lan, and Cinth?

I raised my voice. "Ow, fuck."

Lan flashed me a grin, and I bit my lip against a snort. This was no time to be laughing.

Drake pushed his hand in the air. Rubezahl was moving left?

I nodded. He was searching for me.

"That was my favorite spoon," Cinth said at normal volume.

I cocked a brow, and she cocked one right back.

A gigantic rumble shook the ground, and I wasn't alone in crouching as Underhill shifted. Barely managing not to sprawl on my ass, I waited for her to stop her galactic shuffle before righting myself.

The caves appeared the same from the outside.

But *inside* they had to be different.

I gestured to Lan to switch positions, then shouted. "Is everyone okay?"

Rowan switched with Lan, and Cinth with Drake. I held Rowan's gaze, then Drake's, and held a finger to my lips.

Lan and Cinth called out.

"The caves shift with Underhill," I shouted. "Get out of here."

Drake was listening hard. I tensed, ready for the giant to leap out at me. Although his preference would be to lure me into the caves, he might come out if he thought the caves were claiming the others.

Drake's eyes widened. "Watch out!"

I raised my dagger.

But I was too late. Cinth screamed. My feet were already moving before my mind had caught up. I slowed, heart in my throat as Rubezahl stepped out of the cave, Cinth pressed to his body like a shield. His thumb and forefinger pinched either side of her throat.

The cruel twist of the giant's mouth dropped slightly when he caught sight of Drake and Rowan.

He'd believed our ruse.

"Clever, Queen of Nothing," the giant said mildly. "Perhaps you *can* learn. If only I cared to teach."

I clenched my jaw. "I don't want any more of your lessons, Rubezahl. Release her."

"You are in no position to make demands, Kallik," he said sadly. "You never were. A secret, an orphan, an exile, an unwanted queen."

Pretty accurate. "Your verbal daggers will not work. This ends. We are an even match now, Rubezahl. By now you must know Underhill will not allow for unbalance. Cinth is part of my power and will therefore live whether you like it or not." My friend grounded me, and that *was* power, though not the magical kind. "Stop with the pretense that you have any control over our state when we battle at last."

The giant seemed amused. "You surprise me yet again, young one."

For an odd, weighted moment, I met the giant's twinkling blue gaze. As one person who had to walk to her death to another, we exchanged the knowledge of our impending end.

"I see you understand," I said carefully, more than aware of Lan's heavy focus.

Rubezahl's gaze cut to the harp on Lan's shoulder, showing far too much interest before he forced his focus back to me. "Your ability to explore Underhill's message is impressive, young one. However, your weakness is in believing Underhill is the sole messenger. I am where I am because I decided to write my own message."

I snorted. "Hiding in caves, what's left of your army in my possession, and severely depleted of magic. What I'd give to be in your shoes."

He pinched harder, and Cinth—who'd wisely remained still during our exchange—cried out.

Rowan sent me a white-faced look of panic.

I folded my arms, sliding my feet farther apart. "Tell me your messages, oh great Rubezahl."

"I think not," he answered. "I'd rather write a new one now." He squeezed harder, and Cinth's eyes bugged.

My chest rose, and I forced myself to stay put. "Put Cinth down, and the others leave. We'll make this a fair fight at least."

"Fair," he mused. "Yes, now that is a message I would be happy to pen." His face firmed. "A portal to the Earth realm for her life."

"Agreed." I'd send him to the Triangle. The area was cleared of fae. He couldn't drain anyone to gather power. I could easily join him there.

"To Unimak," he said, the cruel twist of his lips appearing again.

My stomach churned. *Unimak* was a different kettle of red caps. There were plenty of fae to drain there, including the fae from his army, who were confined and in recovery if General Stryk had followed my orders.

The words of my departed spirit sister rang in my ears.

Both of you have a choice as to your eventual meeting place.

A fae bereft of Underhill is a weak fae indeed. For Underhill replenishes our connection to its energy and essence. This is her power. And Rubezahl knows it well.

Rubezahl was separating me from Underhill. He thought she was on my side. Just as I'd misinterpreted her actions in the past to mean she favored him.

Didn't the giant see what I saw? That she favored the need for balance above either of us? The only reason she wanted Rubezahl gone was because he was causing death that upset the scales. If he would only stop, this could all be over.

"Why not stop this madness?" I said softly. He'd loosened his grip, but Cinth's lips were still blue. "Stop throwing off the balance, and Underhill may show you lenience."

There was a flicker in his eyes, or maybe I'd simply wished the ripple of regret into being.

The giant lifted his chin. "Underhill has forsaken me."

I had to wonder if it hadn't been the other way around.

"The portal to Unimak," he hissed. "Now."

The strength of a giant was no joke. And I wasn't about to bluff with Cinth's life on the line. "You'll set Cinth down when the portal is half your size. Take her with you, and I'll follow and bring you right back." Which I'd try to do anyway.

He dipped his head. "Agreed."

Lan joined me, lowering his head. "Alli . . . "

"I know," I said my voice low. Taking the battle close to other fae and possibly humans wasn't ideal. And yet opening this portal felt right. Preordained, almost. The puzzle toy I'd unraveled had contained a portal, and that more than anything was fueling the burning conviction in my gut that this was meant to happen. That it was inevitable.

I'd learned to trust that feeling—or at least to understand that no matter what I did, what was meant to happen would happen despite my actions.

Pulling on my power, I submitted and opened the fabric between realms. The force shook me, and I reached for Lan's hand. The effect was immediate. The jolting power smoothed into a calm channel that flowed from me with ease. I stretched the portal until it was half Rubezahl's size.

Eyes twinkling, he shoved Cinth away. "Until next time, young one."

"Next time, this ends," I told him.

I widened the portal, and he stepped through. I dropped the portal before anyone—including myself—could do something stupid.

Rowan caught Cinth, and I joined them, sending my magic into the vicious bruises around her neck to ease the pain. She clung to Rowan, shaking.

"We're going to Unimak," I announced.

Lan joined us. "What about your connection to Underhill? It will be lessened."

"As will Underhill's connection to Rubezahl." Balance was still present. "The battle could have always been in either realm. I was warned."

"He won't waste time drawing on other fae."

"We don't know that for sure. We leave now."

Cinth coughed a few times. "Devon. The Oracle."

"The Oracle knew," I told her.

Cinth thought it through, then nodded. "Of course. It just seems so sudden."

It did . . . yet it also felt right on some level.

I could just imagine Adair standing beside Uncle Josef, who sat like a puppet on the throne in the meeting chamber. General

Stryk would've had his work cut out for him since returning. He'd probably been yelling at them since I left.

Taking Lan's hand, I pushed a wave of power forward, opening a portal with ease. Oh, how things had changed. I stared through it to the doors of the meeting chamber in the Seelie castle. "Follow me."

I stepped through, not releasing Lan's hand.

The two guards lowered their spears at the sight of me.

"Queen Kallik," one spluttered. "You're dead."

Was I now? "Good to know,' I replied. "Open the doors."

They scrambled to do so as the others appeared behind me, and I released the portal, saying a quick, heartfelt goodbye to the fae realm and those who remained in it.

Shouts echoed out to me, and I took in the purple face of General Stryk, who'd been engaging in the chief of the yelling, then the irritated and bemused expression of my uncle.

Unease twinged in my gut at the resemblance between this scene and the one I'd imagined while in Underhill. My gaze swept to Adair last of all, taking in the slight roundness of her belly under a dress that had been designed to flaunt her pregnancy.

Their shouting match trailed off as they caught sight of me.

The general dropped to a knee. "Queen Kallik, you return."

I smirked and marched into the room. "Thought I'd come back from the dead for a quick visit."

CHAPTER 24

The look on Adair's face gave her away. As if I hadn't already guessed that she was the one telling any fae who would listen that I was dead so she could steal the throne for her unborn child. Of course, the kid couldn't take the actual throne until he or she was of age—sixteen long years under Adair would reduce the courts to shambles.

"Kaa—lik." She stuttered my name, and I raised an eyebrow, waiting. Very slowly, as if it pained her, she dropped into a curtsy, her pale pink skirts pooling around her. Even caught in treachery, she got points for style. "*Queen* Kallik. We thought you were dead."

"Had a party planned, did you?" I strode into the chamber, taking note of the bright swaths of silken material hanging from the ceiling and cascading down the walls. They weren't in typical funerary colors. Nope, these were gold and bright pink. In addition, fake petals floated overhead, interspersed with tiny pink hearts that slowly spun. A party indeed. With hundreds in attendance, surely all of the houses with highest status in the Seelie court.

I blinked, connecting the dots.

This wasn't my funeral. It was a fucking baby shower.

Pink and gold.

So Adair carried my sister. The realization hit me far harder than I'd expected. Aside from wondering how Adair would use the pregnancy against me, I hadn't had time to really connect with the idea of a sibling. A fierce surge of loyalty rose within me now. I had a sister to protect from the woman who'd made my life miserable. This child would need someone in her corner.

And yet, I knew I wouldn't be long for this world.

I pivoted to face her, thinking hard. My sister couldn't rule until she was sixteen, and I needed a regent I could trust. There weren't many of those, and with the battle looming, I had to make a decision quickly. Time was not on my side. With each second that ticked by, Rubezahl was pulling himself together.

Gaining power again.

I pulled one of my short swords clear of its sheath and Adair gasped, putting a delicate hand to her throat as she tumbled—gracefully, no less—onto her ass.

I pointed the sword at her, and the room tensed to a degree that surprised me. "If I die, Adair, let me be crystal fucking clear that you will not rule in your daughter's stead."

She glared at me, eyes sparkling with animosity. No one else could see her face, which is no doubt why she'd given me an honest reaction.

I smiled. "The only Seelie fit to hold this throne as regent is Hyacinth."

Cinth was as startled as anyone else in the room, her jaw dropping as I spun and pointed my sword at her. My smile softened as relief flowered in my chest. I could see Cinth as regent, sitting at the desk that had been mine for mere weeks, bringing everything into order using her experience from the castle kitchens, pouring her heart and logic into each choice. Rowan would be at her side. So clear was the image that I had to shake it off.

I tilted my chin. "With the guidance and help of General Rowan, Hyacinth will hold the throne for my sister until her sixteenth year, should I die battling Rubezahl. *She* is the only person I trust to do the job right."

"I can't!" Cinth whisper-yelled. "You can't actually expect me to—"

I held up a hand, stopping her. Because I had to do this now. I had to provide for everyone. "Cinth, you run a kitchen like a general, and the other cooks respect and maybe even fear that wooden spoon of yours. Ruling a kingdom isn't so different from running a kitchen, no matter what the rich and entitled may wish to believe. And . . ." I paused to compose myself, "I have no doubt that you will rule with a healthy balance of firmness and respect. The people will love you."

Everyone loved her. Most people at the very first meeting. She just had a way about her.

Cinth's eyes welled, but she nodded. "Okay."

She wasn't saying the word in the hopes she'd never have to take up the mantle of regent. Cinth said it *knowing* that what I was asking would come to pass.

The Seelie throne was sorted.

Who the hell could I put on the Unseelie throne? That was another empty spot. Faolan was the obvious choice, but would he take the seat of regent after my death? Would it be cruel of me to ask? To have him occupy the room attached to the balcony where we'd once watched each other across the valley?

My heart said it wouldn't work. That, for a time, his soul would be too broken beyond repair to care about others. I swallowed my sorrow. There was only one other Unseelie that I could see on the throne. I could see him leading the Unseelie for a time, hard-faced but fair.

"General Stryk," I said, loud and clear. "If I go under in battle —" I looked at Adair. "Or fall victim to an assassin's knife. You will become regent for the Unseelie throne until the Oracle names a proper heir."

The general paled. "As you wish, Your Majesty, but—"

I held a hand. "No buts. We know what I face. What we are all facing."

General Stryk stood slowly. "Your Majesty, you speak as if you have no time."

I deliberately didn't look at Lan. I could feel the weight of his gaze and the unasked questions: *Why are you doing this now? Why didn't you name me as regent?* "I don't—*we* don't. We're in a race to save our kingdoms and the giant is on the move."

A group of advisors shuffled forward. Fuck me, I hated advisors.

"Queen Kallik, is this a good time?" One of them found the bravery to ask.

Did it *look* like a good time? "What do you want, Harlin?"

"I'm not Harlin, Your Majesty. My name is—"

My tone sharpened. "*What do you want?*"

He paled. "The human authorities are losing patience. If you have a message to pass on?"

Blood pounded in my ears. This is what I hated about being queen. I didn't have the patience for this political, tentative bullshit. My father and mother would have stood here and calmly rattled off a proper reply. Actually, my father and mother would have thought of the humans sooner and probably wouldn't have needed to be prompted by their advisors to manage relations from that quarter. "Tell the humans that we are approaching an end to these troubling times, and I have the utmost confidence that a peaceful resolution will occur. I will be in touch shortly." *Unlikely.* But hopefully that kept them away for a while until Cinth took up the reins.

Not Harlin bowed and hurried away.

I'd just opened my mouth to speak again when the castle around us rumbled, an earthquake shimmering through the walls. The quake held an edge of power—dark and dangerous—that my very being rejected. A small tug on my own magical reserves had me bracing myself as Rubezahl's power flowed over the room.

The green power reared away from my essence, and when I saw it stealing over the Seelie fae at the back of the chamber, I threw my power out in a wave. Gold covered Lan, Cinth, Rowan, Drake, General Stryk, and Adair in time, but the others in the room slumped where they stood, eyes dulling, skin turning waxy.

"They look like his outcast army," Rowan said, his voice tight as he hovered close to Cinth.

Drake's voice was grim. "He got them."

My calm state was a sign of how much crazy, twisted shit I'd experienced of late. This was just another horrific act from the giant that I had to take down. In a time long since passed, the sadness and anger of seeing these people used—*drained*—might have driven me to my knees.

Not anymore. I'd known that he'd try to tap into the magic of others for his own gain. I just hadn't expected it to happen so fast.

I pushed my gold into the one who was closest to me. Green slapped against my gold, and the two essences locked in battle.

I reigned my power back to the few I'd managed to keep from his control. I couldn't drain myself now by reclaiming these people. But that fucking monster was going to have me ramming my foot so far up his ass he'd be spitting their energy back out.

"We have to get him away from Unimak if we can," Lan said, stepping up beside me. His face didn't show the waxy effects of

Rubezahl pulling energy from him. My power was still protecting him, thank the goddess. "If we can do that, we can limit the damage to the realm and the fae he's drawing from."

Adair gasped, pressing a hand to her cheek. "How dare you assume to tell the Seelie queen—"

"Shut your stupid, gasping face, Adair," I snapped. "Faolan of the Unseelie court, grandson of Lugh, is the other half of my heart and soul. I will not allow you to speak to him as if he has no value. His word is my word."

Okay, that little speech? Yup, that speech flowed out of me like water runs downhill, and it took me a minute to realize what I'd done. The words to bind two hearts together were not so different from what I'd said. Basically, I'd just spit marriage vows out without even thinking about it. *No problem, Kallik. Just announce to the world that you love him with all you have. No big deal.*

I glanced at Lan and drew myself tall. I would not cringe or apologize for what I'd said, not even to him. Even though he probably should have a choice in the matter. "Anyone *else* got a problem with how I feel and who I feel it for?"

I realized that most of the people in the room were pretty waxy right now.

Lan's lips twitched. He gave me a half smile as he bowed from the waist. "As my queen speaks, so shall it be."

I glowered at Adair. "You?"

She shook her head, then opened her mouth. "I would have wanted better for you is all, someone not . . . "

Faolan stepped between us, so I was looking at the harp over his shoulder. He *may* have done it because my sword hand had just twitched in preparation of dropping the weapon to free my hands. Her complete and utter bullshit words were enough to make me want to strangle her, pregnant or not.

His words rang through the room. "Someone not Unseelie?" His voice was carefully neutral. "Is that what you intended to say?"

"The darkness in the Unseelie fae make you unfit for a throne, let alone for any child of the Seelie court to marry," Adair said, sniffing.

I could not believe she possessed the stupidity to make that comment. Didn't she feel how precarious her position was?

I stepped around Lan and touched his arm. "You'll never convince her, Lan. The best we can do is wait for her to die and teach her daughter to be better than her mother. Adair lost herself and her heart long ago." Perhaps it had happened the moment she'd discovered my existence, when she believed I was the result of my father's dalliance with a human. Or maybe she'd uncovered the *real* truth, something I only strongly suspected—that my father had loved the Unseelie queen.

Adair inhaled sharply, as though I'd slapped her. While I wished I could, I didn't have time to wait for her to give birth before doing it.

"We have to go," I ordered. "The giant waits for us."

The castle tilted, and Adair and Cinth cried out. I struggled to keep standing and had just righted myself when a voice boomed through the walls.

"Kallik of No House. Child forgotten. Exiled. Orphaned. Come and meet your fate." Rubezahl's voice echoed through the room, powered by his magic and the magic he was draining from his victims. I could see the threads of his essence woven through the sound. Interesting. I usually had to blink into my magical sight to see such a thing. Now that I thought about it, I hadn't needed to blink into it when his magic had poured into the chamber earlier either.

When had my connection with my magic heightened to this level? I couldn't remember. But I suspected it had happened in the battle by the dragon wings in Underhill. That was when I'd truly understood what being the conduit of her magic meant.

I took a closer look at his essence. *What the . . . ?*

Darker than before, the green was . . . *bleeding* was the only word I could use to identify the way the color leaked. The layer around it was almost black, as if darkness bound his essence—darkness made of hatred and anger. I watched as the black soaked into the green.

Before my eyes, Rubezahl's magic was being destroyed. It was something I'd only heard about in tales of ancient times. Something I'd *never* given credit to—old recounts always seemed half myth, the truth dressed up in wild clothing.

The stories didn't say much about the phenomenon. But from them I knew that his *soul* was destroying his essence. He'd embraced evil too closely. For that, there was a price.

To be Unseelie wasn't to be dark. The same thing could happen to a depraved Seelie. This wasn't a matter of Unseelie magic causing death, balanced by Seelie magic creating life. This wasn't even a matter of an Unseelie and Seelie union draining one of them of their essence until only one victor remained. *This* evil in Rubezahl would consume him, control him, and keep him alive while it tried to spread into other people.

Rubezahl had to die now.

The scales had to be reset, which meant my time was up.

I turned on my heel. "You have my orders. See them through should there be a need. I command all of you to remain here," I said to Cinth, Rowan, Drake, and the general. "Faolan and I will see this battle through."

I tilted my chin. "Don't touch anyone who looks like they do." I jerked a thumb at the dull, motionless figures in the chamber.

Cinth's eyes welled, and I looked away. This was how it had to be. Even knowing that, I hurried away from her. Because I only had so much strength when it came to those I loved.

I turned to Adair, stayed by the thought of the baby girl in her womb. "Don't touch anyone else. If you do, Rubezahl's magic will claim you."

Adair's eyes widened and she cradled the swell of her stomach.

Leaving the others and some of my heart behind, I made my way through the castle with only Lan at my side.

We walked in silence for about 2.4 seconds.

"You going to tell me what all that was about?" Lan asked as we strode through the halls. More than one servant lay slumped against the wall, unmoving but for the slight rise and fall of their chests, eyes dull and unblinking.

Rubezahl would be full up in power if he'd gotten to every fae on Unimak. *Damn it all.*

"Prudence is a virtue," I said.

"That's patience," Lan replied. "What General Stryk said . . . you *are* speaking like you have no time. What's going on, Alli? We're all in this together. Unless there's something you know that you're not telling me."

Did I lie to him? I wanted to lie to him. But I couldn't have him remember me that way either.

I stopped as we reached the lowest level of the castle that led out into the courtyard. "My life has never been a fairy tale. There has never been a happily ever after. And I wouldn't want one, Lan, because my life may have had its trials, but every second of it has been *real.*"

"There's a happily ever after this time, Orphan. We'll face him together, and we'll take him down. Our fates are bound."

But they couldn't be. Not this time.

I slipped my arm around his neck and kissed him, deeper than ever before, as if I could mesh our bodies together. Our magic flared hot around us, and as I pulled back, I felt regret to the center of my bones. Not only my own—it was as if our magic wished we could stay like that too.

"Forever and ever, I'll be with you, Lan. No matter what."

His eyes were shadowed with worry. "Again, you say that like you know something I don't."

I didn't want to lie to him, not in what felt like our last moments together. "I don't see this ending well for me, Lan. Underhill demands that balance be restored. I don't see any other way to finish things."

That was as close as I could get to telling him our time together only numbered in the minutes. *Hours* if we were lucky.

Lan's face looked as though I'd stolen his energy, like Rubezahl had done to the other fae, along with his heart. His very soul.

"Don't—"

I kissed his mouth, silencing him. "We go together now. What happens, happens. I'm doing this to save our people."

Our.

Not mine, not his, ours.

His jaw flexed, and I could see that he was already trying to come up with a way to stymie me. But this wasn't my idea. Underhill was steering this train, and what she wanted, she got.

"You have a plan?" He changed the subject so quickly that I knew he hadn't processed what I'd told him. No, he'd gone straight to utter denial, just like I would have if our situations were reversed. Complete confidence that there had to be another way because the alternative was too horrific to consider. I may work to keep him alive, but he'd do just the same for me. More and more the feeling filled me that Underhill would have the final say on saving Lan's life.

"Rubezahl's power has been claimed. He is now a conduit to evil, and I can't say how much he's even in control at this point." I touched the newly made harp Lan carried on his back. "That evil will do anything to gain a foothold against Underhill."

"You think it's a counterpart to Underhill?"

I thought it reasonable to assume unbalance could take a form just like balance—Underhill—had done. "It's only a theory. But one my gut says is right. We have to lead Rubezahl and the evil that's using him away from here. The harp means more to that evil than the giant's life, I think."

Lan pulled the harp from his back. "You know he—or whatever he's unleashed—will want to make a bargain for this."

"He can bargain all he wants once he follows us through a portal." I took Lan's hand and faced the large doors that led into the courtyard.

A wash of Rubezahl's power attempted to flow over us again. When it contacted Lan and me though, it didn't simply shy away. The magic *shrieked* and pulled away, racing back to its master.

The grunt Rubezahl expelled could be heard even through the thick doors.

"What the hell was that?" Lan asked, his voice shaking.

"I don't think his magic likes it when we touch," I said, part of me unsurprised. "Don't let me go."

Lan looked at me. "Never. And I mean that, Alli. *Never.*"

I glanced away. With my other hand, I called up my indigo magic and wrapped my throat in it, amplifying my voice so that all fae could hear me. "Rubezahl, leave Unimak now or die. I will not allow you to harm another fae."

Before he could answer, I pushed one of the heavy doors to the courtyard open. Bright sunlight flooded the sky and made me blink several times. So strange for the weather to be so beautiful when the world was crashing toward a battle that would define the history of two realms.

Rubezahl stood leaning against a building on the other side of the courtyard, crushing the roof with his weight.

"I do not think I will be the one to die, misbegotten mutt." He smiled, and there was no kindness in it. His eyes were black, just like the evil that had overtaken his very essence.

I'd seen Underhill in Devon's eyes, and now I saw its opposite in Rubezahl.

This was a darkness without limit, and I shivered from its scrutiny.

I wasn't fighting a fae any longer, I was fighting something much, much worse.

Yet fight I must. I took one step and then another.

I opened my mouth to tempt him with the harp, to lure him away as planned.

He stood suddenly, his fist wrapped around the tall wooden staff he carried. "Now you understand the cost of defying me." He slammed the butt of the staff into the cobblestones and the earth erupted, exploding outward as a wave of soil, stone, and houses rippled toward us. Lan yanked me to the side, and we dove to escape the path of the earthen wave.

The wave hit the castle, splitting stone and gold and wood to the top of the highest tower. There was a keening noise, and then we were racing back as the building buckled inward. A building that had stood for nearly a hundred years since the contract with humans was first signed.

"No!" I screamed, reaching for my own magic, but I could already see I was too late. The castle fell before my eyes, crumbling, windows exploding, screams echoing above the crashing of the stones.

Lan held me tightly as I strained against him. "You can't, Alli, you can't!"

"Cinth is in there," I screamed the words, tears flowing. "Cinth is in there—I have to get her out!"

Goddess above and below, let this be a dream, a nightmare, something I could wake up from. Yet as I watched the castle go down, as the dust and debris rained around us, I knew it for what it was—a death blow. Cinth . . . Cinth was gone. Rowan, General Stryck, and Drake were gone. I didn't give a shit about Adair, but the child . . . lost. So many lives, so callously stolen and for what? Spite.

Nothing but spite.

Nothing but senseless, *senseless* darkness.

Lan shook his head. "You can't, Alli. It's what he wants, for you to be distracted and . . . and if you're right about what's coming, then Cinth will wait for us on the other side. We'll be together." He choked on the words, and tears tracked through the dust on his face. "You'll see her soon enough, Alli. We *both* will. Don't think I can't see what you're planning. We live together, or we die together."

My heart clenched. His denial hadn't lasted as long as I'd hoped.

The last, tiny hope that I'd held about somehow saving him flicked and died. I still carried the suspicion that Underhill would intervene on my behalf for the sake of balance, but there was also a glimmer of guilty relief that I might not be alone at the end too.

Hiccupping back a sob, I held my hand out for the harp, and Lan gave it to me. We'd remade it into a completely different shape, but I plucked a string and the sound still rippled outward. It was a beautiful sound, and the very world around us seemed to vibrate.

I'd only intended for the note to gain his attention, but I could *feel* the power thrumming through me.

The beautiful note gave me hope. It gave me courage. And the strength to take the next step.

"You want this back, you oversized motherfucker?" I snarled as I opened a portal to the place where it had all began—the house in the Alaskan Triangle where Rubezahl had first given me a cup of tea.

The giant whom evil had chosen as its conduit leaned forward.

My lips curved. "Come and get it."

The giant surged toward us.

Chapter 25

Lan and I clasped hands and dove through the portal and out of Rubezahl's charging path.

Breaking into a run, we crossed from the east side of the house to the west, keeping the building behind us. There wasn't time to really look at the beautiful wooden home behind me. Or peer at the surrounding trees and think of how I'd once walked through them as an outcast. Yet my eyes had been opened to the magic all around me, and it changed everything. I saw the vibrant green tendrils in the trees and patchy grass. The red energy thrumming hot and deep underground. The earthy warmth in the wood of the giant's home. This spot was awash with magic. The fabric between the realms was weaker here, and the energy had converged in response.

Going inside the house wasn't an option after what Rubezahl had done to the Seelie castle on Unimak. My chest squeezed at the thought of my friends. I'd left them behind to protect them and killed them in doing so. They'd never stood a chance.

"He'll want the harp," I said under my breath, pushing past the pain in my chest. I turned to face the opening we'd created.

Despite the evil force consuming him, Rubezahl pulled up short at the sight of the place that could well have been his home for hundreds of years. Was he reminiscing on the thousands he'd chatted up while numbing their minds and magic with his tea?

I tightened my grip on the harp, then extended it to Lan.

He settled it against his chest. His new multi-hued magic surged up within him, and he began to play.

A humming vibration shook the very ground we stood upon as he strummed. The leaves rustled on the trees in answer, pebbles leaped and jerked underfoot, the foundations of the giant's old home groaned in protest.

Lan plucked several strings at once, and the giant staggered back as though punched.

Whatever he was doing, it was helping.

I drew my twin blades, thinking of the mother I'd never truly known as I did so. Maybe part of that was Elisavanna's fault, but the rest of it was Rubezahl's for taking her from me—and I'd never seen a flicker of remorse for the death of the woman he'd apparently loved either.

I had a giant to slay.

"Look at you," I said to Rubezahl, getting between him and Lan—and the harp. "What happened to the fae who loved a queen once upon a time? Why did you keep turning to evil when there were so many chances to take the right path?"

Rubezahl righted himself against the harp's power, then hunched away from another vibrating chord.

I stalked closer, loosening my wrists with large loops of the swords. "So many lives. So much pain. So much destruction.

And now we come to this moment."

The giant used his enormous wooden staff to prop himself up. "And *I* shall walk away from this moment, young one. Not you."

I smiled sadly, sliding my feet wider as I stopped fifteen feet from him. "You still believe one of us wins this, Rubezahl?"

"You will never wear a crown of petals," he rasped, "Only one of ice."

The giant's eyes were flooded black. He twisted his slackened mouth into a smirk. Throwing back his head, he roared. Magic—entirely black—exploded from him.

I threw up a shield of gold just in time, large enough to protect me and the man at my back. The force of the blow stole my breath, and I leaned into the onslaught, watching through slitted eyes as spears of black magic shattered against my shield.

My feet slid backward on the ground, and when the assault cut off, I almost faceplanted in the opposite direction.

He was on me.

The harp played on as the end of Rubezahl's staff crushed where my head had just been. I swung my swords through the staff, one after the other, cutting it in two.

A massive fist, strengthened with magic, came for me. I ducked closer, digging a sword into the ground to help me deliver a savage kick to the inside of his knee.

I danced back at his howl of pain.

Rubezahl crouched, tossing away his ruined staff.

He didn't have a chance at winning a physical fight. I wasn't saying it would be easy, but the giant had dedicated his life to *magical* knowledge. A large portion of mine had been dedicated to the opposite.

I charged, still between Lan and the giant, and Rubezahl pounded his fists on the ground. Liquid black poured into it, but with what purpose?

I watched as the tendrils wound deeper and deeper. Then the air was sucked from the clearing as the black speared upward.

Not toward me.

Throwing out a wall of gold between Lan and the ground, I was driven to my knees by the force of the rush. The harp music cut off, and Lan fell into my wall of gold.

"Alli," he choked.

A shadow fell over me. I rolled to the side, slashing blindly with my blades. Rubezahl was faster and stronger without the harp playing.

"The music," I shouted, crying out as the giant caught me with a backhand.

I *flew. Crack.* A pine tree caught me, and I tumbled down to a halt on the needles littering the ground as my mind reeled from pain and the sheer force of the blow.

Clutching my ribs, I drew cool blue energy from the rocks deep underground to soothe my wounds. *Thank you.*

"You *did* disappoint me when you decided to become all you could be," Rubezahl was saying to Lan. "It made life far more inconvenient."

Lan didn't answer. He probably couldn't. The harp clearly could not be played without a price. Magic was pouring out of my love. Sweat beaded on his brow and dripped in torrents.

He edged toward me, and I strode toward him. We were more powerful together.

"I think not," the giant said in a new voice.

I didn't stop trekking forward. "Who are you?"

"You know who I am. You feel it in my magic. I was forced out long ago, but nothing lasts forever. For eons I have waited, knowing that what I had created would pay dividends in the end." The voice echoed around us, everywhere at once.

"And what did you create?" I asked, sliding a sword home to pull free the gold dagger strapped to my thigh. Something was telling me I'd need to be as nimble and unburdened with larger weapons as possible.

Unbalance smiled. “I created a divide. I created Unseelie and Seelie. Once, fae were as one. There was no need to compete, to compare. I changed that. And I waited in the knowledge that a time would come when discord would reign, and a foothold would appear once again.”

And Rubezahl had given it to him.

In that same moment, I saw how it could be if he won the day. Visions of chains and waxy-faced, starving fae swam before my eyes. The Triangle would be a smoking wasteland. Soon, Earth would follow. Underhill’s creatures would be slaughtered. The dragon’s wings would be bolted to the ground.

Death.

Despair.

The vision made bile surge in my throat.

“You see the future I speak of,” Unbalance said. “You see what will come to pass.”

What I saw made my decision achingly clear. Giving my life to stop it was as easy a choice as breathing.

There was *no* choice.

I adjusted my grip on the dagger, seeing that Lan’s watchful eyes were taking in the shifting of my weight, something that would bypass the giant completely. “I see a different path too.” I did. And this path shone with gold. It *could* end in the barriers of the two courts dissolving and our race being unified again.

“That will never come to be,” he snarled, and his presence crawled through the forest like a sea of cockroaches.

Uh-huh.

I threw the dagger and didn’t wait to see how it would be blocked—already knowing it would be—as I raced toward Lan.

He ran the same way, stopping his music to run to me.

Boom.

The ground split in two.

No. We couldn’t stop.

I picked up speed as the divide between us lengthened. Summoning every speck of energy that I still possessed, I shoved off the ground in a leap. The ground was eaten away as I soared toward Lan.

He was scrambling back from the edge.

I pushed gold out to protect the ground from more erosion, but it wasn't enough. I wasn't going to make it.

Lan shouted, and a roar filled my ears as he lunged forward, our fingers slipping against each other before mine slipped free.

I fell into the darkness.

Clawing to stop my descent, I fell.

Yet the walls had morphed from rock to an oily slickness. And through my horror and pain as Lan's face disappeared above me, I understood where this pit ended.

The center of evil.

His stronghold.

And I could only feel relief—amidst the pain of our goodbye—that Lan would not join me in this place. Underhill had saved him after all.

Lan would live. Now all that remained was to die and take evil with me.

I pushed off the wall, which was only trying to coat me in hate and agony.

In the middle, free-falling, I gathered the gold magic Underhill was lending me in this battle. And I released it all. I was the sun, a star in this place of depravity. Gold pressing against darkness. Darkness did its best to crawl through the protections granted to me by Underhill.

I was but a channel for her magic. Her battle.

And she flowed from the fae realm through me without stop, a river trying to cover a cracked wasteland.

A thrum began.

A distant part of me felt the walls closing in. As they did, I continued to fall, the black compressing, thickening and concentrating. My body shook. Her gold wavered.

And the vision of death I'd seen surged to the forefront of my mind as gold began to lose the fight against evil. Shrinking, buckling, cracking, the black wedged and rammed against the last beacon of hope both realms had.

In this place, Underhill was weaker than Unbalance.

Against Rubezahl, my life would have been enough. In this battle of entities, it couldn't hope to prevail.

Arms wrapped around me. Lan spun me in the air, and my heart shattered even as it took flight when his lips pressed to mine. He'd leaped into the yawning fissure to die with me? The fool.

My fool.

What else was left to do in this moment except cling to these last fleeting touches. I fisted his tunic in my hands, legs hooking around his hips as our mouths clashed in a desperate kiss, the harp digging into my breasts and hips as it wedged between us.

I pulled back, wanting to look at him in our final moments—needing it—but wonder was lighting his features. Peering down, I blinked at my body. Because I wasn't just emitting gold anymore.

I *was* gold.

Raising my head, I sucked in a breath at the sight of gold beating at the black, gaining lost ground, pressing against the closing walls. I rested my cheek against Lan's as weariness seeped into my bones.

"I've got you, Alli," he whispered, his voice reaching me through the thrumming, screeching din.

I smiled. *I know.*

The gold was holding, but that slimy black layer coating this endless fissure in the earth wouldn't give. Even now, even with us touching, it wasn't enough.

"The harp," I rasped, unable to even lift my head. "Play."

He pushed me back slightly, and my fingers, which had been curled around his hip, swung forward. Extending them to the closest string, I strummed pathetically.

The note was taken up, stretching, amplifying. Eviscerating the ugly thrumming of Unbalance. My vision started to blur as I rested against Lan's shoulder, gold flooding from me.

Underhill punctured the last defenses of her counterpart. She rammed and drilled without mercy. Because the entity that had protected us from this evil had no mercy.

She *couldn't* have any.

Unbalance, what was left of him, screamed, crumbling to dust and pieces that were no match for the supernova that was *me*.

In a last, desperate move, the darkness pushed out from the walls of the fissure in the earth, taking the form of a face that had nearly ruined two realms. Black dripped from his nose and eyes. Fissures were spreading through his face—just as Devon's had been doing but on a sped-up scale. Rubezahl was disintegrating before my eyes.

His mouth moved, evil's voice coming out. "You will never truly win, *Styrterya*. Our children will always reject peace when enough time lapses between wars."

And *her* voice rocketed from my lips. "That is why I am here. That is why I will always be here. Begone, *Istyrteryas*, once more to your pit."

She retreated again.

Rubezahl's face disappeared, fragmented in a silent scream.

And though I didn't scream—though I wasn't in pain, this was my end too. In my soul, my heart, I felt it approach. The path of death and evil grew smaller and smaller, and the path my father and mother had created me for grew larger. Gilded in gold.

I smiled at it.

Welcomed it.

My blinks were heavy as the harp began to evaporate into flecks that settled over Lan's skin, sinking into him. Freed from the dissolving harp, the fiery spear reformed, then dissolved also, the flecks whisking away from us—a sacrifice against Unbalance in its own right. Just one more thing we'd needed to tip the scales to victory.

Fae would live on.

Maybe not anyone who'd helped to make it so.

But the rest of our people would survive.

"I love you, Lan." My voice wasn't even a whisper as we continued to fall through the fissure. Eventually it would end, and when it did, we would be gone. I accepted this fate. I was powerless to do anything else.

Underhill made sure he heard me.

Lan squeezed me tight, suffused with gold, his voice as weary as mine from the part he'd had to play. "Don't be afraid. We'll be together soon."

I wasn't afraid. Not in his arms.

I closed my eyes.

CHAPTER 26

Death was not what I expected, not at all. I surely did not expect to end up back in the Oracle's valley, staring at her home. Only . . . it wasn't the way I remembered it.

The windows were shattered, the gardens around it scorched, the plants closest to me dead. A cold wind swirled from the space where the door had been, and I found myself fearing for my life, which was ridiculous. I was dead.

I took a step, and a burst of tiny birds swept up and around me in a windstorm of wings and song that tugged gently at my clothing and hair, a tingle of gold magic swirling with them, warming my skin.

I closed my eyes and let the sensation pass through me. Whatever this moment was—Death, life, limbo—I would take it one second at a time. With my eyes closed, I reached for Faolan, seeing him at my side in my mind's eye. *Please let him be here. Please.*

Strong fingers tangled with mine, and I smiled as I turned, choosing to ignore the confusing, empty shell of the Oracle's house for now. Lan stood next to me, dressed in a pair of cream-colored, loose-fitting pants and a matching shirt, as though he'd stepped off a beach somewhere warm. I looked down at my own body. The dress flowing around my legs and torso felt like spun spider silk. It was of the same cream-colored material worn by Faolan.

"The color seems understated for someone who's dead," I muttered, plucking at it with my free hand.

"What were you expecting?" Lan laughed softly.

"I don't know. Some red leather? A set of horns?" I grinned at him. "Something fitting for a mutt like me."

He frowned. "Don't talk about the woman I love like that." With a quick pull, he tugged me into his arms. "But in all seriousness, doesn't it seem odd to you that we died and came to a version of Underhill?"

I shrugged and leaned into him. "Are we sure this isn't what comes after life? Maybe the spirits of our ancestors are here too. For all we know, Lugh could show up again. Mind you, he might be pissed."

"Because we destroyed his spear?" Lan held me tighter. "A small sacrifice in the scheme of things, I think, when you think of all we had to offer to restore balance."

"His spear *and* his harp," I said, remembering both the artifacts dissolving.

Lan frowned though, rubbing his fingertips together. "I don't know about that. I have a feeling the harp is still with me."

Absorbing a harp wasn't the weirdest thing to happen today.

We looked back at what had been the Oracle's home. Or what it still *was* in the version of Underhill kept for living fae. "What happened here? Or is this normal?"

He shook his head. "I don't know, but it feels off."

A groan rippled out of the gaping doorway, and a voice whispered out. I couldn't quite understand it, but I *knew* that voice. It was dead as we were too.

I'd just *fought* it.

Unbalance lay in those ruins.

I untangled myself from Lan, and we turned from the cold wind and the voice that I would have preferred to never hear again. Instead, I looked past Unbalance to the valley where the alicorns and the land kelpie had grazed. The meadow was empty of the equines, and the grasses and flowers blowing in the wind appeared lonely. "I feel like this is . . . an echo." I said, struggling to find the right term. "Like it's not quite real. It could be an in-between place? Or maybe I just want to think that."

Because Lan was right. Something about this place was off . . .

"And here I thought you were stupid."

We both spun as the Oracle emerged, not from the house but from a portal. I peered past her and through the portal, but the space behind her was as black as the dead of night. She looked far better than when I'd last seen her.

In fact . . .

"You have both your eyes, and they're normal!" I blurted out.

"Balor's left nut, you can't figure it out, can you?" She raised her brows and snorted.

Of course I could. If she was here with us, then . . . "You're dead."

"That I am. Took all I had to stay alive long enough to guide you," She pointed her walking stick at me, but I doubted she needed it now. Her gait was sure as she strode toward us, and I could see with each step that her body straightened and grew stronger. Younger. More supple.

She stopped right in front of us and bowed from the waist. "You two gave your lives for the world of the fae. You truly are queen of all, Kallik of No House. Even if you are occasionally thick."

"She has a house," Lan said softly. "She is of House Gold."

The Oracle snapped upright and waved a hand right in front of his face, then bopped him on the nose with her cane. Perhaps that was why she'd decided to keep it. "House of Gold may have produced her, but she has always been Kallik of *No* House. That is the only way she could be of all fae—by not being subject to prejudices. Idiot. Though I suppose queen was never really what you were meant to be. That path was too small for you from the start. The fae needed you as queen just long enough to do the job that no one else wanted to do." She pursed her lips and looked hard at me. "Or could do. Now that job is done, at least."

Nope, I did not like the look in her eyes. It looked like scheming to me. Fuck, wasn't dying enough?

I tightened my arm around Lan, definitely sensing the Oracle wanted something more. "I'm dead. You know that, right? I'm done with your tasks and riddles. My people are safe, and I'm ready for a nap." Or a lot of afterlife sex with Lan.

"Death is a state that can be and not be at the same time." I turned toward the speaker, not surprised to hear her voice. Underhill had killed her just as surely as Unbalance had killed Rubezahl—by using her up.

A flurry of the tiny birds blurred a space close by, and when they fluttered away, Devon was there, dressed as she always had been, except her eyes were bright and her skin glowed with health. The blood fae looked great.

Death was seriously underrated. They should bottle this shit.

"Devon." I couldn't help the way my voice sharpened. She'd screwed us over, and so many more lives could have been saved if we'd been allowed to kill Rubezahl on that first battlefield. Maybe Lan and I could have lived too, if things had ended at that moment. I couldn't help feeling bitter about that.

"Do not be angry with me." Her voice was a gentle rebuke. "I see in your eyes that you believe you would have won the battle had you killed the giant. But if Rubezahl had died then, Istyrteryas would have left him and gone into another body. His evil had already been released. Then the cycle would have started again. From what the Oracle could see, *that* cycle would have ended the world in the dark way you saw. The battle had to take place as it did, so that Istyrteryas was beaten, not *just* the giant. Both had to be trumped in order for there to be peace for the fae." She paused. "For a time at least."

Lan drew a shallow breath. "What do you mean *for a time*?'

The Oracle swept her hand through the air, and the tiny birds followed her hands as she lifted and lowered them. "Life is cyclical, boy. The good and the bad, the up and down, this is the balance that Underhill and her mate agreed upon when they came into existence. Between the ups and downs—" she paused her hands, and a row of the tiny birds flew through them, "—there is peace for a time. You two, despite your failings, have managed to give that to the fae."

The Oracle and Devon shared a look, and the Oracle shook her head. "No, I don't think that's a good idea. You saw the outcome as well as I did. This is the way it must be. The work must continue."

Devon hummed low, and I found myself pushing on Lan, backing us away from the two women who'd been at the center of many of the trials we'd faced. They might not be evil like Rubezahl, but they'd used us as pawns to make sure things happened in the way they thought best. Manipulation was not something I wanted to deal with in death, too, thank you very fucking much.

"Time to go," I whispered.

"Where to, exactly?" Lan said as I dragged him away. "They're dead, we're dead, where can we run to?"

I didn't know, but I had every intention of trying. The Oracle wasn't done with me. I could feel it in my bones and *see* it in my head. She had another use for me.

My bare feet sunk into the soft moss of the valley as I began to run, the long grass tickling my legs. Lan was beside me.

"Where do those two think they are going?" the Oracle barked, her voice as close as if she stood right behind us.

I fed more of the gold magic into my indigo, looping it around Lan and me, cloaking us as we ran. Faster and faster. I knew we could outrun them. That had always been my strength.

"Does she think we can't see her?"

"I guess. The question is why is she running?" Devon answered quietly. "She does not even understand what is being offered."

Devon was so quiet, and yet I heard her.

Lan glanced at me as the landscape changed, and we ran barefoot across a desert, the hot sand sliding through our toes. Then the sand changed, and we were on the shore of the raging purple ocean.

I slid to a stop, barely panting.

I turned to see the Oracle and Devon still behind us.

"Lugh be damned!" I yelled. "The both of you can just fuck off! I don't want another task! Can't I just be dead in peace and quiet?"

The Oracle's lips swept upward. "Those with great gifts don't get peace and quiet. Not even when they are dead. Look at Lugh. He had to help his nincompoop of a grandson. Look at me. Still trying to deal with a dumdum." She sighed and snapped her fingers. A well-padded chair appeared behind her, and she slumped backward into it. "Perhaps I *will* get some peace and quiet once you are dealt with, but I doubt it. Underhill is a demanding mistress even after so very long.

Tension flowed through me, hot and angry. What more could I do? I just wanted to go find Cinth and the other friends I'd lost.

I'd better still be able to taste Cinth's cooking. If I had to go without ever tasting those beetroot tickles again, there would be hell to pay.

"This is not the death I was expecting," I yelled at the ocean, as if the waves of purple would have an answer. "Where the hell is my happily ever after? And where is Cinth?"

Lan groaned. "Maybe this is our punishment?"

"For what? Saving all of fae?" I snorted and forced myself to turn back to the Oracle.

Devon stood beside her, as calm as the ocean was furious. They were waiting on me to finish my meltdown.

I ran a hand through my hair. "All right. I'm done for now. Spit it out."

"Cinth is not dead." Devon said. "Rowan saved her. Love can do that."

The words could not have shaken me harder. She was *alive*?

And I was dead.

I clutched at Lan just in case he was snatched away too. I was happy Cinth was alive. I was. It meant she had a chance to have babies and to have a real life. I just . . . I'd thought we'd be together here.

"Anything else?" I choked out.

The Oracle tossed me her stick. I caught it out of reflex.

"You were never meant to be queen," she said. "Not in the long run. You chose wisely for the Unseelie throne. The general will remain at the helm of the Unseelie for years. And the Seelie court could not have a better leader than Hyacinth, between her heart and her understanding of the fae. I could not have chosen better myself."

I held onto her walking stick and stared at her. "So?"

The Oracle rolled both her eyes, but Devon stepped forward. The weight of her gaze changed as Underhill spoke through her.

"The balance must be put right." She tipped her head to the side, glancing at Lan. "Too much good has died. An offer I will make. A chance, yes. A single hope, yes. Give and take, yes."

I blinked at her messed-up speech. "Lan *wasn't* meant to die. I knew it!" Turning, I jabbed a finger in his chest. "You messed up the sum of things."

"Don't care." He shrugged a shoulder.

Underhill smiled, and I watched her closely. Had she hoped that Lan would die with me?

She snapped her fingers, and the world inverted, twisting around me as if I had been wrapped in rope and then spun about like a child's top. I landed on my knees next to Lan. We were at the entrance to the Oracle's home. The cold wind slid around me, cooling the sweat on my skin.

The voice of Unbalance still whispered inside and that, more than the wind, made me shiver.

"The Oracle chose her path to death when she decided to give you more information than she should have," Devon said, in control of her voice once more. "In doing so, she widened a future path for you—the only path that would allow you to live on. The world needs an Oracle. Underhill has chosen you. Faolan's death means that too much good was lost in the final battle. Yet to restore both of your lives would result in too much good remaining. The burden of becoming an Oracle mitigates this good in part, but there must be a further sacrifice made if you are to both return. There *must* be balance to prevent evil gaining an easy foothold back into the realms. So, to return to the land of the living as my Oracle, you must negotiate with my other half—with Istyrteryas. You must find a way to keep the scales even."

I stared into the dark hole, felt the whispering of Unbalance within. "And Lan?"

"He must negotiate with Istyrteryas also. Your fates are bound in life and death."

We could both live again. We could see Cinth and the others. We *could* be together again.

I clutched the staff. "And if I refuse?"

"There will not be balance. Istyrteryas won't need to wait to begin his work again. Another Oracle will be born. The fae will need to wait for guidance, and once again, we could face the dark future you saw," Underhill said. "Choose now."

So many things suddenly made sense. The odd visions I'd been having. The large and small paths that had appeared to me. The Oracle had been preparing to leave the world, and Underhill had lain the groundwork for me to fill her robes.

My mind whirled, connecting the dots, seizing onto answers and releasing them so it could snatch at questions I knew better than to ask.

"Life?" I asked Lan.

This wasn't just my choice.

"Life." He didn't smile. We didn't know the price yet.

I stood and held out a hand to Lan. Once more we locked fingers, and together we walked through the doorway.

Darkness swamped me immediately, and I closed my eyes.

Istyrteryas laughed. "You think you have anything to offer me worth your life? A life for a life. *That* is the only true balance. You killed my slave, so you, too, shall remain dead."

But Underhill had said to negotiate. There had to be a way. She wouldn't have sent me in here otherwise.

The world fuzzed, and I could see Lan and me starting a family on Unimak. A little girl who looked a great deal like me, her eyes dark like her father's and full of innocence.

"Mama? Why are you sad?" Her fingers tightened on mine.

I struggled to breathe around the pain in my heart.

A life for a life, he'd said.

Yet to give up a child, even one who did not yet exist, was a cut so cruel that it was unacceptable. Better to be dead than to lose her, to *willingly* choose to lose her.

Beside me, Lan gasped. "Orphan, that price is too high. I do not think I can do it."

I started to step away, but the images inside my mind shifted, and I saw two paths. One where we stayed dead. The fae survived, they lived on, but they continued to dwindle, their numbers sliding away. Hundreds of unborn children waited in the darkness. *Hundreds* who would never find their way into their mother's arms. I couldn't fathom why us living or dying would affect how many children were born, but it was clear from the pathways in my mind that it would.

And if we gave up our precious one? The pathway changed, flickering gold and purple. The fae flourished, and the children of the fae were beyond numerous. Those hundreds that would not otherwise have been born found their way home.

Cinth and Rowan were on that path with not one, but *two* children. Twins.

I looked to the other path again.

Cinth had no children there.

A sob crept out of me as I struggled to weigh the cost. Cinth's happiness was on the line. Could I take that from her?

If I went back, not only would I be in her life, but she would have the babies she'd always dreamed of. So many mothers would be blessed with babies.

I would not be.

"The balance must be maintained." Underhill's voice was rough and perhaps even thick with tears on my behalf. "What chose you?"

"I am with you," Lan whispered in my ear. "I will follow where you lead, Kallik of All Fae. I trust you and what you see."

Swallowing hard, I nodded and fought to find the right words. But there were none— there were no right words for giving up a child.

"Fuck you, Istyrteryas," I said to the cold, whispering evil. "We go back to Unimak."

CHAPTER 27

I cracked open an eyelid and peeked at my clothing. The softly woven garments of the Between were gone, and I was dressed in an outfit that trumped gold armor and queenly dresses any day.

Supple brown leather leggings and a forest green tunic. I wiggled my toes and felt the leather boots move easily with my feet.

Bliss.

Turning my head at the rustling of grass, I met Lan's gaze. He was dressed in similar clothing of a different color, and his expression matched mine.

Bittersweet joy filled my chest. The laughter of the unborn baby girl rang in my ears and heart, even as that same heart soared at the thought of being back here. Alive. At the price of any future children we might have had.

"Where are we?" Lan asked in a rough voice.

Sitting up, I scanned our surroundings. We'd been deposited in a shallow cave, slightly raised off the ground, that overlooked a stream. Trees, snow, and a deep thrum of silence. Not much else was needed for me to hazard a guess. "The Triangle." I stood. "Come on. We better get back. I need to check on Cinth."

"Cinth and Rowan are alive," Lan said, staying put. "She has just become queen."

I pulled a face. "Right. My presence will confuse everyone. But she doesn't know we're alive. She'll be grieving."

"She'll know the truth soon enough. Don't rob her of the chance to win the hearts of the Seelie. Or General Stryk of the chance to establish himself either. Let's start a fire and take some time to process everything. It's not every day you die, negotiate with evil itself, and are restored to life."

See? I hadn't just latched onto this fella for his bod.

Sighing, I sat again. "Now that we know why Unseelie and Seelie courts exist at all, it doesn't seem right to allow the two separate courts to exist." I blinked as two pathways of equal size blinked into being in my mind, stretching out into the not-too-distant future. A person lay sleeping at the mouth of the pathways, the person that would walk one of the paths, and a smile came to my lips when I recognized who it was.

Lan snorted. "I'm gonna have to get used to that knowing smile, aren't I?"

"Yep," I quipped. "I need you by my side." A tickling awareness had me turning left to another path, this one stretching *back* in time. Instinct prompted me to search for any smaller branches that were still attached to this main vein. There were none, and my gut told me that meant I could speak of what that pathway had held.

I said slowly, "Your Unseelie magic with the Seelie magic you absorbed from the harp is needed to augment my own balance. Until I strengthen over the centuries, I'll require your help to open portals so as not to drain my essence." I blinked again, and dozens of pathways literally filled my vision. Tiny ones, wide ones, twisted and smooth ones, dark, light, you name it. "We're both gonna have things to get used to."

"You'll only need me for a few centuries, huh?" Lan said, sitting too. "That gives me more than enough time to think up another reason to convince you to let me stay afterward."

I cocked a brow. "I don't know. It'll need to be good. I *will* be an all-powerful Oracle, after all."

He rolled to his feet and started collecting wood from inside the cave. It wasn't as dry as was ideal, but Lan poured magic into it, drawing red from the ground, until the wood caught.

I edged closer to the warmth, and my feet snagged on a thick, black cloak. It was folded neatly, and beside it lay a cane. "Looks like my uniform made it back too."

Lan glanced over. "Guess it's important for fae to continue believing absolutely in the Oracle, huh?"

Guess so. In her negotiations with Istyrteryas, the Oracle had simply needed to sacrifice an eye to keep balance and take up her post. Far less than the sacrifice I'd had to make, but then she'd become Oracle in a simpler time, perhaps.

As I looked at the previous Oracle's path, I saw that her walk had always had an end date. She'd lost the man she needed to augment her power. Not immediately, but early on in her service. After that, opening portals had started to drain her essence, aging her and setting her death date.

I tracked a small path that linked up with a *huge* path—the one I'd just walked. My heart squeezed. She'd chosen an earlier death to help me. I could see that her path had burned into another's—one I saw had belonged to my mother. The Oracle had helped Elisavanna at one point. My eyes rounded. The twin blades. The hints along the way via Lan. The puzzle game. Those had all been the Oracle's doing. Even then, she could have lived. But when she'd actively helped me instead of remaining an impartial bystander, *that* was when she'd chosen an early passing.

Or maybe she'd chosen it as a mercy for herself.

Her fate and life were a warning to me to never get complacent about Lan's presence. As if I'd needed one.

I spread out the thick robes before the fire. "Come here," I said quietly.

Lan sat, and for a time we just looked at the steadily strengthening fire, feeding it as needed. When warmth licked the walls of the shallow cave, I rose to my knees.

Dark eyes filled with every hue fixed on me as I drew the cord of leather from my dark chestnut hair. Wherever we'd just been had left my skin glowing and hair gleaming, and the silken strands slithered over my shoulders, curling gently over my breasts.

Our breathing synced as we stared at each other and the last, desperate, uncertain months dropped away. My fingers went to the buttons of my tunic, and I undid them without any trace of haste.

For the first time, I felt a hint of gratitude that we'd been interrupted in Underhill. If we'd come together then, it would have happened out of fear.

It wouldn't have been just me and Lan.

I pulled the tunic off and heard the soft thump of it hitting the ground. A tight bandeau contained my breasts, and I started on the buttons of that. Lan swallowed as they bounced free, and I dropped the bandeau on top of the tunic.

"You're beautiful, Alli," he whispered hoarsely.

And though I'd always considered myself more a warrior than a beauty, I *did* feel like a goddess when he looked at me. I smiled and straddled his lap.

His hands gripped my hips, then inched up my sides, fingers splaying over my ribs. As he roamed, I set to work on his tunic, exposing his firm chest and ridged abdomen.

Lan brushed the underside of my breasts and hissed low as my nipples pebbled more in response. I shoved off his tunic, then he took me in his iron grasp again, his mouth closing over one nipple.

Despite the fire's warmth, a slight sting of cold still licked my skin, but it only made the heat of his mouth and tongue more delectable. I gasped as he pulled slightly, my hips circling on his lap without conscious intention on my part. He kissed between the swells of my chest, moving to the other nipple as I gave my hands free reign over his shoulders and back. I threaded my fingers through his dark hair, gripping the strands tightly as he nipped softly against my sensitive skin.

Indigo whispered down my arms, tangling with his magic of every hue.

I ground into Lan's hardness, and he clamped down on my hips, raising his head.

"I love you, Alli," he said, gaze hooded.

Lifting my hand, I touched gentle fingertips to his jaw and lips. "I love you, too, Lan. I can't believe we made it."

I can't believe we get to be together.

Leaning forward, I touched my lips to his, and our power burst out in a tidal wave that shook the very ground. But not a single worry infringed on my thoughts as our mouths moved against each other, the contact slow and firm. His touches were soft, however. A hand moving through my hair, fingertips playing my spine, a thumb brushing over my nipples.

Lan swiped me up and lay me back on the thick, black robe. After removing my boots, he touched his lips to mine again before straddling *my* hips. He drew the top of my leather leggings down, kissing as he went. Moving the leggings down over my ass, he peered up at me as he slipped his tongue down through my folds.

I jerked, automatically trying to widen my legs.

But they were confined by my leggings and his thighs on either side of mine.

"Clothes off," I urged, wiggling.

Lan reached up and pinned my wrists to the ground in response, then returned to his station. He probed between my folds with his tongue again, delving as deeply as he could with my legs still pressed together before drawing up again, gliding past my clit with wide, sweeping laps that had me desperate to widen for him.

Up and down he bobbed as I lay there, only able to arch my hips upward by a tiny degree to keep his tongue on my sweet spot for a half second longer.

He was fucking me with his mouth, and I felt a telling heat creep over my jaw and across my chest as he picked up speed and roughness.

A growl slipped from him, and the vibrations of his voice and magic shuddered through my body.

Up and down.

I cried out, trying to grind against his face. But pleasure crept up from between my legs to claim me. A languidness spread to my toes, to the crown of my head too. I stopped grinding and arching and could only urge him on with soft, wordless, cries.

"Fuck," he groaned.

Lan ripped off my leggings and pressed my thighs to the ground with a suddenness I didn't have time to register before his mouth was on *all* of me.

Half-sitting up, I screamed at the intensity of the onslaught and then slapped my hands on the ground as my chest arched up. He didn't show any mercy, licking between my thighs like a man starved and half-mad.

"Scream for me," he said against me.

And I did, his name tearing from my lips as the orgasm I'd approached with slow, languid certainty only a moment before crashed over me, catapulting me into mind-shattering, body-clenching pleasure that had me clutching his face to my core and wrapping my legs around his torso to hold him there.

He didn't stop sucking and laving through the aftershocks. Not until my hands slid from his hair and my thighs fell open. Only then did he slow his pace. He moved his tongue in lazy strokes, kissing and kneading my inner thighs with his hands.

A delicious shiver rocked me again. He kissed my clit one last time, then raised to look at me.

No walls.

No impending death and doom.

I was Alli, and he was Lan. It was what I'd dreamed of for so long, and part of me couldn't regret what it had taken to get here.

"Seems you figured out a pretty good reason for me to keep you around," I rasped.

Chin gleaming, he winked, and my focus dipped to the front of his pants.

"You better get those off before you split the seams," I said.

He stood, and I rolled up to a crouch before him, holding his gaze as I dragged them downward. His erection sprung free, and I hurried to push his pants down so he couldn't kick them off.

Gripping his ass, I fixed my mouth over his bobbing head and flattened my tongue to take him deep.

His hiss filled my ears as his hips jerked.

Yeah. It was my turn to torture him.

Keeping my movements slow, I drew my nails down his ass, kneading the back of his thighs before drawing one hand back to grip the base of his shaft.

I jolted as something tweaked my nipples.

My eyes flew to his, immediately tracked the threads of magic extending down to my breasts. They circled my nipples, brushing over the tips.

Lan's eyes were dark enough to devour me whole, and as I swirled my tongue around his tip before plunging forward, he released another tendril, a small smile playing on his lips. My breath caught as the tendril inched downward between my breasts and over my stomach. I groaned as it slipped between my folds, much as his tongue had done. His magic flicked over my core for a time before it began to vibrate with tiny, furious shakes.

I shouted, the sound muffled by Lan's cock in my mouth.

I pressed on his thigh to brace myself as the shaking sensations took hold of me. My thighs trembled as I doubled the speed of my sucking movements, my hand pumping in tandem.

Two can play that game.

Indigo crept from me, and I peeked up to make sure Lan hadn't spotted it. Flattening my magic, I licked it against the firm sack hanging between his legs, pressing and rolling.

His shout brought a curve to my lips.

Of course, it only served to ramp up his efforts. Two more dark, multi-hued tendrils shot out, and I only had the warning of them circling my entrance before they entered me and began to piston.

My magic shot out, covering his body, stroking, digging, and pushing his hips against my mouth.

I cried out as the shaking of my thighs spread through my body, the tendrils pulsing in and out of me ramping up. Lan had gathered my hair into a ponytail and was all but fucking my mouth, just as I'd done with his.

My throat relaxed, along with every other part of me.

My magic draped over him like a blanket as I was once again consumed with a heat that rocked me to my very core.

Lan drew out of my mouth, and I rested my cheek against his thigh as his magic retreated from my core. Holding my shoulders to keep me upright, my Unseelie lowered to sit on his haunches and drew me up onto his lap. We were both panting hard, and I lifted my head, still half in the throes of orgasm, to take him in.

The muscles in his neck were taut, his dark eyes wild and almost furious with the need to be inside me.

And I felt that same need down to my very soul.

Reaching down, I gripped his rock-hard erection and settled him at my entrance. Caught in the moment, barely aware of our physical bodies, I slid down onto him until he was buried all the way within me.

We both shuddered as we became one.

At last.

Gripping his shoulders, I began to rock in tiny, slow, grinds. "Forever, Lan," I whispered against his lips before claiming them.

He tilted my chin when our kiss ended. "Forever, my Alli."

Placing his hands on my ass, he helped me rock against him. Our heartbeats were synced. Our breaths hitched in tandem. Our magic was a supernova that could surely be seen and felt for miles around.

My tempo increased, and I whimpered at the friction as my core ground on his thighs and stomach with every return journey.

Lan captured my wrists and held them at the small of my back. With him holding me upright, I rocked and bounced, chasing the pleasure waiting for us both. He moaned low and pressed his forehead against my breasts.

His grip shifted to my elbows, and he thrust into me from below. Our movements would probably look blurred and perhaps savage to the human eye.

"Lan," I pleaded.

He looked at me, the wildness draining from his gaze as our movements slowed. Our breath, our heartbeat, the awareness of being in our bodies stopped as I lowered one last time.

As indigo and rainbow darkness merged.

As we came apart, completely together.

CHAPTER 28

We may have stayed in that lovely, warm, solitary cave for more than a night. Possibly even a week, but to be honest I'm not sure. Mostly because of all the nakedness, the days and nights rolled into a never-ending glorious feast of sensuality.

At some point though, I came back to myself. The warmth of a spring sun cut across my face, waking me up slowly, leisurely. I rolled in Lan's arms and tucked my nose into the crook of his neck, breathing him in. He smelled like fresh snow, pine trees, and sex. I licked up the side of his neck to nibble on his ear, drawing a low groan from him.

"No more, woman. I need to sleep." He tightened his hold on me, even as his cock stood up and pressed against my inner thigh, making a liar of him.

I smiled. "I'm just making up for some serious lost time, Lan. Years of suppression, of making do with mediocre dick. It's no way to live."

He pulled back. "Mediocre dick?"

"At best," I pulled a face. His brows were furrowed. "You'd better claim the same, my friend."

"That all I got was mediocre dick?"

His grin was infectious, and I started laughing. "No. that . . . you . . . never mind."

The past was the past, and though I could see some of the threads that had tried to tie themselves to Lan, they were weak and ineffective compared with the love he'd held for me all the years we'd spent apart.

He rolled so he was on his back, and I was splayed across his chest, our heat warming each other better than any fire. I looked past him, out of the cave's entrance and for the first time, really looked.

"What time of year did we fight Rubezahl?"

Lan stroked his hands down my back and over my ass cheeks, smoothing away the goosebumps that were slowly rising. "Summer, why?"

Summer.

Outside of the cave, the *first* of summer's flowers had appeared, and the last of spring's show was fading. It wasn't possible! I scrambled to my feet. "The time. It passed like crazy while we were dead."

I was up and pulling my clothes on, suddenly frantic as I did the math in my head. We'd been gone a year, give or take. Cinth had been grieving for so long . . . "We've gotta go!"

Lan dressed quickly and held out a hand to me. "Take a breath, Alli. Put your robe on, grab your whacking stick, and make a portal. You are the Oracle now. You can go wherever you want, whenever you want. And we don't have to run there."

I yanked up the long black robe and settled it over my shoulders, held my hand out, and called the long walking stick to me with my magic. The thick wood hit my skin with a resounding smack, and I settled the end of the stick into the ground. "Damn skippy. . . Can you tell who I am?"

"If I hadn't seen you put the robe on, I'd think I was looking at the old Oracle." He grimaced. "Kind of unsettling actually." He held out a hand.

I took it, and my indigo magic flared, reaching for his dark rainbow power. Trickling through our comingled power and extending out to the spear on Lan's back was a thin strand of gold, connecting our essence tightly.

I thought about where on Unimak I wanted to go, and the answer came in an instant.

Focusing on the image in my mind, I swung the staff, and a small portal opened at the mouth of the cave. Lan and I stepped through it together, the air changing and warming. Unimak was south of the Triangle, and the temperature difference was apparent, even on the outskirts of the fae realm. I let Lan go. This part was for me alone, and he stepped back, giving me space.

My mother's grave lay at my feet, and I knelt before it, resting my staff across my knees. I bent at the waist and pressed my forehead to the ground. I breathed in the smell of the earth, of the stones and the salty air as my childhood memories swirled through me.

My mother had walked a hard path, but she'd done it willingly, knowing I would appease the spirits if I was strong enough. Tears gathered in my eyes as I saw her pathway not as only as the Oracle but as her daughter. She'd been determined to give me a childhood full of love. Even if my blood wasn't hers.

"You did good, mama," I whispered. "I always knew you loved me."

Lifting my head, I blinked away tears as her spirit came into view. Her smile crinkled the edges of her eyes, and her round cheeks were pink as if she stood in the wind. Other spirits came into view around her, indistinct forms whispering in Tlingit.

You have brought us peace. The children of the moon are gone. Balance is restored. Well done, Daughter of All.

The voices tumbled over one another, but I heard them clearly, and my heart filled to bursting. "Thank you for choosing me."

As I said the words, I realized that I truly was grateful. If not for all the shit I'd gone through, all the hardships I'd faced, I would not be here in this moment with Lan and a life ahead of me.

She understands.

Those two words were said in a sigh of relief, and the spirits slowly dissipated, the indistinct forms disappearing one by one until only my mother remained. "I won't see you again, will I?"

She shook her head. *No, my precious one. But I will be with you always.*

I stared at her form as she too began to disappear, blurring as my tears fell. "I love you."

And I will always love you, the daughter who was mine, even when she was not.

And then she too, was gone.

Catching the sob before it could escape me, I stood up. Lan tucked an arm around me and tugged me tightly to him. He didn't say a word . . . he didn't need to. I just leaned into him as the tears fell, as the goodbye settled over me.

I brushed my face clean of the tears and stepped back. "Ready?"

"You just want to run so you can prove how much faster you are than me," he said, lifting an eyebrow.

I laughed, as I was sure was his intention. "No. I want to walk. I want to feel Unimak under my feet now that I'm the Oracle."

Lan bowed from the waist. "As you wish, my love."

Linking arms with him, I turned away from the grave and started toward the Seelie side of the island. I would visit General Stryk, but first I needed to see Hyacinth.

I grinned at the thought. She was going to shit a damn brick. Maybe two.

As we crossed the invisible line between the human and fae realms, the urge to run washed over me, and I couldn't help but pick up speed for a moment.

Lan laughed. "I thought we were walking?"

"Speed walking is still walking," I pointed out, even though I did try to slow. All around us the forests were bursting with colors that drew my eyes. Brilliant purples, pinks, blues, and greens dominated the flora. Some of the flowers floated upward and spun out into birds that sung, their songs bright and clear.

"Someone paid attention when they were in Underhill," Lan said.

I nodded and kept up the pace. It wasn't long before we were hiking up through the tiers of the Seelie fae. Only . . . they weren't the same as they'd been.

The sections had been blended, the obvious lines between the haves and have nots obliterated. At least every other house in the lower tiers had been cleaned, repaired, and given a new look. I tugged up my hood as the fae around us took note of our passing.

Some of them might remember my face. Some would certainly know Lan. But in this robe, they would see who they'd always seen. The Oracle.

I'd prefer not to explain myself to anyone before I saw my friend.

But I couldn't stand it. I had to know what had happened to create a better place for the fae. The simple fact that torrents of humans were *everywhere* and not just in the areas surrounding the castle was a huge sign of change—and hopefully that meant relations between our races was improving too.

"Hey, what's going on, dingdong?" I yelled at one of the laborers who was standing to the side of a half-built house, doing fuck all.

Lan snorted.

The laborer startled and spun. "I'm working!"

"Bullshit, dumdum, and what is this," I waved the stick at the house, and he went to his knees as if I'd clobbered him in the head.

"Oracle. I didn't realize! I do this with the blessing of our regent, Hyacinth. She said the city needed to have a better recipe, and for that we needed more—"

"Blending." I grinned underneath my hood. Fucking right. I'd known Cinth would be able to lead.

"Yes, blending is what she said," There was a heavy pause while he wrung his hands, and then he reached out to me. "Can you tell me . . . will I find a wife soon?"

Lan startled almost as much as I did. Shit, I guess this was part of the gig, wasn't it? I took a step forward and then grabbed his hand. The pathway for him was not forked. He was not destined for adventure, but he would find a wife. Though she was not the one he was looking at.

"Stop pursuing the woman you believe to be your match and let your true match find you," I said. "And when she tells you that you are going to marry her, I'd suggest that you listen." An image of a rolling pin came into view, and I nodded in appreciation. "She's a good cook, so don't piss her off."

He grunted as though I'd kicked him in the balls. "Lallybell can't cook worth shit. Does that mean—"

Lan pulled my hand away. "That she's not the one. Listen to your Oracle, boy." He hung onto me tightly as he led us up the steep road. "Did that tire you?"

I shook my head. "No, not at all. But maybe that's because you're here."

We didn't speak again until we reached the first tier. Both of us were awed by all the changes to our childhood home. The Seelie realm had always been beautiful, but there had been a dreamlike quality to it, as if it weren't quite real.

Whatever Cinth was doing had brought a solidity to the realm, adding substance to the beauty.

I could see her now, sitting down and looking at the tiers as if they were ingredients. Her brow would furrow as she dug into how to best meld them into a cohesive . . .

Her brow furrowed deeper and a scream ripped from her mouth.

"Cinth!" I was running before her name was fully out of my mouth. All I could see was her screaming, crying, as if she were being tortured.

Killed.

No, no, no! This was not happening, not now! I turned on the speed, knowing I was leaving Lan behind, but he'd catch up to me. All I could see was the pain rippling across my friend's face.

I hit the main doors of a rebuilt castle, barely acknowledging that they'd done a good job. My magic raced ahead of me, opening doors and literally throwing people out of my way. I whispered my thanks as I pulled energy from the earth and the stone around me to funnel my strength.

Her screams went from inside my head to my ears, and I found myself pulling more magic, more energy from the world around me. My hands hummed with it as I prepped to do whatever was needed to save her.

A bunch of women clustered around a door in the hallway. They took one look at me in my long black cloak and knelt, thinking I was the Oracle. I mean, I was, but why weren't they helping Cinth?

My mind couldn't put the pieces together: I didn't register the white aprons, the surgical gloves, the equipment. Not until I burst through the door did it all click.

Cinth was on her back, belly huge under a white sheet, her hands gripping the edges as she groaned. Rowan stood at her side, holding her hand as the groan turned into a scream.

A fae woman with white hair and deep-set blue-green eyes sat between Cinth's feet. "You must push, Your Highness. The babes are big, thanks to that knobbly-headed man you decided you couldn't live without."

A sob rippled out of Cinth. "I can't. I'm too tired, I can't push any more—" Her eyes lifted to mine, and I knew she couldn't see me. That was the beauty of the hood. I crouched next to her and took her hand as I smiled, tears gathering at the corners of my eyes.

"Cinth."

She blinked, and her eyes focused on me as I lifted one hand and pulled the hood back. Her scream was immediate, and then I was sitting on the edge of the bed as she sobbed, and I sobbed with her, and it was pretty much just a giant mess of emotion.

I pulled back so I could just see her face. "You've been . . . busy?"

Her body tensed, and a low moan slid from her. "It hasn't been . . . what I expected."

I glanced up at Rowan as I felt Lan enter the room. Rowan was pale, and he was sinking to his knees. "I don't understand," he muttered, looking as if he'd seen a ghost and not just his dead friend.

"Let's get Cinth through this, discussions later," I said as I took her hand and fed some of my magic into her, the indigo and gold blending into her soft pink.

"Breathe, Cinth," I whispered. "I'm here, and I'm not leaving you again." She squeezed my hand tightly, her smile wobbly. Mine wasn't much better as I squeezed her back. "You've got this."

An hour and fourteen minutes later, the first of the twins was born. A boy with a bellow that matched his father's shout for joy. His sister would have none of him taking the spotlight and followed him out less than a minute later, screaming at the top of her lungs.

"Spicy," I whispered to Cinth as she cried and held her two babies. I kissed them both on the tops of their heads, kissed Cinth, and then backed out of the room.

"Don't leave!" Cinth said.

"I'm just going to get cleaned up," I lifted a hand. "Then we can talk."

As soon as we were clear of the room and in a side hall, Lan tugged me into his arms, and I let my tears fall. I was so happy for her, but my heart broke at the thought of the girl with the dark chestnut curls and dark eyes. My girl that would never be. I breathed through the pain and let it flow instead of pretending it didn't hurt.

"It's worth the cost," I mumbled into his chest. "But it still cuts."

He held me a little tighter, his heart beating a tad too fast, his voice thick with emotion. "I know."

I leaned back and stared up into his face, seeing the echoes of a child who would never be. It would always hurt, I knew that. The ache of knowing her for even that split second had been enough to fill me with the knowledge that she was my daughter, even though she would never take a breath.

"We'll get through this too," Lan said. I wiped a tear off his cheek.

"I don't think it's a matter of getting through it, so much as living with it," I said. "For what it's worth, I don't want to forget her. I want to honor what could have been."

Lan nodded and closed his eyes. "Yes." Just that. One word, and I knew that he was right. We'd see each other through this too.

"Let's go get something to eat," he said, then cleared his throat. "I'm starving. And if we're lucky, Cinth will have taught some of her cooks how to make her beetroot tickles."

I smiled up at him, pulled his head down, and kissed one of his closed eyelids. "Yes."

The next few days flew by in a blur.

It turned out that when Lan and I had finally gotten naked together after regenerating, we were still technically in a version of Underhill and time was acting . . .strange. The magic we'd unleashed had impacted the entire fae population of Unimak. Not only had we gotten busy, but everyone else had too.

Our magical explosion had literally caused a fae orgy. Kind of proud of that, not gonna lie.

The result was a baby boom that was still rippling through our race. The maternity fae were overrun helping new babies enter the world daily—an unheard-of precedent given our low reproduction rates.

This was what I'd seen when I'd bargained with Unbalance—a baby boom. But I hadn't realized that Lan and I would be the cause of it.

"Think it will happen every time we have sex?" Lan whispered to me on our second night in Unimak, and I grimaced.

"I don't think Cinth will forgive me if we're the cause of a second pregnancy with another set of twins." I grinned, and Lan chuckled as he moved over me.

"Just in case. We'd best be sure," He murmured into my mouth as he took control and brought me to a climax that had me struggling to remain coherent.

The next morning, we made an appearance in the Unseelie court to check on General Stryk, who immediately tried to hand me the throne.

"No, that path is no longer mine to walk," I let my eyes flutter to half mast, seeing his path clearly. "Your first born will take the throne when he is of age."

"I'm not married," he grumped.

I turned and looked behind us. "You bang a middle-aged widow eight months ago?"

He paled and his eyes went wide. "You . . . can see backward too?"

"Get ready for a son," I grinned at him and slapped him on the shoulder. "He's going to be a strong-willed one, handsome as the devil and—" I paused as I looked at his son's potential pathways. He could be serious trouble, but he could also be as legendary as Lugh, depending on how things turned out, and which paths he chose. "—I'll be keeping an eye on him, too."

General Stryk bowed from the waist. "Your Majesty."

I shook my head, "Not anymore. Just Kallik is fine."

From there, we visited Drake and his pack, who'd settled on the Unseelie side of Unimak. He'd found a nice girl, and they were expecting a child too, on the next full moon. A changeling child, no doubt.

Knowing so many children would be born to others, but never to me, the pain in my own heart could have increased. It didn't. I found that the more time I spent with others, with Cinth's and Rowan's twins . . . the pain changed. It didn't go away, but it shifted into something else.

On the eighth night, after another night full of laughter, stories, and beetroot tickles, I lay content in Lan's arms and stared up at the ceiling above us.

The paths of our friends were simple—very few had forks in them, and I understood why the Oracle had taken an interest in me. When I looked back on my own path, the forks were numerous, all on top of each other, stacked three and four deep in places. Each choice I'd made had narrowed the rest, but in many cases it had added more.

Lan and I would stay in Unimak and set up a house that we would build over the river, bridging the two halves of the fae. Maybe we could find a way to bridge that gap in a more meaningful way, but for now . . . for now an Oracle who stood on both sides would have to be enough.

"It's shocking that we made it through, that we won," I mumbled sleepily against his chest. "There were so many times we nearly died. So many choices that hung by a kelpie's strand of hair." I laughed softly, "Literally, I guess."

With my new ability to look backward, I understood that the way I'd been treated in my formative years had ensured my survival. As much as it had sucked, it had made me strong enough, resilient enough, to do what no one else could.

Lan mumbled something in his sleep, and I lifted up to see he was out cold. There was one more person I had to visit.

I slipped out of our room, pulling the long black cloak around me as I slid through the halls of the new palace and then stepped out onto the grounds. My feet led me to the eastern slope, where the sun would rise and cast its light on the graves of those who had fallen before me.

First was my father's grave. "You did a shit thing. But it turned out okay in the end. It was still a shit thing."

Yup, that about summed up our relationship. No goodbyes. No I love yous.

I started to turn away but found myself staring at my stepmother's grave.

"Adair," I didn't touch her grave. She'd died when Rubezahl had pulled the old castle down. He'd done it out of spite, to hurt me. All he'd done was take out one of the people who hated me most. Next to her grave was a smaller marker.

Princess Cathara. I blinked at the name. Adair must have picked it out for her before her death.

Feeling wistful, I put my hand to her tiny grave, wondering who she would have been. Would we have been friends, or would she have been like Adair? Pathways burst out in front of me in way I hadn't expected and didn't understand.

The dead didn't have paths to follow. Only the living.

"Well, Dandelion, you found one last secret. But that isn't your path to follow. You see? Your paths won't cross for a long, long time."

I didn't turn to look at the old Oracle. I didn't need to. Her spirit was there, pressing against me.

"She doesn't need me." I couldn't help the hurt in my voice, at least until I saw the moment our paths would cross. "Not yet."

"Not yet, Dandelion," the old Oracle whispered. "But in time, you will find your sister. And she will need you to teach her how to live. Until then—" her voice began to fade, "—I suggest you enjoy the peace and quiet. For when your sister finds you . . ."

I nodded, seeing the disaster that would arise with the arrival of the girl who would be queen. "She'll be a fucking monster."

I sighed and ran a hand over my face and then shook it off. No. No more worry, no more stress. I was going to bed, and I was going to enjoy the years I had before I had to deal with the creature that Adair had created. Until then . . . until then I would live. I would love.

And I would eat all the beetroot tickles I bloody well could.

EXPLORE MORE WORLDS FROM

Shannon Mayer

SHANNONMAYER.COM

&

Kelly St. Clare

KELLYSTCLARE.COM

Printed in Great Britain
by Amazon